Tainted

Tainted

Blacc Topp

www.urbanbooks.net

Urban Books, LLC
300 Farmingdale Road, N.Y.-Route 109
Farmingdale, NY 11735

ISBN 13: 978-1-64556-463-8
ISBN 10: 1-64556-463-0

First Trade Paperback Printing March 2023
Printed in the United States of America

10 9 8 7 6 5 4 3 2 1

Distributed by Kensington Publishing Corp.
Submit Orders to:
Customer Service
400 Hahn Road
Westminster, MD 21157-4627
Phone: 1-800-733-3000
Fax: 1-800-659-2436

Prologue

At thirteen years old, Monica was already a very beautiful young lady, but the attention that she received was neither appropriate nor appreciated. She wanted to be a *good girl,* and to her, that meant good grades and faithful service in church. She had been elated when her parents coughed up the money for her to go on her church's teen retreat. Monica would have the chance to bond with girls her own age. At home, she only had her parents and her seven-year-old sister to associate with, so the retreat would be a nice getaway for the young girl.

Monica's parents were avid drug users, and it bothered her to no end, but at thirteen, there was very little that she could do. She obeyed her parents and did everything that was asked of her because her pastor had told her on many occasions that children are supposed to honor thy mother and father.

Monica was in her arts and crafts class when she heard her name bellowed across the loudspeaker. "Monica Dietrich to the chaplain's office, Monica Dietrich to the chaplain's office," the voice said.

Monica entered the chaplain's office, unaware of what lay ahead. She sauntered into the office and plopped down in the high-back leather chair, as she had done on numerous occasions.

"You called for me, sir?" she asked politely, looking around at the Christian artwork hanging on every wall.

"Yes, child. I called for you. Do you believe that the Lord loves you, Monica?"

"Yes, sir, I do."

"And do you believe that Jesus died for our sins so that we may have everlasting life?"

"Yes, I do, but—"

The preacher cut her off before she could finish. "I want to pray with you, Monica. Would that be okay?"

"Yes, sir, that's fine," she said as she dropped to her knees.

The chaplain came around his desk to join the young girl on her knees. "Lord, I ask that you put a veil of protection over this child. Lord, I ask that you work in her life . . ."

Monica's mind wasn't on prayer, though. She was anxious to know why the chaplain had called her to his office. They prayed enough during the day in groups for her to not need a private prayer session. She could only think of one reason why the pastor would call her into the office alone, and her stomach lurched.

As the man finished his prayer, Monica grasped his hand tightly. "Father, please tell me why you've called me here. We could have prayed anywhere. Is there something wrong?"

"There has been a tragedy, and you should thank the Lord that you were not there, child." The chaplain studied the girl's face. He could see the confusion in her expression, and his heart began to ache. "Have a seat, Monica."

She staggered back to her chair. "What kind of tragedy sir?"

"Your mother and your father both overdosed on drugs. There hasn't been much information released, but what I can tell you is that the police are actively searching for your little sister," he said.

"My little sister? What's happened to Jasmine?" she asked frantically.

"They don't know if she's been kidnapped, but she wasn't in the house when your parents' bodies were found," he said with an eerie calmness.

Monica's hands trembled, and she started to sweat. She stumbled and nearly lost her footing, but the Chaplain caught her. Monica wept quietly, unable to control the rumble in her chest. Although her sister annoyed her, she loved the little girl. Jasmine Dietrich was her heartstring, and she would do anything for the young girl. The thought of her baby sister missing filled Monica with a sense of dread.

"There will be a sheriff here to take you back to the city shortly. Take as much time as you need." The chaplain exited the office, closing the door behind him.

Monica sat and silently prayed that her sister was okay. Jasmine was a very innocent and sweet girl. Monica couldn't think of any reason why someone would want to kidnap her, unless her parents had gotten involved with the wrong people.

There was a light tap on the door, and Monica managed a weak, "Come in."

A female sheriff's officer entered the office and placed her hand on the young girl's shoulder. "Monica, I am Sheriff Harper. How are you holding up, baby?" Her tone was soft and caring, as if she was a mother herself who could sympathize with the grieving child.

"I'm okay. Miss Harper, can you tell me what happened?" Monica asked through her sobs.

"We will talk about it more when I take you to your grandfather. He is very anxious to see you, my love."

Sheriff Harper escorted the girl to her squad car and buckled her into the front seat. As they drove, the policewoman had a hard time telling the girl exactly what had happened to her parents and her sister. She wanted to do it in a tasteful way, but with the subject being as touchy as it was, that was going to be next to impossible.

"Baby, what I am about to tell you is a terrible, terrible thing, but I want you to know the truth. Your mother and father, as you have probably heard, died of drug overdoses."

Monica nodded but remained silent.

"Well, the drugs that they got were too strong, and they died. They were able to get those drugs by selling your little sister to the drug dealers. We found your little sister, but she's been badly hurt. She is in the hospital now with your grandfather," Officer Harper said.

Monica shrieked in horror. The policewoman reached across the seat and patted her knee.

"I'm sorry, honey."

They rode in silence except for Monica's quiet sobs.

Upon reaching Parkland Memorial Hospital, they entered through the emergency room. Her grandfather stood and greeted the pair as they rounded the corner. He embraced his granddaughter and tried to absorb her pain. He felt partly responsible for her loss, but mostly he blamed his no-good son-in-law. He had always felt that his daughter was too good for the man, but she was in love and couldn't be kept away from him. He cried with his oldest grandchild, his tears running down his cheeks into her long, wavy hair.

She looked up at her grandfather through teary eyes. "Pop Pop, where's Jazzy?"

"She was sleepin' last time I was in the room, baby. She ain't herself, though. It's like them devils sucked the soul right outta my Jazzy Bell." He shook his head.

Her grandfather pulled her closer. "Baby girl, I'ma always be in your corner. We can get past this mess that's been made. All we hafta do is have faith."

A portly nurse came into the waiting room. "The family of Jasmine Dietrich?" she said.

Monica and her grandfather braced for the worst. With the day going as badly as it started, another tragedy would kill them both.

"I'm her grandfather, and this is her sister."

"Well, sir, your granddaughter is still in a state of shock. We've had some of this hospital's best physicians examine her and there has been no change. She won't speak, or look at anyone. Maybe if she sees family it will pull her out of her trance. If we can't get her to come back to us, and our psychiatrists determine that the trauma she's suffered has caused irreparable damage, then she will be placed in the psychiatric ward of the Buckner Home for Youth until we can determine it's safe for her to return home."

Monica and her grandfather were led into the room where Jasmine lay in her hospital bed. Her face was badly bruised, and her eyes were hollow pits where her soul had once shined through. She lay on her back with her hands cupped across her stomach. She stared at the ceiling blankly, not blinking and not feeling.

Monica moved along the side of Jasmine's bed and took her hand. Their grandfather stood motionless on the other side of the bed, staring down at his granddaughter, his baby, his Jazzy Bell.

If I was younger, I'd kill those bastards myself, he thought.

"Jazzy, are you okay?" Monica asked, but there was no reply.

Her sister merely gazed out into space, no sign of life showing in her young face. The only indication of life within the girl was her shallow breathing and the slow, rhythmic up-and-down movement of her stomach.

"Jazzy Bell, it's Pop Pop, darling. I know you're in there. Come on back to us, baby," the old man pleaded.

Still there was no answer. Monica ran her little sister's hair through her fingers. She was angry, but at such a young age, unsure of whom that anger should be directed toward. She sighed in disbelief, looking at her sister. How could anybody hurt a child so beautiful?

Monica looked at her younger sister. If not for the age difference, they would have surely been twins. They were both gorgeous, a product of their white father and black mother, children of an interracial love that had produced a beautiful result.

Then, both sets of those jade green eyes interlocked as if in some kind of cosmic conversation. Jasmine held her sister's gaze as she clenched her hand, searching her eyes for comfort. Jasmine's green eyes formed puddles of lucid despair, calling silently, almost begging for an explanation. Finally, she spoke.

"Why did you let the bad men hurt me, Moni? You said you would protect me. Why did you let the bad men hurt me?" she asked over and over again, calmly at first, and then frantically, until her voice reached a feverish pitch. "Why did you let them hurt me, Monica?" she screamed.

The nurse rushed back into the room, accompanied by two male security guards to restrain the agitated little girl. Once they had her restrained and the family was safely out of the way, the nurse filled a syringe with haloperidol and thumped the cylinder violently to dissipate the air bubbles. She injected the tiny-framed girl, and almost instantly, the child fell silent.

Monica bent down over her sister and kissed her forehead. She could feel the slight heave of her chest and the soft whisper of her gentle breath. Monica silently promised her sister that someone would pay for what they had done to their family, and she meant to make good on that promise.

Chapter 1

Ten Years Later

Monica Dietrich had been voted the best and brightest to come out of Hampton University in the year of her graduation. She had finished four years of studying criminal justice, and she'd applied to both the Dallas Police Department and the Drug Enforcement Agency. Monica was accepted into the DEA, but not the DPD.

Now, at twenty-three years old, Monica sat in the waiting room of the DEA branch office in Dallas for a meeting that was long overdue. A thin but curvy brunette sat behind a desk, eyeing Monica curiously. She twirled a pencil between her brightly painted red fingernails as she tossed her long straight hair behind her shoulders. Monica wondered where the girl's ambitions lay. She was probably the type that thought a pretty face and cute smile meant that she was going somewhere, but unfortunately, that wasn't the case for most. From experience, Monica knew that hard work and dedication were the only things that definitively worked. Women historically needed to work twice as hard, if not harder, to achieve what men were granted free of charge.

The brunette's phone rang, momentarily snapping her out of her daydream. "Yes, sir, right away," she said. "Miss Dietrich, they will see you now." She walked around the desk and opened the door leading to the conference room.

Monica stepped into the room and was greeted by an elderly white man. He was sparsely built, only 5 feet 5 inches tall and maybe 140 pounds. His hair was graying, but it was surprisingly thick for his age. His skin was weathered from either too many days in the field or from too many minutes dedicated to a tanning bed. At any rate, his skin looked tough like leather.

Senior Agent Muldoon introduced each man seated in the room by their respective titles. Each agent present was senior in their respective divisions. The DEA; DPF; Bureau of Alcohol, Tobacco, Firearms, and Explosives; and Federal Bureau of Investigations all had officials present for the meeting, and that in itself made Monica antsy. She was beyond nervous, but she refused to let it show. This was the opportunity of a lifetime, and she wouldn't let a case of the jitters keep her from it. In every agency, there was always the star—that person that got the perfect case that would define their career, and Monica hoped that this would be that case for her.

"Okay, Agent Dietrich. You've met every agent here today, so let's cut to the chase. I want to explain what we are up against in dealing with this case. First of all, this is a joint effort, as you can see by the presence of multiple agencies. You were chosen not only for a certain level of brilliance, but, for a lack of a better phrase, your attributes," Muldoon said.

The small man dimmed the lights and started a projector. "This is Kochese Mills, also known as King. He owns and operates numerous drug houses throughout the Dallas metropolitan area, but his operation spans as far as Miami. His name has been mentioned in the investigation of at least ten murders, but we don't have enough evidence to convict this son of a bitch. He uses his legitimate businesses to try to mask his illegal empire. This is where you come in, Miss Dietrich."

Every agent present turned in unison to look at Monica. It made her fidget. She could tell by the stern faces present that this was her rising star, her *golden goose,* as they called it in the academy.

Muldoon turned the lights up and walked over to Monica and placed his hands on her shoulders. "Monica, you're one of the smartest and most gifted agents I have here in the DEA, but this is a very dangerous and sensitive case, so if you feel as though it's too much, I will completely understand."

Monica could hear the apprehension in his voice. He looked shaken, but it only served to heighten her curiosity. She did, however, wonder how many other young agents he had given that same lecture to.

"No, sir, I have no problems with it. I'm with you one hundred percent. What do I need to do?"

"Well, the problem is that every time we think that we are close to indicting him, our agent comes up missing. This time, we were able to flip a man inside of his organization. He is King's second in command, and although his intel has been invaluable to us, unfortunately, we cannot use his testimony. He is a convicted felon and an informant, and we cannot take the chance of King walking on a technicality."

Muldoon then walked over to another agent and whispered in his ear. The agent got up from his seat and disappeared into the hallway. He returned a few moments later with a young Black man in tow. If Monica had to guess, the man was no older than twenty-four or twenty-five years old. He was exceptionally handsome, except for the long scar creasing the length of his face. It started at his temple and ended at the corner of his mouth. He was tall and well built, 6 feet 4 inches, maybe 200 pounds. He had teenage-smooth skin, and the hair on his face had barely begun to grow. His hair was cropped short and faded.

Muldoon noticed the look of interest in the young woman's eyes and decided to quiet those interests before they started. "This is Calvin Bircher, aka Bird to those that know him, Agent Dietrich. He has been in King's organization for ten years, the last five of which he has held a position of prominence."

The lead agent for the FBI stood. "Between our surveillance of the suspect and Mr. Bircher's intel, we have amassed quite a profile, but it's just that: a profile. We have nothing concrete that will hold up in court."

"Again, where do I come in?" Monica asked. Her curiosity was piqued, and she wished they would get down to the meat of the situation.

"Gentlemen, if I may," Bird said to the agents. "I know this cat better than I know my own brother, and he has one weakness, and that weakness is bitches—pardon me, his weakness is women."

Monica didn't flinch. She was nobody's bitch, but she could be one if and when the need presented itself. The look that Monica shot Bird made him choose his next words carefully. Her green eyes burned through him angrily, and if looks could kill, he would've been dead.

"Listen, all I'm saying is that Kochese is a very private dude, and as close to him as I think I am, there are still things that he won't even put me down with. If anybody can get close to him, it'll have to be you," Bird said to Monica.

"And how do you propose that I do that, Mr. Bircher?" Monica asked sarcastically.

"You're the expert, Miss Dietrich. You tell me."

Agent Muldoon could see the fire in Monica's eyes. If Bird and Monica were going to work together, they would have to learn to get along. He would have to find a way to defuse the situation before it got out of hand.

"Monica, it's no accident that you were chosen for this assignment. Before you graduated from the academy, we were planning to bring you into this case. The truth of the matter is, in examining King's profile, we found that his taste in women matched your profile. Your body type, your skin tone, even down to your eye color."

"With all due respect, sir, don't you think King will get suspicious if, out of nowhere, his perfect woman comes strolling along?" she asked.

"Not really, because for months now, Bird has been talking to King about his cousin Monica, aka Money, coming down from North Carolina. When you make your appearance, King will already be expecting you," Muldoon said. "We have it set up where you will start low level in his organization and hopefully work your way up."

"So, you expect me to stand out on the corner and sell drugs?" Monica asked, surprised.

"In all actuality, Agent Dietrich, I expect you to do whatever is necessary to bring King down," Muldoon said. "If it takes selling drugs to do so, then so be it. If you have to kill to prove that you're down for him, so be it. If you have to smoke a joint, snort coke, or suck his dick in the back of a crowded theater, I expect you to do your job with no hesitation."

"You're basically telling me to compromise my integrity for the sake of winning a case, then?"

"No, I'm basically telling you to grow up. This case, our mission, is larger than any one person."

Monica sat, petrified by the thought of selling her soul for the sake of winning a case. She'd lived a life free of drugs and drama for as long as she could remember. Even after everything she had been through with her family, she had somehow come out on top. She had some heavy decision making to do, and it terrified her.

"If you don't mind, sir, I would like to take a little time to assess the situation and give it further thought."

The Senior Agent of the ATF had remained quiet during the whole meeting process, but now he addressed Monica directly. “Agent Dietrich, I can totally understand your apprehension. I’m sure these other gentlemen have read your file, as I have, so I can sympathize with your hesitation. However, keep in mind that this man is a cancer on our society, and his terror goes far beyond selling a few nickel and dime rocks on the corner. King has his hands in just about every aspect of illegal activity in Dallas and beyond. He is selling everything from marijuana to automatic weapons. This is the definition of a drug kingpin. Think of how many kids you could save if you bring this asshole down.”

“I will consider everything that I have heard today, sir. Thank you for your patience.”

“Well, it’s settled then. We will conclude this meeting until tomorrow, when, hopefully, Agent Dietrich will have good news for us,” Muldoon said.

Chapter 2

My Sister's Keeper

The next morning, Monica walked into the Buckner Home for Youth with a lot on her mind. Her little sister, now a teenager, had been in the youth home for ten years and still didn't show any signs of regaining her mental functions. The rape had caused mental damage to the young girl so severe that it baffled the psychiatrists working at the home. She was withdrawn and mute. She never spoke again after that tragic day ten years earlier. Her daily routine was always the same. She would walk to the window, sit down in a chair, and rock.

As Monica made her way down the long hallway, her high-heeled Prada shoes clicked and clacked against the immaculately polished tile floors. As she neared the front desk, she greeted a young nurse, who seemed to always be on duty when she came to visit.

"Hey, Miss Dietrich, good morning. How are you today?" the nurse sang.

She was a little too chipper for Monica's particular taste, but Monica managed a "Thank you, likewise," to not seem rude.

The nurse escorted Monica to the recreation room of the youth home where her sister waited for her. The recreation room wasn't a recreation room at all, though. It was more of a room filled with lifeless zombies. The assortment of kids ranged in age from as young as eleven all the way to eighteen. Children milled about voiceless, some playing checkers, some playing cards, but most of them sat quietly roaming inside of their own heads.

Jasmine sat alone on the window sill, clutching a plush blanket, staring blankly into the forest below. Monica placed her hand gently on her sister's shoulder.

"Jazzy," she said softly, but the girl didn't move. She took a seat in front of her sister and took her hand. To see Jasmine unresponsive was devastating. Monica felt helpless because no matter how hard she tried, she could not bring Jasmine back to the lively girl that she had once been.

She grabbed her sister's hand and led her to a nearby couch. Monica removed a brush from her purse and brushed Jasmine's hair. Even in her current condition, she was still beautiful. Her hair hung in unkempt silky locks that flowed past her frail shoulders. As she brushed Jasmine's hair, she talked to her sister as she always had. It was more venting than actual conversation. Monica hoped to free the girl from her mental prison.

"So, I made it into the DEA, and my first big case is bringing down some mega kingpin. I think that I can handle it, though. I am going to use my position to make those grimy drug dealers pay, sis. I'm going to get some payback for Mommy and Daddy. What do you think?" She waited for a reply. "Hopefully when you're better, you will be able to come and live with me. Would you like that?"

Out of the corner of her eye, she saw the nurses pushing the pill carts. *That's probably why she's like this; because they are pumping her full of pills.*

Monica looked at her sister affectionately. Jasmine was the only family that she had left. Her grandfather had smoked for as long as she could remember, and cancer had taken him hard and quick. She'd watched him waste away to nothing. A once burly man of more than 200 pounds had dwindled to less than 130 by the time he died.

Monica kissed her sister on her forehead and took her face into her hands. "I love you, Jasmine Dietrich. Don't you ever forget that."

Monica stood to leave, but Jasmine wouldn't release her hand. Jasmine stood up and wrapped her arms around Monica's neck. She didn't utter a word, but this was more progress than her sister had made in her entire stay at the youth home. Monica was beyond surprised.

"I will never give up on you, Jazzy. Trust and believe." She kissed her sister again and walked away.

Monica was sad to leave her, but she was excited to share the news with Jasmine's doctor. She made the short trek to his office and tapped lightly at his door. The doctor stood as Monica entered.

"Monica, so nice to see you. How are things?" he asked politely.

"Things are great, Dr. Myers. I was hoping that we could discuss Jasmine's progress."

"By all means, please have a seat."

"Do you have any idea when Jazz might be going home with me?"

"Well, Monica, as soon as Jasmine shows some real progress, I don't see that being a problem. Emotionally, I want to let her go home immediately, but clinically, I have a moral obligation to Jasmine and my profession to make sure that she's well before I release her."

"That's understood. What if I told you that she hugged me today and wouldn't release my hand?"

The doctor looked at Monica in dazed astonishment. He'd been working with Jasmine for the entire time she'd been there, and she hadn't once shown any progress. "If this is true, then this would be just the break that we have been looking for! Let's keep working with her and experimenting with dosages until we get her completely stable. I'm not convinced just yet. Let's see if a new regimen will open her up more."

"Maybe we should try that then, Dr. Myers."

The doctor stood up as if to excuse Monica from his presence and extended his hand. "That is exactly what we will do then."

Monica smiled weakly at the doctor. It sounded good, almost too good to be true, but anything was worth a shot. She shook his hand and exited his office. The next stop on her agenda was the DEA headquarters to let Agent Muldoon know that she was most definitely going to take the assignment.

Monica drove the short distance to the DEA office. She parked in the underground parking garage and sat in her car, quietly thinking. This was a life-changing decision for the young agent, but she was up for the challenge.

Monica smiled to herself. Going undercover, especially with this case, was going to be very interesting. The only thing that weighed heavily on her mind was the fact that once she went undercover, she wouldn't be able to spend as much time with Jasmine. It was going to be a necessary sacrifice to do what she deemed as her calling.

As she exited the elevator and entered the reception area, the brunette secretary looked at Monica as though she was her biggest fan. The young receptionist now seemed to have a newfound respect for the agent.

"They have been expecting you, Miss Dietrich," she said anxiously.

Monica walked through the doors of the office and greeted Muldoon. Every agent that had been there the previous day was present for the new meeting. Bird was there as well. He sat leaning in the leather chair, not showing any sign of emotion.

As she made her way to her seat, Monica could feel the eyes of the men in the room glued to her. They were waiting anxiously for Monica's decision. If she refused to take the case, then they would have to return to the drawing board to formulate another plan. The success of their case depended on Monica's cooperation.

"Miss Dietrich, I'm sure that I speak for everyone here when I say that we are very anxious to hear what decision you've made," Muldoon said.

"Well, Senior Agent, I have decided to take the case. I believe that I can truly be an asset in this particular case, and I am looking forward to doing my part to bring Kochese Mills to justice."

An air of excitement floated through the room. The sound of papers being shuffled could be heard over the whispers and muffled applause. Bird nodded his head in approval. He was happy that Monica had taken the assignment. He would finally get the chance to get rid of King Kochese. He had been working for the man for the last ten years, and he wanted out. He had all the money he needed, but King's organization didn't have a retirement plan. You worked until you were either killed or you caught a case. In some instances, if you caught a case, you were killed to silence you anyway, so it was a no-win situation in King's camp. If King was indicted, Bird had plans to move somewhere far away with his money and never step foot inside Dallas city limits again.

"This is very exciting news, Agent Dietrich," Muldoon said. "Let us begin with the case prep, shall we?"

The ATF agent said, "I don't think you understand how big of an asset you are in this case, Monica. If you pull this off, I'm sure there is a promotion on the horizon for you. Would you agree, Agent Muldoon?"

Muldoon smiled at Monica, who understood that a lot was riding on her undercover work, and she was more than excited about getting started. Agent Muldoon gave everyone present a file marked CONFIDENTIAL in red lettering. They went over the file with laser focus, line by line. The agents discussed Kochese's likes and dislikes, his tastes in women, where he went, what he ate, when he showered, and more. For hours, they talked about the suspect and the best way to execute their plan. By the time they were finished, Monica had transformed herself into Money, the streetwise, drug-dealing hood chick from North Carolina.

"If you don't mind me asking, Bird, what's in this for you?" Monica asked.

"Nah, it's no problem, Money. I'm tired of sellin' fuckin' drugs. I want a normal life, and Kochese isn't willing to let that happen. I remember when I graduated from high school a few years back and Kochese took me to Pappadeaux Restaurant for dinner. He rented a VIP dinner suite and everything. He asked me what my plans were now that I'd graduated, and I told him I was planning to go to college and then play a little ball overseas. Ruthless muhfucka looked at me and smiled, stood up, walked up behind me, and cut my fuckin' face from my lip to my temple. He tossed me a goddamned napkin and told me to clean myself up. He sat across from me while I was bleedin' like a muhfucka and continued eating his bloody-ass steak like nothing had happened.

"After he finished eating, he took me to the hospital. The whole ride, he kept mumbling about how this family was a marriage and wasn't no divorces and all that. The nigga's a killer, and I for one won't be sad to see his heartless ass leave the game. That is what's in it for me, Money. I'm done. I want out."

Monica gained a measure of respect for the young man. It wasn't often that a drug dealer, especially a successful drug dealer, chose to get out of the game. He had made his mistakes and wanted a different life, which was to be commended.

"I'm sorry that happened to you, Bird. We will get this son of a bitch. I promise. I'm not sure what kind of deal you've made, but if you hold up on your end, I will most definitely do my part. I'm all in."

Bird nodded. He knew that it was a very risky and dangerous deal, but he had faith in Monica. She seemed as though she was really passionate about the case.

"Kochese don't trust nan muhfucka, so we are gonna hafta time this shit just right. You will have to go to North Carolina and ride the bus back just to cover our tracks, because knowing him, he will have someone watching me when I come to pick you up. If I pick you up from some random location around town, he will get suspicious. You can stay with me for a little while until you find a place."

Monica took in everything that he said and nodded. Muldoon slid a manila envelope across the table to Monica. Inside was a fake North Carolina driver's license for Monica Bircher. There was also a cell phone and $10,000 for expenses.

"Miss Dietrich, are you ready to take this asshole down?" Muldoon asked.

"You muhfuckin' right, daddy. I'ma have his bitch ass sprung on dis good pussy in no time," Monica said as she winked at Muldoon.

An eruption of hearty laughter pierced the room. With Monica's level of intelligence, everyone present knew that she was stepping into her role to demonstrate her level of expertise in the field of undercover work. She had taken her role on full steam. Or, as Monica put it, she was *all in*.

Chapter 3

King Kochese

Kochese Mills knew he was a handsome man, but handsome didn't play into his personality. He used his looks for one thing and one thing only, and that was to bed women. Everything else about him was gangster, and he liked that. From the way he dressed to the way he carried himself, he was a true thug. He had expensive tastes in everything that he did. From cars to women, his preferences were exquisite, but he never hesitated when it came to pulling the trigger.

Kochese took pleasure in his ruthless reputation. It was indeed true that nice guys finished last, because he was the world's biggest asshole, and it paid very well. He had amassed a fortune due in part to the fact that he was known to pop that tool. Even if the mood struck him to not shoot, he could always hire someone to do the shooting for him. He paid his workers extremely well, and they wouldn't give it a second thought if he asked. Some of them would do it out of respect and loyalty, some of them would do it because of the desperate need to impress Kochese, but ultimately, they all did it for the money.

His contracts never started below $10,000 and could exceed $150,000 depending on the target. At certain times, he would just pay to have a man kidnapped and brought to him for the mark's disposal. Today was one of those times. H had given a half kilo front to Shawt Dawg and hadn't had a return on his money after three months. He had tried to be understanding with Shawt Dawg, but the streets didn't lie, and Shawt Dawg had been talking reckless in the streets. Kochese was a reasonable man, and all Shawt Dawg had to do was come to him and make some type of arrangement, but he had been dodging Kochese, and that angered the man.

At six feet even, 230 pounds, Kochese wasn't a little man, but he was borderline pretty, and it was often taken for weakness. He was the son of a prostitute, and Kochese had never known his father because he was a trick baby. Kochese had long, wavy hair that lay in layers all the way past his shoulders. He kept it in a long ponytail. His eyes were ice blue, and his pupils were irregularly large and black, making him look like a cat.

He was fair-skinned, and people had often mistaken Kochese for Hispanic, but in his mind, he was all black. He hated his white roots because of the way he had been conceived. He felt like his bloodline had been tainted by his sperm donor, and he wanted no part of it.

These fools can take me for weak if they wanna. I murder niggas for sport, he thought.

Enough thinking. He had business to handle. One of his goons had hit him on his cell and told him that they'd caught up with Shawt Dawg.

"Hold that bitch nigga at the spot. I will be there shortly!" Kochese barked into the phone.

Minutes later, he pulled into King's Korner, the strip mall that he owned. It housed an assortment of businesses: a beauty shop, barber shop, liquor store, storage unit, nail salon, corner store, and a couple of clothing stores. In the back of the strip mall was his pride and joy, a massive 5,000-square-foot warehouse that housed his prized pedigree pit bulls. He called it King's Kennel.

He pulled his black Range Rover around the building and parked among the assortment of cars. The chrome on the rims shone brightly against the candy paint and low-profile tires. King Kochese stepped out of the Range and smoothed the ruffles out of his crisp white T-shirt.

Kochese was a gangster's gangster. He kept his dress code simple, but his jewelry was a different matter. Kochese wore a white diamond-encrusted crown charm with the word *KING* in blue diamonds, hanging from a diamond chain that almost reached his waist. He also wore matching diamond pinky rings on his pinkies. A diamond watch on his left wrist and a diamond bracelet on his right wrist completed his ensemble. He stayed icy, and he dared anybody to try to get his jewelry because he kept his .45 Desi close by. Plus, he was well-known and well-liked because he didn't mind taking care of his people. Anybody could go to Kochese, and he would look out for them at any given time.

Kochese walked around to the back of his Range Rover and lifted the back hatch. He put a leash on his best friend, a muscular albino pit bull named Noisy Boy. The dog was snow white. The only color present was in his eyes. They held the exact same bluish hue as King Kochese's. The dog was a trained killer. No one could get close to his master unless invited by Kochese. He kept his dog spoiled. Noisy Boy sported a diamond-encrusted collar, and his fangs were 18K gold.

Kochese walked into the kennel amped. He had been waiting to catch up with Shawt Dawg. Now that his boys had him, he wanted to see if the man would still talk reckless in his face.

The sound of barking and growling put Noisy Boy on high alert. King could see the tension in the dog's body. His sinuous muscles flexed as if he were readying himself for attack. To calm him, King kneeled and stroked Noisy Boy's back from head to tail.

"Shhh. Cool down, big daddy. You're good. Chill, my dude, chill," he said to his puppy.

King undid the leash to let the dog run freely about the warehouse. Noisy Boy walked slowly from cage to cage, inspecting its occupants carefully. He knew that he was the alpha dog, but he was always on the lookout for a bitch in heat.

"So, where is this pussy Shawt Dawg?" King said loudly.

One of King's young soldiers chimed in, "We got this roach over here chained up, King." It was Lucky, a short, dark kid who wore too much jewelry for King's taste, but the boy was extremely loyal. He had been with King since he was ten years old. At fourteen, he had taken five slugs that were meant for King, but the boy hadn't died, and since that day, everyone had started calling him a little lucky motherfucker, so the nickname stuck.

As Kochese got closer, he could see that his boys had stripped Shawt Dawg down to his boxers. They had taken one of his socks and shoved it in his mouth to muffle his screams. He was chained as though he were about to be crucified, spreadeagle and suspended in midair.

Kochese walked up to the man as his boys stood around watching, wondering what their leader's next move would be.

"So, what's good, my nigga? Word on the street is you've been talkin' reckless as a muhfucka," Kochese said.

The man mumbled, trying to plead his case.

"What's that? I can't hear you, fuck boy. Say it again."

The change in Kochese's tone made Noisy Boy run to his side and immediately start to growl viciously.

"Take that gag out of his muhfuckin' mouth so he can tell me something," Kochese ordered. Another one of his boys walked up and snatched the sock out of the terrified man's mouth.

"King, man, I been tryna find you, dawg. I-I-I—" Shawt Dawg stuttered.

"Nigga, you's a goddamned lie. I been hittin' your cell, hittin' all of your spots, and you been straight dodging a nigga. So what up, Shawt? Where's my paper, mane?" Kochese asked. His words dripped venom.

Shawt Dawg knew that even if he had Kochese's money, he would kill him on principle anyway. He didn't have the money, though. He had tricked it off, trying to be a baller. He had gotten so caught up with trying to impress the strippers at Club Concise that before he knew it, he had spent all of the profit. Shawt Dawg had tried to get the money back by flipping what he owed King, but it hadn't worked out as planned. He had to toss the dope to keep from catching a case.

"King, we go way back, man. I had to toss the dope to keep from bein' jammed up, dawg. Straight up!" Shawt Dawg said anxiously.

King examined the man's face carefully. Either he was extremely stupid, or he thought that King was a fool.

"Nah, bitch nigga, I'ma tell you what happened," Kochese said. "Your punk ass was going to the strip club, trickin' my fuckin' money off. You got caught up in trying to look like you had paper instead of staying in your fuckin' lane gettin' money. You woke up one morning and realized that King was gonna kill your bitch ass, and you decided to hide for a little minute. Your dumb ass obviously don't pay attention in the streets, 'cause if you did, then you would know that nothing happens in these muhfuckin' streets without King knowing about it, my nigga."

"Kochese, I swear on my mama, dawg, I didn't trick your money off. I'ma get that paper for you, man. I swear!" Shawt Dawg begged.

"Nah, you're good, playa. Don't even worry about that paper. I don't want it, nigga. I want your life."

Kochese looked at the man curiously. He couldn't understand why people couldn't just stay loyal and do their part. Shawt Dawg had been on his ass when he came to King, begging for him to give him a front. He hated fronting dope, but he understood Shawt Dawg's dilemma. He was fresh out of prison, and before he'd gone in, he had been "that nigga." When he got out, he'd come straight to King. Kochese had offered to give him his own block, but Shawt Dawg wanted to control his own shit and be his own boss. King was reluctant but had agreed.

"Don't fuck my money up, Shawt Dawg. Any problems, let me know and we will handle it, but I want my bread come hell or high water," King had said to him.

"Nigga, I'm a thoroughbred. I got this. I will move this shit in a few weeks and be copping kilos from you in no time," Shawt Dawg answered enthusiastically.

Now they were in King's warehouse, and Shawt Dawg was begging for his life.

"Kochese man, please! How long have we known each other, my brother? You know I'm good for it, man."

Kochese laughed loudly. "Why is it that when niggas know that they've fucked up, they want to be your brother? Nigga, you ain't my goddamned brother!" King spat vehemently.

The sound of the front door opening caught King's attention. He turned to see Bird coming through the entryway. His facial expression said that he wasn't pleased with Bird's tardiness. He turned his attention back to Shawt Dawg.

"I ain't gonna kill you, my nigga. Stop cryin' like a little bitch," he said. King could see the relief in the young man's face. "Let this pussy down and throw him in the cage with Beast!"

Lucky lowered the chains, and two soldiers snatched Shawt Dawg up and tossed him into the chain-link tomb with Beast. The sounds of Shawt Dawg's horrified screams could be heard as Beast ripped into his exposed flesh.

"Oh my God!" Shawt Dawg screamed in terror as Beast bit a chunk out of his thigh.

"That's right, nigga. Call on him. Maybe God will save you, 'cause I ain't," King said as he turned to leave.

The massive dog devoured the first few bites of the man quickly, but grew tired of Shawt Dawg squirming and fighting and went for his throat.

"Ple—" was all that he was able to get out before his world went black.

Bird was so used to seeing the scenario that it didn't even bother him anymore.

"Where the fuck you been, nigga? I've been trying to get hold of you since noon," King said to him.

"Man, my little cousin will be here tonight, so I went to the mall tryna get some shit to make sure she's comfortable when she gets here."

"Oh, okay. I forgot you told me your fam was coming down. What's the plan?"

"I guess I'ma hafta put her on my squad. I keep tryna tell her to model or some shit and leave these streets alone, but she a hustler, mane. She want that fast paper."

"A model, huh? Damn, she bad enough to be a model?"

"Man, not on no incest shit, but my little cousin badder than a muhfucka. If she wasn't my cousin, it'd be on and popping," Bird said.

"What time are you s'posed to pick her up?"

"Her bus comes in from North Carolina tonight at nine o'clock, but I will have my cell with me if you need me, my nigga."

"That's what's up. Handle your business. And Bird?"

“Yeah, Kochese, what’s happening?”

“You can put your cousin on, but if she fucks up my paper, nigga, it’s your debt. You know how I feel about that family in the workplace bullshit.”

“Yeah, I know, my nigga. She straight, though. I wouldn’t be puttin’ her down if she wasn’t ’bout that life.”

King led Bird to his office. Bird took a seat on the overstuffed plush burgundy leather couch as King walked to a huge safe behind his desk. He started the combination and looked back over his shoulder to make sure Bird was still seated. King opened the safe and pulled out two perfectly wrapped kilos of cocaine.

“I need you to deliver these two chickens, Bird. One of them is for Junior and his squad, the other one is for Nay. Nay and her little Bad Bitch Clique running through a kilo every two days. Shit, you might wanna consider puttin’ your little cousin on her team. Them hoes getting paper over there, nigga.”

“I don’t know yet. We will see how shit goes. They pretty tight with their squad. Introducing an outsider might upset their flow, you feel me?”

“Yeah, I feel you, and you’re right. I’m making too much paper with these hoes to have shit fucked up. Besides, if you put her with Nay and she as bad as you say, Nay gonna eat that pussy up. I think that dyke bitch gets more pussy than me.”

Both men laughed at the thought. Most people didn’t even know Nay was a woman unless they *knew* her. She was good for King’s business, though. Her money was always right, and she ruled over the females that worked for her with unbridled brutality.

“All right, nigga. I’ma go and make these deliveries and then do my pickups,” Bird said. “If that little nigga Corey short this time when I go pick up, how do you want me to handle it?”

"Like I would, fool," King said, laughing.

Bird nodded and left the office. He walked outside into the warm May sun. He hit the auto start on his white BMW 750i and felt a cold chill run down his spine. His Spidey senses were tingling like someone was watching him. He turned to see Kochese standing in his upstairs office window, staring down at him.

This evil-ass muhfucka creeps me the fuck out. Nigga hate every goddamn body, Bird thought as he got into his car. He cranked his system up as he backed out of the parking space. He had a nasty stereo system and knew it. With four 15-inch i-pipe woofers in the trunk, his mids and highs were sick, and he always played the videos that went with the song so that his screens in the headrests were on. The system boomed and clicked.

I'm on my New York shit; I think I'm hot, son. White girl starin' at me, lookin' like she lost sum'n, Plies rapped as Bird peeled out from the strip mall.

King watched the man drive away and shook his head. He had a certain amount of respect and love for Bird, but he wouldn't hesitate to dead his ass if Bird got out of line. He knew his protégé wanted out of the game, but why he wanted to leave when there was so much money to get confused King.

He shrugged as he sat down behind his desk. He pulled a blunt from a cigar box on his desk and lit it. As he leaned back in his leather chair, he smiled.

Shit, the nigga can get out whenever he wants, but the only way out is in a body bag, he thought as the potent hydro smoke filled his lungs and swirled about the room in grayish-white clouds.

Chapter 4

Birds of a Feather

Bird drove toward the small dope house on Collins Avenue. Nay had trap houses all over the east side of Dallas. The neighborhood was gang-infested, but Nay didn't gangbang. She was strictly about her money. The only color that mattered to the lesbian was green, and Bird liked that.

When Bird pulled up, Nay stood on the steps of the tiny wood frame house, spitting some of her best game to a young girl who couldn't have been any older than eighteen.

"What it do, Bird?" Nay said. "But yeah, baby girl, like I was saying, if you let me suck that pussy, I guarantee you won't never want another dick. I'm gettin' money. You need to let a bitch spoil you."

"Unh-uh, I'm strictly dickly. I don't get down like that," the girl said. "I'm just over here waitin' on my cousin."

"Yeah, that's cool. I'm just saying a nigga don't know what your body needs like another woman know, baby. Don't knock it 'til you try it," Nay said flirtatiously.

"Yeah, I hear you, Nay," the girl said, trying not to show her frustration with the subject.

The teenager's cousin walked out of the house, moving quickly. The girl fell into stride right behind the young man as they made their way down Collins Avenue headed toward Lagow Road.

"Bird, my nigga, what brings you my way?" Nay asked, knowing full well what Bird was doing there.

"I got that work. You got them ends?" Bird said.

"Yeah, hell yeah, fa sho. Come inside," she said, holding the screen door open for him. "Man, we can't keep enough of this shit around here for these dope fiends, Bird. King tell you we running through two keys a week?"

"Yeah, he told me that shit today. You making some major moves, huh?" Bird asked.

"Oh, hell yeah. Shit, I'm 'bout a dollar, bruh. Believe that."

"That's what's good. Shit, the nigga King is thoroughly impressed. Here's a chicken. We are scoring some more shit tonight, so I should have another one for you by tomorrow evening."

"No doubt. Say, bitch, go get that paper," Nay said to a petite, brown-skinned girl. Then she said to Bird, "I got sixty stacks from those last two thangs, mane."

Bird simply nodded. There was no need to count it because Nay was never short with her count.

A short time later, the girl emerged from a back room carrying a Louis Vuitton duffle bag stuffed with money. Nay looked at the girl with angry eyes.

"Man, you hoes slipping, mama. I told you to bundle that bread up. It better all be there, too, or we gonna have a major problem," Nay said.

This bitch must be new, Bird thought, because none of the girls he'd met that worked for Nay would've dared to suck their teeth and roll their eyes at her.

"Sorry about that shit, Bird. I can bundle this shit up if you need me to, though."

"Nah, you're straight. I still got another drop to make," Bird said as he gave Nay dap on his way out of the house.

He tossed the duffle bag into the trunk and sped off. His next pickup was clear across town. He drove down the highway, careful to obey the speed limit.

Bird pulled into a gated community, parked just outside the gate, and called Junior from his cellphone. "Hey, Junior, it's Bird. Open the gate, dawg," Bird said into the receiver.

A few seconds later, the gate slid open, revealing plush landscaping and manicured lawns. Junior had the white clientele in Mesquite, Texas, on lock. He didn't even bother to sell rocks. He went through a kilo a week just moving powder to the rich doctors and lawyers in the suburbs.

The wealthy social elite loved to do blow. To them, it was a status symbol. Crack, in their eyes, was a poor person's drug. They drove expensive cars and held down prestigious positions but were more of dope fiends than the average crackhead walking the block.

Their children were an altogether different matter. The kids would do any drug that they could get their anxious little hands on—X, crack, meth, powder, oxy, roxies, percs. It didn't matter. They just wanted a high, and Junior was more than happy to supply their every need. The young white girls would do anything for a high, and Junior pushed the limits trying to see just how far they would go.

Bird rang the doorbell to Junior's house, impatiently waiting for the man to answer. He curiously glanced at his watch, wondering why it was taking him so long. He knew that Bird was on his way up, so why not be waiting at the door? Alarms in Bird's head started to sound, wondering if Junior was trying to set him up, until the front door opened and two young white girls came strolling past. Junior stood in the doorway in his boxer shorts.

"Aye, y'all need to come back later on and holla at me. We gonna have a party," Junior said slyly. "Bird, c'mon in, mane. Sorry 'bout that shit, bro. Them little hoes freaky as a muhfucka, dawg. The blonde one is nineteen.

The other one is her sister, man. Today her eighteenth birthday. That bitch's pussy tight as a muhfucka." Junior massaged his crotch, obviously still aroused by the thought.

"Man, I don't wanna hear 'bout your sexual conquests, nigga. We got business to attend."

"All right, man. Let me throw something on, dawg. You need to lighten up, my nigga. All work and no play makes Bird a boring muhfucka, mane."

"Yeah, whatever. Just get that paper together. Aye, you talked to that little nigga Corey?"

"Nah, I ain't seen him lately, bro. Why?" Junior yelled from another room.

"I just asked. Look out, hurry up, man. I got shit to do."

Junior emerged with a large brown paper sack filled with money. "I put that shit in thousand-dollar stacks just the way King likes it, man. I'ma need some more X pills, too, man, so when you bring me my re-up, keep that in mind. I think a thousand tabs should be okay. That right there is thirty thousand dollars." Junior stood proudly. He didn't sell much crack, but he held his own selling everything else. There was nothing that King could give him that he couldn't sell.

"I'm on top of it, man. It's a thousand tabs, a kilo, and five pounds of 'dro in that duffle. Do I need to count this bread?"

"Don't even try me like that, nigga." Junior laughed. "I might trick off with these hoes, but I'm 'bout my business."

The men gave each other dap as Bird left. He had a few more pickups to make before he went to the bus station to pick up Monica. As he drove, he wondered whether she could handle it. He didn't know anything about Monica, but he did know King, and if the kingpin suspected for one second that Monica was anything besides a hustling country girl, he wouldn't hesitate to have both her and Bird murdered.

She *was* fine, though. There was no denying that. Bird had been with a lot of women in his short twenty-five years, but he had never been even remotely close to a woman as fine as Monica. Everything about her was official. She was sexy and she was smart. The latter was a definite plus, but King was nobody's dummy. If the plan was going to work, she would have to bring her A-game.

As Bird turned onto Grand Avenue, he thought about how much he hated this part of South Dallas. It had an overabundance of dope fiends, and the neighborhood hustlers were still in the stone ages. It didn't matter what kind of car rolled up; they had the same routine. They would run up to the car, waiting for a person to roll the window down, and when the driver *did* roll his window down, the dealers would all thrust their hands into the car as if begging the driver to choose *their* rocks. The thought made Bird cringe.

Everywhere he looked, he saw trash. It was bad at night, but in the daytime, it was worse. Broken bottles and paper littered the streets, dope fiends wandered about aimlessly looking for their next hit, and the police patrolled the streets as if enforcing martial law.

Bird parked his car near Corey's front door. He would have Corey come outside. There was no way he was leaving his car unattended in this neighborhood with all of the money he had in his trunk. He knocked and waited.

Corey came out looking nervous and paranoid. His eyes were bloodshot red, and he smelled as though he hadn't showered in days.

"What up, Corey? Come outside, dawg," Bird said.

Corey looked around warily. He was grinding on his teeth so hard Bird swore he could hear it.

"Bird, what's up, boss? What's good?" Corey asked.

Something in the youngster's demeanor made Bird suspicious. He was fidgety and agitated, as if he had gotten hold of something that he shouldn't have.

"You got that paper, Corey man?" Bird knew exactly what his response would be.

"I got some of it, Bird. Man, you ain't gonna believe this shit, dawg," Corey said excitedly. The boy was scratching and shifting from foot to foot. He launched into world-class game. "Man, you 'member my dopefiend-ass cousin Nikki? Yeah, man, that bitch ran off with all my shit! I been looking for that ho, man. Soon as I find her, she gonna hafta see about me, dawg. So, it's gonna take me a little time, but I'ma get that paper to you soon."

Bird pulled out his pistol and put it in the boy's face. "Nigga, you think I'm stupid? You smoked that work, fool. That's why you're tweakin' and shit. Why you playin' with me about this nigga King's fetti?"

Corey couldn't think of anything remotely effective to say. He just hoped that Bird wouldn't kill him. He never meant to start smoking, had only tried it to prove that the smoker controlled the high, not the other way around, and he had been sorely mistaken. Corey had instantly fallen in love with the crack-induced high. Now it would more than likely cost him his life.

Bird slapped Corey across the bridge of his nose violently with his gun. Blood gushed from the gaping wound as Corey sank to his knees. Bird hit him again, this time on the top of his head with the butt of the pistol.

He kneeled down next to Corey and whispered in his ear, "You got a week, Corey. Heaven can't hide you, playboy, if you don't have that cheese."

Bird wiped the blood from his pistol onto the boy's tattered shirt. He hopped off of the porch and jumped into his BMW. He only had twenty minutes to make it downtown to pick up Monica, but he couldn't rush because he still had a trunk full of drug money.

Bird reached the Greyhound bus station ten minutes late. He parked and put two quarters in the meter and walked toward the entrance of the bus station. Monica was standing outside, leaning against the wall. The streetlight above her head made Monica's skin glow, and Bird was taken aback by her appearance. When they'd first met, she was all business in a gray business suit, flat black shoes, and her hair in an updo. Now she looked like a woman straight out of a rap video. She was gorgeous, and the shorts that she wore made Bird's nature rise. Monica had on a half tee with the word *JUICY* in green gemstones that seemed to hug her ample breasts perfectly. She wore her hair in a perfect ponytail, save for a lone curl hanging in front. She wore white shorts with green stitching that accentuated her curvy body.

Monica noticed Bird staring at her and turned to walk in his direction. Her shorts were so tight that it looked as though her coochie was balled up in a knot inside her shorts. Bird watched as she strutted toward him, her hips swaying seductively as if some invisible melody were playing in her head. Monica was perfectly manicured and pedicured.

Goddamn, she got some pretty-ass feet, Bird thought.

Monica had gone so far as to have her navel pierced with a diamond stud. She was playing the sexy hood rat to the tee, and it turned Bird on.

"Hey, cuzz!" Monica said loudly as she thrust her arms around Bird's neck. His arousal was evident as Monica pressed her body firmly against his manhood. "You're going to have to learn to control your little friend if we're supposed to be cousins, Bird," she whispered as she took a step back.

"What up, cuzzo? Did you have a safe trip?" he said, trying hard to hide his embarrassment. Bird picked up Monica's luggage and headed toward his car.

King, true to form, had sent his head henchman, Drak, to keep an eye on Bird and his cousin. Drak sat a block away, facing the couple. King had given him a T.O.S.—terminate on sight—order, if everything didn't seem to be on the up and up.

There was nothing out of the ordinary about the meeting. Just two cousins greeting one another. Drak hissed and sighed. He was somewhat disappointed by the boring reunion. Disappointment aside, the only news that he had to report to King was how absolutely fine Bird's cousin was. Drak put his '77 Glasshouse Impala into drive and sped off toward King's estate.

Once Bird and Monica were in his car safely on their way to his condo, he relaxed.

"You know we were being watched, right?" Bird asked.

"Yeah, I figured as much. I think we did pretty good. I mean, except for your dick getting hard."

"Whatever. Shit, you're the one that got off of the bus with them little-bitty-ass coochie cutters on."

"If I'd have known we weren't going to King's, I would've worn something entirely different. Trust me."

"Oh, trust and believe me, as soon as Drak gets to King's crib, he will give him a full report on how fuckin' sexy you are," Bird said.

"You think I'm sexy? Well, that's not how cousins see each other, so you need to dead that shit 'cause ain't no incest shit going on over here, playboy," Monica said. They both laughed as if a joke was told between old friends.

The condominium exceeded Monica's expectations. She didn't expect Bird to live like a peasant, but she hadn't expected to pull up in a complex in Thousand Oaks either. The Dallas Cowboys practiced in the area, and outside of well-to-do professionals, most people simply couldn't afford to live there.

“Damn, cuzz, this is nice,” Monica said.

“You must have thought I was a scrub or something,” Bird said jokingly.

She didn’t think that he was a scrub, but she had mixed emotions about the subject. The low-level dope boys never wanted to leave the hood. The big boys and kingpins got major money in the hood but felt that because they removed themselves from the ghetto, they were somehow untainted. It was better for their egos when they didn’t have to bear the guilt of seeing the destruction that they caused firsthand.

Bird unlocked the door to his condo and walked inside. He loved his place. It was his fortress of solitude. He owned it outright and took great pride in his financial accomplishments. He took solace in knowing that he was the king of his castle, and inside the walls of his home, he answered to no one.

“Since we are going to be roomies, let me show you around the place,” Bird said.

Bird started in the living room. It was huge, and the theme screamed Euro-chic. It was a mixture of earth tones throughout, with oddly shaped furniture accented by deep curves and soft edges. A 60-inch flat panel television was recessed into the far wall. To Monica, it looked remarkably like a large portrait.

He directed Monica to the kitchen. It was also very large, almost too large for a bachelor always on the go. The appliances were stainless steel, which only served to bring out the beauty of the marble countertops and backsplash. Monica fell in love with the kitchen instantly.

Bird then took Monica into his bedroom. She stepped inside and let out an audible gasp. His room was beyond gorgeous. His carpet was white mink, and the bed would easily sleep six people. There was a white European-inspired couch tucked neatly in a corner of the bedroom facing the bed. On the opposite side of the room was an in-ground Roman tub that was both deep and spacious. A terrazzo tile walkway framed the tub, with a path leading from the tub to the bathroom. There were black and white still-life photos on every wall. What struck Monica as both unique and odd was that although the poster-sized photos were black and white, there was a splash of red in every picture. Whether it was the lips of the women or an article of clothing, the only color visible was a vibrant red.

"Are you a gang member or something, Bird?" Monica asked.

"Nah," Bird laughed. "I had them add the color so my room wouldn't be so bland."

He escorted Monica to her bedroom. She tried to contain her excitement from the sheer beauty of the room, but her lively eyes and smile belied her cool demeanor. Bird noticed her excitement but decided against calling her out on it.

"Do you like it? Muldoon wouldn't let me see your file, but he did, however, give me some general information concerning your likes and dislikes," Bird said.

Monica looked at Bird much like a confused puppy, her green eyes beaming, searching the man's face with her head cocked slightly to one side. "Like what?" she asked.

"Like your favorite colors, favorite foods, shit like that."

Monica was a girly girl, and she stared at the room in disbelief, for she was in pink heaven. Bird had decorated the room in every shade of pink imaginable. Soft cotton candy pinks and bubblegum pinks with sprinkles of fuchsia flowed through the room seamlessly. The princess canopy bed with its sheer pink curtains cascaded down to the plush pink goose-down comforter. Monica's room had the same white mink carpet as Bird's room, except he'd added soft pink mink throw rugs to this room.

"Come here. Let me show you something else," Bird said, grabbing Monica's hand and leading her to the bathroom.

The bathroom was an elegant mixture of stones and wood, giving it a rustic natural look. The tub and shower were in one room, while the toilet and sink were in another. They were separated by a thick pane of frosted glass. "I didn't decorate this bathroom because I figured that you might want to add your own touch since it's yours, but I did pick up some things that I thought you might need." He had taken the time to shop for Monica's favorite lotions, shampoo, conditioner, and soap.

"Thank you, Bird, but may I ask you a question?"

"Yeah, what's up?"

"Why are you doing all of this for me? I mean, what's your goal?"

"There is no goal, Monica. I owe you this much. You're putting your life on the line to not only bust King but to give me my life back, and for that, I'm eternally grateful. I will leave you to get settled."

As he turned to leave, he looked back at Monica and smiled softly. "Just because I'm a drug dealer doesn't mean that I don't know how to treat a woman. I do have a mother, you know."

Chapter 5

King's Court

"What's poppin', Drak?" King asked.

"Slow motion, Kochese mane. Little baby fine as a muhfucka, straight up."

"Nigga, I couldn't care less about how fine that bitch is. Did you see anything suspicious about the broad?"

"Nah, Bird picked her up, he gave her a quick hug like kinfolk do, and bounced. Nothing suspicious, but . . ."

"But what, playa? Spit it out," King said.

"Man, that little muhfucka is fine as hell, dawg."

Both men laughed.

King would have to see the girl for himself. Drak was old school, but he was still relatively young. King knew his enforcer well, and as long as they'd been acquainted, Drak had never been a pussy hound. He was more content with murder than romance, so for him to be so adamant about the young lady, she had to be drop dead gorgeous.

The next day, King called a meeting of all of his generals. They needed to do their weekly tallies of profits for all of their illegal businesses. He had no idea how much profit they had generated for the week, but if it was anything like the last few weeks, he would have to follow through on his plans for expansion.

His Mexican general, Chongo, would be coming up from Houston with the week's profits from the syrup and meth sales. Little Whoadie would come from New Orleans with money from the marijuana and ecstasy sales. His Florida connection was heavy and very profitable. King had a set of triplets who controlled the territory in Florida from Orlando down to Miami and everything in between.

The triplets ran a full gamut of schemes, scams, and capers. They were three of the most ruthless women that King had ever met, and they used their beauty and brains to their advantage. They had a wide variety of girls that stripped for them at clubs in major cities across Florida. They had a monopoly on the skin industry in Florida with their stock of beautiful women. Miami, Ft. Lauderdale, Tampa, Orlando, and West Palm Beach all bowed under the thumb of the triplets. The very same women that stripped for the triplets were easily available for escorts through any number of websites run solely by the sisters. They also sold crack, powder, weed, and pills, so King knew they would come with major money.

Bond was a college-educated white boy with more brains than anyone King had ever met. Everyone called him Bond because he dressed like the movie spy 007 no matter where he went. He was a dapper man, deeply immersed in the underworld, and he just happened to be King's defense attorney and gun dealer. It was mandatory in King's organization that his men traded their guns every ninety days to be *washed*, meaning they got new guns to eliminate the possibility of being caught with a weapon with a body on it.

King's Dallas squad would be in attendance as well. He knew from experience that they would bring in at least three quarters of a million for the week.

King Kochese had really come into his own. He was a long way away from the scrawny little kid that had scrambled for Michael Ross and his crew years earlier. He wanted to do something special for his people. King was neither sentimental nor soft, but he was appreciative of his crew. King had a squad of killers, knuckleheads, misfits, outcasts, and thoroughbreds. They made King a lot of money, and he in turn had made the smart ones in his crew very wealthy men and women. His wages were higher than average, and King liked it like that. He truly believed that money either bred loyalty or treachery, with no middle ground.

The meeting that he was putting together was going to be different. King had a whole weekend planned out for his squad. After they tallied their money, they would hit Beamers Nightclub. He'd made plans to rent out the entire club and invite some of the most influential hustlers in the city. He was also having some big-name rappers come in to perform. He planned a lavish picnic for his squad at Rochester Park with full catering for the following day. King even had activities like a kickball game and a softball game planned. If things went according to King's plan, then the weekend would be a huge success for him and his people.

That was coming up quickly, but he had pressing business to deal with, though. It was okay that Drak had reported back to him about Bird and his cousin Money, but he didn't trust anybody and wanted to see for himself. King walked out of his living room with Drak following close behind.

"So, what's up now, boss? What you need from me?" Drak asked curiously.

"Ain't shit tonight. I'ma get some sleep, but be over here bright and early in the morning. We need to ride out and handle some business before the troops start rolling in."

"Fa sho, Kochese man. 'Bout seven cool?" Drac said, puzzled.

"Hell naw, nigga. You knock on my door at seven in the morning, I will shoot your big ass myself," King said jokingly. "Just be here about ten or eleven, dawg."

Both men laughed as King Kochese showed Drak to the door.

Kochese Mills was a kingpin by trade. He had mountains of money, and it felt extremely good to be able to buy what he wanted when he wanted. He stayed in an exquisite estate that sprawled across ten acres of Lake Ray Hubbard. He had an array of automobiles, each of which was rimmed up. He had everything that any man could want, all types of cars from an old school Chevy to a Lamborghini. He had motorcycles and Jet Skis. He even had scooters. If he wanted it, he bought it. King had it all. He was truly at the top of his game.

The sound of his Louis Vuitton slippers echoed through the halls of his large home. King made his way to his master bathroom and started a bath. He sat on the side of the tub, running his hands underneath the water to gauge the temperature.

This ain't living, he thought. King had been feeling like that lately, like something was missing. There were a number of girls that he bedded on a regular that shot the same conversation at him. "I wanna have your baby," they would say. "You need a son to carry on your name," they would say. "You got good hair. I bet our baby would be pretty," they would say. "I hope our baby has your eyes," they would say. It was the same conversation no matter who the female was, and it was getting old. He wanted one woman to call his own, but he didn't want a gold digger. With his looks and money, that was going to be next to impossible to find.

He disrobed and climbed into the large Roman tub. The steamy water instantly relaxed the hardened thug. Money was nice, but it wasn't everything. He longed for something that he'd never in his life experienced: family.

After he'd soaked and bathed, he walked to Noisy Boy's room. His pit bull lay sleeping on a king-sized bed with a white down comforter. King entered the room, and the dog stretched and yawned lazily.

"Wake up, playa. You're on duty. Did you know you're the best friend I got, boy? You're loyal to daddy, huh, boy?" he said affectionately as he scratched the back of the puppy's ear.

There was no denying that Noisy Boy was the only thing on God's green earth that King cared about or trusted. Every man that he met wanted to be him, and every woman that he met wanted to get into his pockets.

Kochese and Noisy Boy walked to the kitchen, where he had the canine's favorite meal waiting for him. There was raw veal cutlet, cooked carrots, and watered-down Dom Perignon. He knew that his dog was spoiled, but considering that Noisy Boy was the closest thing to a child or family that he had, he didn't mind at all.

"I'm going to go to bed, boy. Watch the house."

Noisy Boy gave a quick yelp and lowered his head back into his food bowl as King Kochese walked toward his room. He lay in bed with his hands folded behind his head, staring at the ceiling. His thoughts drifted to his mother. He had tried to love her, but it was next to impossible to love someone that didn't love you back. She'd loved her crack pipe more than she could ever have loved Kochese.

There was a lot on his mind, but it would have to wait. The *click-clack* of the albino pit bull's nails echoed through the halls, and King drifted off to sleep.

Chapter 6

Money Over Everything

It had been a very long time since Monica had had a peaceful night's sleep. She sat up in bed and looked around, trying to figure out where she was. She was still sleepy, but the smell of home cooking had brought her out of a deep slumber. Monica wiped the grogginess from her eyes and made her way to the bathroom to start the shower. Steam from the hot water swirled and filled the room, awakening a sense of invigoration in the young woman. She breathed the steam in deeply as she stepped into the shower. The water ran over the top of her head and cascaded in clear beads down her olive-colored skin. She turned off the shower and stepped out. Water dripped from her curvaceous body, and her hair lay in jet-black ringlets around her shoulders.

Monica wrapped a plush terry cloth towel around her body and went into her bedroom. She dropped her towel and stood naked in the full-length mirror hanging from her closet door. She examined her curves critically. Monica knew that her body was banging, but she was harder on herself than anybody.

You need to hit the gym, fat girl, she thought to herself. She rubbed Sheer Love lotion from Victoria's Secret over her entire body. It was her favorite scent and reminded her of money.

There was a light tap at the door, and Bird walked in. "You gonna sleep all day? Damn, I thought you were still asleep. My bad," he said, letting his eyes roam over her body. Her skin was silky smooth, and everything about her body was perfect. Her breasts were uncommonly firm, and her nipples jutted from them like two perfect Hershey's kisses. Her stomach was flat, as if she spent every moment of her time in the gym. Her ass was a picturesque half-moon that cupped where her butt and hamstring met. He tried to be inconspicuous, but she was gorgeous from head to toe.

Monica stood firm, still lotioning her body. "You don't know how to wait for a person to say come in?" she said, grinning.

Bird smiled. His embarrassment was evident, and he stuttered as he tried to apologize. "M-my bad, I-I thought you were still sleeping."

"Why are you stammering? Look, we're both grown, and I'm comfortable with my body. You should be, too." She winked.

"A'ight, no doubt. Breakfast is ready."

Bird turned and walked out of the room. The exchange had been awkward and uncomfortable. He didn't know how to take what Monica had said. He was attracted to her, but he didn't want to jeopardize the case by complicating their relationship.

Monica came into the dining room wearing silk shorts and a cropped tee. She exuded sexuality, and it was hard for Bird to decipher where the character of Money began and ended.

"Money, if we're going to be cousins, you can't be wearing shit like that around the house."

"Do I make you uncomfortable, Bird?"

"Excuse my language, but hell naw, you make my shit hard as a muhfucka!"

"Well damn, mister sensitivity."

"I'm just being real. Shit, I'm human, and you're sexy as fuck."

"Okay, I will wear granny panties and thick house coats from now on."

"That won't help."

They burst into raucous laughter. The sexual tension was thick in the small dining room, but business was business. Monica looked at the young man. Under different circumstances, she could see herself with Bird, but she was a rookie DEA agent, and he was a drug dealer trying to go straight. Not an ideal match made in heaven.

Bird noticed her staring at him, "What's on your mind, miss lady?"

"What do you mean?"

"You're staring at me like you're trying to look into my soul or something."

"Anyways, what's the plan, boss man? I'm ready to get it in."

"First things first, you won't be able to wear a wire, so how do you plan to get the info that you need to prosecute King?"

"I have my ways. You let me worry about that."

"Okay, cool. Second thing is, you really have to be careful. If I know King the way that I think I do, he's going to send goons to test you. If you show weakness, Money, you're done."

"Trust me, I got this, little daddy. Are we going to the block today?"

"Yeah, I'ma take you out to meet a few people and put you on a crew. Most likely the Go Getta Crew. Those fools are strictly about that paper."

"Okay. I'ma go and put on my hustlin' clothes. What time do you want to leave?"

"We will leave in a little bit. Eat your food and get dressed."

Bird and Monica walked to his garage in silence. They had both agreed to never talk about DEA business outside of the condo. They didn't want to take any unnecessary chances, because King had eyes and ears everywhere.

"Nah, we taking this car," Bird said to Monica, noticing that she had headed toward his BMW. He unlocked the doors to a royal blue Dodge Magnum. The face of Papa Smurf winked menacingly from the hood of the car beneath multiple coats of clear enamel. Chrome twenty-six-inch rims with hints of royal blue completed the exterior's candy finish.

Monica sat inside the car and looked at the interior. The inside was cocaine white with blue trim, and the character of Papa Smurf was stitched into the headrests. He started the car, and the digital dash sprang to life. Every LED light in the Magnum had been replaced with blue bulbs, giving the car a bluish glow.

"Oh, you gettin' it like this, huh? I like it," Money said.

"I'm doing a little something something," Bird said as he winked at her.

They drove toward the South Oak Cliff section of Dallas. She gazed out of the window, lost in her own world. It was barely eleven o'clock in the morning, but children were already outside playing. A few kids walked in the direction of Big L swimming pool clad in flip-flops and swimming trunks with large beach towels thrown across their shoulders. As they drove, the lush green grasses of the well-to-do neighborhoods of Oak Cliff gave way to unkempt, litter-strewn yards and broken-down cars.

They pulled into the parking lot of a large apartment complex. Gangsters ranging in ages from thirteen to their early twenties milled about in front of one particular section of the apartments. Some were shooting dice, some leaning against the brick structure passing a blunt and sipping from plastic cups. A baby-faced, dark-skinned kid made his way over to Bird's car.

"B, what it do, my nigga?" the kid said.

"What's up, Face?"

"Shit, slow motion on my end. Just out here tryna get this paper, playa. You know how it go."

"Fa sho. Say, this is my little cousin Money. Money, this is Baby Face. Face to all of his friends."

"That's what's up. Nice to meet you, Face," Money said.

"Oh, you calling me Face. Does that mean you're gonna be my friend?"

"Hopefully, yeah," Money said, winking at him.

"Hold up, swole up. Like I said, this is my little cousin, so don't get no ideas. I'ma put her on your crew as a scrambler for the GGC, so I don't want you muhfuckas tryna get in her pants."

"Man, I'm just shootin' the shit. I got you, bro. We will take care of her."

Bird's cell phone vibrated in his cup holder. He looked at the screen. King Kochese was calling.

"What's up, King? What's good, playboy?"

"Yo, what up, pimp? Where you at, dawg?"

"Over in the Cliffs, settin' my cousin up with Baby Face and the GGC."

"A'ight, stay there. I'm 'bout to roll through."

"Fa sho."

Bird looked at Monica and Baby Face carrying on some random conversation. Before he could let them know that their boss was on his way, King's Range Rover pulled up next to the Magnum.

King hopped out with his signature chain, looking crisp and clean. In true King fashion, he sported gray

Dickies and a baby blue T-shirt with baby blue and gray Jordans. He had baby blue rubber bands spaced perfectly running the length of his long ponytail. The blueness of his T-shirt made his eyes sparkle like new diamonds. He walked around to the back of his SUV and put Noisy Boy on his leash.

Bird got out of his car and leaned against his hood. "What's crackin', boss man?" he said.

King looked at Bird and smiled. They had known each other so long that they had the same taste in clothes. Bird had on the exact same clothes as King, except his outfit was black and gray.

Bird looked down to see Noisy Boy sniffing around his feet. "What's up, ol' spoiled-ass little boy?" he said to the dog, who was wagging his tail feverishly as he sniffed Bird's hand.

"Yo, come here, Money." Bird held his hand out for Monica to come over and take position beside him. "King Kochese, this is Money. Money, this is King Kochese. King to those of us that know him."

"Nice to meet you, Kochese. Thank you for the opportunity, 'cause it wasn't shit poppin' in North Cacca," she said.

"Yeah, no doubt. Just stay loyal, keep ten toes down, and have that paper right, and you should be straight."

Money simply nodded in agreement as she kneeled down to pet Noisy Boy. "Well, aren't you just the prettiest little thang? Yeah, look at those eyes."

Noisy Boy dropped his head and began wagging his tail fanatically.

"That's crazy, man!" Bird said as he and King both stared at one another in amazement.

"What's that?" Money asked out of curiosity.

King looked the young girl up and down. "This little evil albino muhfucka don't like nobody. I think he'd bite

Jesus himself if He came down, but he bowing down to you like he's known you his whole life."

"I hope that's a good thing," she said as she rose to her feet.

"We will see, shawty. We will see. Bird, I'ma need everybody out at the crib tomorrow, bruh. Everybody."

"Okay, man. What's the occasion if you don't mind me asking?"

"It's time to tally that paper, and I have an announcement to make," King said dismissively.

King put Noisy Boy in the Range Rover and drove off.

"What was that all about, man?" Baby Face said to Bird.

"You know it's that time of the month to tally that paper. I don't know what that other shit was about. I guess we will see when we get there, huh?"

"Yeah, I guess so, B."

"So, check it out. I'ma leave Money with you cats, and I'ma go and handle some business," Bird said, climbing into his car.

He sped off with what felt like the weight of the world on his shoulders. He had set into motion a series of events that could go a multitude of ways. King had people that were extremely loyal to him, and most of them were willing to kill just to make a name for themselves in the organization. If he and Monica couldn't pull off this ruse, then they could both cancel Christmas. Bird had a lot of living to do and had no plans on dying anytime soon.

Chapter 7

Muldoon

Muldoon hadn't heard from his rookie agent in a few weeks, but he wasn't worried about her safety. He was more worried about the man known as Bird keeping his composure. Monica was a rookie, but she had an axe to grind, and Muldoon knew that. Agents with a cause often made the best undercover operatives.

He sat in his office, staring at his computer screen. King's face was plastered across the screen with the words dead or alive scrolling across it. He wasn't actually wanted dead or alive, but that was Muldoon's attitude toward the situation. He wanted King Kochese Mills brought to justice, but he would rather lose a drug dealer than an agent with potential. He'd made an agreement with her to keep an eye on her sister while she was undercover. The risk of King having eyes on her and finding out her true identity was a risk he wasn't willing to take. Muldoon knew that Monica could be great, and he was going to take her under his wing to make her one hell of an agent.

I'm getting ahead of myself. First we have to get her out alive and well, he thought. He wasn't sure what Monica's plan was, but in order for them to ensure her safety, King would literally have to never see the light of day again. If he got a short federal sentence, there was no doubt in anybody's mind that neither Monica nor Bird would ever be safe. Even if he got life in federal prison, with his street connections, he could still reach out and have them touched.

Muldoon sighed. Monica would have to make damned certain that whatever she got on King stuck like Crazy Glue. He was beyond nervous because he knew Kochese's reputation. If the stories that Muldoon had heard were true, then his suspect was a merciless killer with no conscience. He dropped his head and said a silent prayer for Monica. She would need it.

He grabbed his suit jacket and headed for the door. Jasmine would be waiting for him at the Buckner Home. Even though he didn't know the young girl personally, she had taken a liking to him, and him to her. Age and career had kept him from having children, and he was drawn to both Monica and Jasmine.

Her doctors had been surprised and relieved after his first visit because Jasmine had made some real progress. She'd dressed herself the morning after Muldoon's visit. She had also taken her meds, attempted to comb her hair, and smiled at her doctor. That was a breakthrough compared to the disheveled, unkempt girl with the blank stare that had come into the Buckner Home. With Jasmine showing signs of improvement, he knew that the news would be an incentive for Monica to come home safe and sound.

Muldoon sped along I-35, heading toward the Pleasant Grove section of Dallas. He wanted to make it to the Buckner Home before lunch, when Jasmine would be more lucid and talkative. Muldoon personally believed that she was past the point of needing medication, but he wasn't a doctor either, and if her physician felt it was necessary, then he had no room to argue.

He pulled into the parking lot of the youth center just before 11 A.M. He was excited to see Jasmine. If the doctors approved, he would take her outside and walk with her. He believed that sunlight was a good form of therapy. It had always helped him when he felt down and depressed, so hopefully, the sun would be good medicine for her also.

"I am here to see Miss Jasmine Dietrich," he said to the receptionist as he signed into the visitation log.

The young lady never even glanced up to make eye contact. She pointed in the direction of Jasmine's room and kept reading her book. Muldoon looked at the secretary in disdain. He was all about professionalism, and evidently the girl had no idea what that was. He would deal with her later. He was anxious to see Jazz.

He gave a light tap at her room door and walked in. She was standing at her window, looking out onto the courtyard, and swaying back and forth.

"Jazzy Bell, is everything okay, dear?" he asked.

Jasmine turned to face the agent with a wide grin. Her smile was bright and radiant as if she didn't have a care in the world. Even approaching eighteen years old, her soft features and innocent demeanor belied her age. Her aura and vibe was more of a nine- or ten-year-old, most likely due to the many years that she had spent confined to the mental ward of the youth home.

Muldoon walked to her and wrapped his arms around her innocence. "I was thinking that maybe we could take a walk outside through the courtyard, kiddo. What do you think?"

Again, she nodded yes and smiled. Jasmine took his hand and led him out of her room. They reached the courtyard and made their way through the maze of lush green hedges and colorful flowers. Jasmine stopped and raised her head to the sky. She closed her eyes and took a deep breath. The rays of the sun beamed down on her face, giving her a sense of energy and refreshed vigor. Her smile broadened as she lifted her arms and twirled like a ballerina.

"I take it you like the feeling of the sun, huh, Jazzy?" Agent Muldoon said, smiling at the young, fresh-faced girl.

"It feels soooo good to be outside. The sun makes me feel free!"

"Well, well, well, it's good to hear your voice, my dear. I knew that there was a real live person in there. Your sister will be glad to know you're coming around."

"Where is she? It seems as if I haven't seen her in forever."

"She's on a special mission, so she's unable to come at the moment, but soon, very soon, Jazzy."

"Pop Pop used to call me that." She had taken a somber tone, and tears flowed from her eyes.

Muldoon embraced the girl tightly. "I know it makes you sad, my love, but I'm here for you if you need me, and soon this will all be over."

"I know. I guess I'm just tired of living like I'm crazy. Do you know why I haven't spoken? It's not because I couldn't. It's because there was never anyone that I felt truly understood me besides Moni. Then you came along, and you're so much like my grandfather that I feel close to you." She cried softly. "I just want my life back."

Muldoon didn't know what to say. He wanted to comfort her, but he knew that the only thing that would truly comfort her was a reunion with her sister.

Agent Muldoon's cellphone rang, breaking the conversation. "Speak on it," he said into his iPhone.

"It's Money. I don't have a lot of time. I just wanted you to know that I've made contact with King and that I am on a crew. I should have more information for you the next time that we speak. Just keep in mind that the deeper undercover that I go, the less you'll hear from me. Don't panic. You will either hear from me or Bird one way or another."

"Okay, has he shown any interest in you as a woman?"

"It's hard to tell. I mean, we've only met once so far."

"Gotcha. Well, on a brighter note—" he started, but before he could finish his sentence, Jasmine touched his arm gently, shaking her head no with a sad look in her eyes. For reasons unknown to Muldoon, she seemed to not want her sister to know of her progress.

Muldoon nodded in approval and continued his conversation. "Sorry, on a brighter note, I think I'm going to stop smoking cigarettes. It's taking a toll on my body," he lied.

"Well, good for you. Smoking kills, and—"

Muldoon wondered why Monica had cut her conversation short until he heard muffled speech and laughter in the background. It got louder as if right on top of Monica.

"Yo' ass on the phone cakin'. I betcha that nigga ain't gettin' paper like this," a deep voice said from the other end of the phone.

"Boy, this my granddaddy. Watch your mouth. Well, Grampy, my rude friend Baby Face is back with our food. I will talk to you later. Kiss Memaw for me."

Muldoon ended the call and smiled to himself. Monica had handled herself like a seasoned vet. Maybe he was worrying about her for no reason. She had gone from agent to hood rat in a split second.

He turned to Jasmine and looked into her eyes deeply, searching for the answer to an unasked question. "So, why didn't you want me to tell Monica about your progress?"

"You said that she's on a dangerous mission, and I don't want to cloud her mind with thoughts of me."

"Don't you think that her knowing that you're well would be more incentive for her to come home safely?"

"I will be fine until she is done. Please don't say anything to her."

"Your wish is my command, Jazzy Bell."

Chapter 8

King's Money

King sat across the street from the apartment complex, watching his workers. Money worked the dope fiends like she had been selling dope her whole life. She moved gracefully from one crackhead to the next, serving twenty and fifty pieces as though her life depended on it. King smiled devilishly behind blackened tint. Noisy Boy lay across the front seat with his head resting lazily in King's lap. Kochese gently stroked the dog's head, talking to him as if the canine somehow understood every word that he spoke. "She a down little bitch, Noisy, but she look too fuckin' good to be corner hustlin', mane." Noisy Boy whimpered quietly in agreement. "King Kochese might hafta change all that shit."

His loyal dog gave a quick yelp to let his master know that he approved. King stepped out of his black Lexus LFA and put Noisy Boy on his leash. The smell of stale urine mixed with the sweet, rancid aroma of burning crack assaulted his nostrils.

"What's up, King? When you gonna put me down, dawg, and lemme grind for you?" a sullen-faced crackhead asked.

"DirtBag, man, what the fuck make you think I would take a chance fucking with yo' crackhead ass, mane? I give you a package and you run off, dawg. You already know what it is. Why would you wanna go out like that, my nigga?"

"I already know how you get down, boss. I'm just tryna come up like everybody else. I'm tired of living like this for real. Lemme show you I still got hustle, man." DirtBag had been a big-time hustler back in the day, but he had broken the number one rule in the game: *Don't get high off your own supply*. He had been turned out on his own dope by a young, fresh-faced girl barely out of high school. Now he was a broke junky roaming from gas station to gas station in hopes that someone would allow him to pump their gas for a dollar or two.

"I tell you what, Dirty. I will give you a try under one condition," King said.

"Yeah? And what's that, boss?"

"I will start you out at two hunnit a week to look out, and for every week that you stay clean, I will increase your pay until you get to two stacks a week, but you have to be drug-free, nigga!"

The fiend looked into the distance, pondering the young kingpin's offer. He would have to shit or get off of the pot, and he knew it. If he took the job and got clean, then there was nowhere to go but up. If he took the job and relapsed, he knew for certain that King would have him killed. There was no middle ground in dealing with Kochese; business with him was a one-way trip to hell. DirtBag was desperate, though, and as sad as his life was at the moment, he was willing to sell his soul to the devil to do better.

"That sounds like a bet, dawg. Thank you, and I promise I won't let you down."

"Yeah, if you know like I know, muhfucka, you better not." King turned to walk away, but DirtBag put his hand on King's shoulder to stop his stride.

"King, I know I just started, but can I get an advance?" DirtBag asked. King flashed his sinister grin, reached into his pocket, and peeled off two crispy one-hundred-dollar bills. "Don't smoke it up, fool."

"Naw, man, I wanna get me a room and some clothes. I gotta represent," DirtBag said as he scurried off into a nearby breezeway.

Kochese eased across the street toward a group of hustlers that included Money and Baby Face. Most of the young hustlers began to scramble when they saw King. He was strictly business, and he expected his workers to drum up business much like street telemarketers. He wanted his workers to be out scouting fiends and running off the competition. If any other hustlers were in the area moving work and they didn't work for King, they were dealt with swiftly and severely. He walked over to the porch where Baby Face and Money were sitting, but when he approached, Money stood and walked away.

"What's crackin', Face?"

"Shit, slow motion, King. What's good, boss?"

"Slow motion is better than no motion," King said. He watched Money walk away. Her hips swayed to some invisible rhythm as she moved into the shadows of the complex to serve a fiend. "What's her problem, my nigga?"

"Who, Money? She straight, man. Bitch is about her paper; I know that. She ain't missed a beat since she started."

"That's good. That little muhfucka fine as fuck. I might hafta scoop her up and run this dick up in her," King said huskily.

Baby Face laughed. King was known as a ladies' man, but Money didn't strike him as the type of female that was just giving her pussy away like that. From the conversations that they'd had, King would have to come with a lot more than money and a pretty smile.

"Nigga, what's so muhfuckin' funny?" King asked. His irritation was obvious.

"I'm just laughing because honestly, dawg, she is different. She not like these sack chasers that we fuck on a regular. Baby girl is strictly about her fetti, but I mean, you might be able to get her."

"Nigga, you know my pedigree. I *am* fetti, playboy," King stated harshly.

"Dawg, why you gettin' heated? I'm just saying Money is not like the rest of these broads, bruh. Shit, if she was, then I woulda been done fucked by now." Both men laughed. King knew that his young friend was right. Besides King, Baby Face was one of the only people that he associated with that always had a different girl.

"Ay, Face, have you seen Bird today?" King asked

"Yeah, he came through to drop off Money and to check on work, then he dipped. I think he said something about going over to the south side to holler at that nigga Corey."

King gave Face dap and disappeared toward his Lexus. His mind was on what Face had told him. There weren't many women he couldn't have when he put his mind to it, and Money was no exception. He would have the young girl if it was the last thing he did.

As he crossed the busy street dividing the houses and apartments, he could still smell the sweetness of her perfume. The smell was a welcomed visitor that effortlessly drowned the stench of stale cigarettes and warm piss. Noisy Boy's tail began to wag frantically as his master made his way back to his Lexus. The canine sat guarding the car as if his life depended on it.

"How's daddy's boy, huh? How's daddy's boy?" King asked as he approached the car. He reached into the vehicle and grabbed his Blackberry.

"Yo, Drak, what's poppin'?"

"Slow boogie, boss. What's good?"

"Man, I just saw Bird's little cousin. Dawg, you were right. That little bitch is tight work."

Drak laughed uncontrollably into the cell phone. "I told you, nigga, I told you. Baby fine as frog hair, huh?"

"You damn skippy. I gotta have her, mane. I need her on my team."

"Damn, King. I ain't ever heard you talking about no broad like this."

"Yeah, and you probably never will again, but as it stands right now, playboy, I'm on a mission."

King ended their conversation with a click. After he hung up the phone, he was slightly embarrassed at his lack of composure with his older friend. Although embarrassing, King didn't believe in sugar coating shit. It was true that he wanted her. The girl's beauty was remarkable, and the fact that she had all but ignored him twice made his blood boil. The first day that he'd talked to her, he had looked at Money like every other female that worked for him. Seeing her this time was different. Her eyes hadn't lit up like most women when he'd come around. It seemed to King that he was invisible to her, and that intrigued the young drug dealer.

As it stood, though, King had more pressing business to attend. He had given Bird orders to deal with Corey, and if he hadn't, there would be hell to pay. He had a reputation to uphold, and he expected everyone in his organization to do their part. The minute he started letting his workers run off with money and drugs, the underworld would eat him alive.

King dropped his Lexus into fifth gear as he headed toward South Dallas. He dialed Bird's cell number, but it went directly to voicemail. *Where this nigga at, man?* he wondered as he punched the V12 harder. He dialed again, with still no answer as he exited the freeway by Fair Park. He made a right onto Grand Avenue and headed for the apartment that Corey shared with his crackhead mother and alcoholic sister. He was just about to call Bird again when his cell rang

"Nigga, where the fuck you at? I been calling you like a muhfucka!" King screamed into the phone.

"First of all, dawg, chill out. Second of all, I'm tryna take care of this Corey situation. Damn."

"So where you at, nigga? You know, Bird, you make a nigga wonder about you sometimes, bruh. You snitchin', fool?"

"Man, don't even try me like that. Goddamn, my nigga, I been with you since I was a youngster, and you still treatin' me like a nigga off the street? You are unreal, mane."

"Bird, don't talk to me about loyalty, playboy, and you still haven't answered my question."

"Whatever, dawg. I'm at the warehouse."

King ended the call and ran his hand across his unkempt braids. His brow furrowed, and he wondered why it was so hard to get Bird on the phone. When people were hard to get in contact with, the first thing that came to mind was snitching. He had witnessed the scenario play out too many times before.

He pulled into his warehouse parking lot and saw Bird's car. It was dark except for the overhead light that shone brightly against the candy paint of Bird's Magnum. King walked inside to find Bird circling Corey's bloody body. He was tied to a chair, and Bird wielded a large leather belt in one hand, and a set of brass knuckles adorned the other hand.

"Where the muhfuckin' money at, Corey?"

Bird spat as he struck the man violently across the bridge of his nose.

King's eyes lit up. He loved violence, but even more, he loved to see violence carried out on his behalf. "Why this nigga ain't dead yet, B? You slackin', my nigga," King said as he emerged from the shadows.

Bird jumped with a start and threw the belt down like a guilty child. "You scared the shit outta me, dawg. Man, this dopefiend-ass nigga thinks this shit is a game," he said as he punched the man again.

"You going about this shit all wrong, playa. That's why he's not talking. You feel me?"

"Nah, I don't feel you. I done just about beat this nigga silly, and he still ain't saying shit!" Bird wore his frustration on his sleeve, and it showed.

King smiled at his young protégé. He had been in the game long enough to know that you could beat a crack-head within inches of their life and they wouldn't budge, but the prospect of getting free dope was enough to make the information flow freely from their lips. He pulled a large bag of $30 crack slabs from his pocket. He dangled the drugs in front of the man's face.

"Is this what you want, fuck boy? Look at these slabs, pussy!"

Corey lifted his head. Even through the bloody mess on his face, King could see the boy salivating. His mouth watered with anticipation. The thought of crack filling his lungs made him stir uneasily in his chair. Corey began to sob uncontrollably, sniffling and coughing up a mixture of snot and blood.

"I fucked up, man. I was fucking with this little bitch, and she wanted to experiment with the shit. At first, we just smoked a couple of primos, but then the urges got stronger, and we smoked the shit straight." He was crying heavily now.

King looked at the man in disdain, but Bird understood, and his heart went out to him.

Corey rambled on. “I kept smoking until my pack was damn near gone, and when I realized how much I had smoked, I tried to flip what I had left, but it was too late. This shit got me, dawg, and if you niggas kill me, on some real shit, y’all gon’ be doing me a favor.”

“So you smoked all my shit, Corey?” King asked. He pulled his .45 caliber Desert Eagle from his waistband and cocked it.

Bird had seen this scenario play out a thousand times since becoming a member of King’s squad. Corey would die tonight, and King would make sure that they each had a hand in it to cover his own ass. If they both participated in the murder, then in King’s eyes, Bird would be less likely to turn him in.

“Man, as soon as my sister gets her income tax, she is going to give me the money to pay you back, King. I swear, my nigga.”

“Muhfucka, you expect me to wait until next year to get my paper? No thank you, bitch boy. I prefer to get it my way.”

King smiled widely, exposing his perfectly straight white teeth. His mouth smiled, but he had blood in his eyes. King handed his gun to Bird.

“Put a bullet in this nigga’s head, B.”

Bird took aim and let off one shot between Corey’s eyes. The back of his head exploded violently, blowing chunks of brain matter onto the floor behind them.

King was beside himself with glee. “Yeah, now that’s how you do a muhfucka. Walk up on him and *pow*!” He jumped around as if he’d just won the lotto. He walked up behind Corey’s lifeless body and tilted the dead man’s head back.

King looked into his empty eyes and smiled. “Just say nope to dope, dumb-ass little boy.” He pulled a knife from his back pocket and slit Corey’s throat.

Bird winced. It was bad enough that they'd killed the boy, but this was adding insult to injury. "Man, the nigga already dead. What you doing that for?"

"You ain't seen shit yet, B," King said as he began cutting the dead man's head from his shoulders, all the while keeping his gaze focused on Bird.

King was a sick man, and Bird knew it. Murder came naturally to King. He lived for it. King's knife ripped through the skin of Corey's neck, and after he was satisfied that it was completely severed, he let it dangle as he turned to walk to a downstairs office.

King returned moments later with a clear trash bag and a pair of bolt cutters. "Come hold this bag, nigga," he barked.

Bird stood frozen in shock. *This muhfucka is psycho*, Bird thought as he stared at the sight before him.

"Bird!" King screamed. "Grab this bag, bruh."

Bird took the trash bag and watched as his mentor used the bolt cutters to cut through the brittle bone of Corey's esophagus. The detached head dropped and rolled a few feet from Bird. "Bag this bitch nigga's head up and drop it on his mammy's porch, and clean this shit up before you go, bruh."

"Will do, boss," Bird said sarcastically.

Truth be told, Bird was tired of King's constant arrogance. Bird carried out his duties like he was expected to, but it was getting old. Still, he was intelligent enough to realize that if he challenged his mentor, it would mean an all-out war. He would have to kill King in order to live his life. Bird wanted out of the game. He had everything that anyone in the drug game wished for—a fat-ass bank account, nice cars, property, and more. The only thing missing was safety.

He put Corey's head into a second bag so that it wouldn't leak into the back of his car. As he closed the trunk, he thought he noticed someone watching him out of the corner of his eye, but when he looked in that direction, there was no one there. Bird laughed to himself. He was allowing King to make him paranoid. He'd been more paranoid than normal lately, partly because he knew King's reputation, but mostly because he'd never been a snitch, and what he had put into play could, and probably would, get him killed if things went wrong.

Money needs to hurry the fuck up, he thought. If she couldn't pull it off and get the conviction, it was highly likely that Bird would die in prison. The DEA had a solid case against him. Someone had snitched on him months earlier, and their surveillance team had captured him on more than one occasion conducting business. When they'd come to him about the charges, the agents had made it known that to them, he was the low man on the totem pole. They wanted King, and he could either help with the investigation, or he could rot in prison *after* they let King know that his right-hand man was trying to cut a deal. Kochese Mills had a long reach, and prison walls were no exception. If he wanted you dead, you might as well cancel Christmas, and he had a real gift for keeping himself insulated from prosecution.

Bird put those thoughts out of his head just as quickly as they started. He knew in his heart having a normal life filled with something other than drugs and violence wasn't much to ask for. For all of the wrong that he had done and pain that he had caused, he still had infinite faith in God. He prayed regularly, and if having faith meant anything at all, then everything would be all right. His faith was in God, but he trusted the fact that the Almighty was working through Monica Dietrich. He wanted to believe that. He *had* to believe that.

Chapter 9

Drak's Bond

King had an estate that most people would kill for. It was modern-chic and seemed to go on for acres. Bond and Drak pulled through the security gate onto the circular gravel driveway at the exact same time.

"Good morning, Mr. Drak. How is life treating you this fine, money-filled morning?" Bond asked.

"Another day, another dollar, bro. Same shit, different day. You know."

"You're in for a treat today, my man. I have information for King that promises to get shit really stirred up, and truthfully, I'm not sure how he will handle it."

"And what might that be?" Drak asked. He was puzzled, with Bond being both King's attorney and his gun dealer. This conversation could go either way. "You will just have to wait until we are all together. You know how angry he gets when he gets secondhand information."

From the looks of things, the hustlers had already started to arrive. There was a vast assortment of cars in the driveway. Every luxury car imaginable seemed to litter the immense gravel drive. They reached the huge wooden door leading to the foyer of King's mansion and rang the doorbell. A petite Mexican woman wearing a maid's uniform answered the door and showed the two men into a large dining room with a massive mahogany table. The table was at least thirty feet long, and the few hustlers that had arrived talked amongst themselves, exchanging war stories about the drug trade. Both men took seats closest to the head of the table, careful to leave a seat open for Bird. That was the order of things: there was always King at the head of the table, Bird to his immediate right, Drak to his left, and Bond seated next to Drak. The seating was arranged according order of importance. King weighed the order of importance by the amount of money per week that the captains raked in.

Bird and Money pulled into the driveway of King's estate, not really sure what to expect. Bird had started to sweat, and his hands trembled as he gripped the steering wheel, looking anxious and nervous. Money put her hand on his forearm to relax him.

"You look edgy, Bird. Are you okay?"

"Yeah, I'm straight. I'm just not sure how this shit is going to play out. It always makes me jumpy when I go to these meetings, especially when I see both Drak and Bond. Those two muhfuckas are cutthroat, and since King has money out the ass, they are always up his ass."

"It'll be okay. Trust me. I will handle my part if you hold it together and do yours."

Bird took a deep breath, nodded, and exited the vehicle with Money following closely behind him. They walked into the meeting and said their hellos to everyone present. Drak's eyes followed Monica's rear end as she walked past. He shook his head. *This bitch is too fine for her own good,* he thought. As everyone talked amongst themselves, the last of the hustlers trickled in and were seated in their proper order. Baby Face came in and took the seat between Money and Bird. As always, his young face was glowing and sported a friendly smile.

"What up, B? What up, Money?" he asked.

"Hey, Face. Why you always smiling, daddy?" Money asked, putting on her cutest voice.

"Yeah, nigga. Why you always so muhfuckin' happy?"

"Shit, why not? I got paper, I got mad bitches, and I'm free. What's not to smile about?"

Before either could answer the young man's question, King entered the room with Noisy Boy leading the way on his leash. He was dressed from head to toe in white linen; his white Gucci slippers, Gucci belt, and signature chain completed his ensemble. King looked like money, and his position was undeniable.

"Good muhfuckin' morning, ladies and gents. Welcome to the crib. Hope everybody's paper is straight," King said as he walked into the dining room, releasing Noisy Boy to stroll around the room.

Bond stood and shook King's hand, pulling him close and whispering in his ear. "You and I need to talk, and I think that it is important that we do it before the meeting begins."

"Okay, bet," King whispered back. He cleared his throat and addressed his people. "You cats enjoy yourselves and get comfortable. I need to see Bond, Drak, and Bird in my office."

Bird got up hesitantly. He wasn't very fond of Bond, and he was even less fond of whispering. If Bond was in King's ear, it couldn't be good news. They had often joked about Bond's affinity for being the bearer of bad news, even going so far as to nickname him the Grim Reaper.

Bird was the last man to enter King's office, and his boss's irritation was already showing.

"Close the door, nigga!" King barked. Nearby, Noisy Boy's head rose to the sound of his master's sharp tone. "What's so urgent, Bond?" he asked, turning to the sharply dressed white man.

"Well, you know I've been fucking that little intern down at the federal building, right?" Bond bragged.

"Man, just get to the point. Nobody is interested in hearing about your sexual conquests," King replied briskly.

Bond bristled from the venomous tone. “Anyway, she was telling me during some pillow talk that she overheard your name on the lips of some Feds. So, it seems that a little birdy is singing in your organization, King. No pun intended,” Bond said, staring at Bird.

“What the fuck is that shit supposed to mean, white boy?” Bird snapped. “It sounds like you’re trying to imply that I’m snitchin’ or something.”

“Calm yo’ ass down, Bird. Did the man say that it was you who was talking? Fuck you so nervous fo’, my nigga?” King spat.

“I’m not nervous about shit, Kochese! This dude comes waltzing up in this muhfucka making his little accusations, staring at me, and I’m supposed to be okay with that?”

“Look out, playboy. First thing you need to do is lower your goddamned voice in my home. Second, as I said before, nobody said it was you, so calm yo’ ass down.”

“Mr. Bircher, I never said that it was you,” Bond said. “I have some theories, but I don’t think you’re foolish enough to cross Mr. Mills, so you’re excluded. Your so-called cousin, on the other hand, is a totally different matter.”

Bird was horrified. The mere implication would start King’s wheels turning. King looked from Bird to Bond and back again.

“It is rather funny that all of this bullshit jumps off as soon as this broad comes into the family, my nigga,” Drak chimed in.

“That ‘broad,’ as you call her, is my cousin, so watch your mouth. And nigga, just so you know, she ain’t nobody’s snitch,” Bird countered.

King studied Bird’s face for a second. He knew the young man better than just about anybody, and one thing he knew about Bird was that he was a skillful liar. King nodded in Drak’s direction without uttering a word. After working together for so long, King and Drak had a way of communicating without speaking. Drak nodded and disappeared through the oversized oak doors.

"Bird, I need you to understand something. If I run your cousin and she's not who you say she is, I'm going to kill her while you watch, and then I'm going to kill you," King said.

The calmness in King's voice caused Bird's skin to crawl. King was usually very hyper—almost too hyper, as if he had ADHD. Even when he was high on marijuana, he was still keyed up. Bird refused to protest, knowing that arguing with King was futile. He would either talk over you, thereby winning the argument, or he would have you murdered for insubordination. Either way, there was no winning with Kochese. It was better for Bird to keep his mouth shut and let the subject die.

Moments later, Drak reappeared with Monica in tow. Bird quickly glanced in her direction. Monica's demeanor was calm, which made Bird even more nervous. She stood among the men present, with her hands on her ample hips, glaring in King's direction. She burned holes into his soul with her jade-green eyes. The years that she'd spent playing the staring game with her grandfather had come in handy. Monica didn't move and didn't blink. King's blue eyes met Monica's green eyes in some sort of cosmic retinal battle for control, but Monica was unwavering. King shifted from foot to foot. He wasn't used to anyone meeting his gaze, let alone being stared down by a woman. His features softened.

"Why are you looking at a nigga like you wanna rip my head off?"

"That's just how I look, but on the real, I feel like I've been summoned to the principal's office," Monica said.

"Are you a snitch, Money?" King asked.

"Man, miss me with that bullshit. Hell naw, I ain't no snitch."

King didn't utter a word. He turned toward his desk and slid the computer mouse across the desktop. The screen sprang to life, revealing Monica's picture plastered across the 23-inch flat-screen monitor. Bird's jaw dropped. He couldn't believe that King had been so thorough. In the photo, Monica looked disheveled, like she'd been up all night. Her hair was matted to the side of her head, and she wasn't wearing makeup. Her eyes were swollen as if she'd been crying just before the photo was taken. In her hands, she held a placard that read: MONICA BIRCHER #665144 WAKE COUNTY DETENTION CENTER, WAKE COUNTY, NORTH CAROLINA. Underneath the photo was a long list of charges ranging from petty drug charges to armed robbery.

"According to your record, Moni, you're a thoroughbred that doesn't mind popping that pistol," King said.

Monica glanced at the computer screen and then back to King. She had never been worried about her time undercover because she was confident that Muldoon had taken care of his business, but King made her leery. There was no soul present in the man. Even when he smiled, it was a lifeless smile, devoid of feeling. The fact that he already had her information made her somewhat nervous because it showed a level of technological sophistication in King's organization that she had grossly underestimated.

"I'm not a thoroughbred. I'm a thorough bitch, and I'm all in, big daddy. I'ma ride wit' ya 'til the wheels fall off," Monica said with a syrupy Southern drawl.

"Well, shit. Now that that's settled, let's go and finish this business. And Monica?"

"Yes, King?" Monica asked.

"Later on, I wanna know about your being a *thorough bitch*."

Chapter 10

Dirty Money

DirtBag lay in his dank motel room, staring at the ceiling. He planned to use the opportunity that King had given him to get clean and restore himself to his position of prominence. Years earlier, he had awakened in his jail cell to find his cellmate, Yellow Shoes, dead. Initially, he had been blamed for the pimp's death but was quickly cleared. The sheer massiveness of the handprinted bruises on Yellow Shoes' neck had been enough to clear DirtBag of the murder.

The humming drone of the dusty box fan that he'd positioned in the motel window circulated the hot, musty air from outside. Muffled moans of faux pleasure could be heard through the paper-thin walls. It was more than likely the five-dollar crack whore by the name of Precious that occupied the room next to him. She would turn trick after trick in her motel room for five dollars a lay, or ten dollars if the trick happened to be a white boy, and by DirtBag's calculations, she was clearing at least $200 a day. That was $1400 a week if she did it every day—not a bad take for a week's work by any standard—but Precious would spend it just as soon as she made it. Day after day, her salary would be lost in a cloud of milky white crack smoke, and on more than one occasion, DirtBag had lain with Precious.

In his current mental state, the thought of lying with the fiendish woman made his skin crawl. There was something about weaning himself off of the drugs that gave him a certain amount of clarity. His thoughts had never been so lucid. He wanted more from life than waking up in the morning looking forward to getting high. DirtBag sat up and reached for his cigarette pack, seeing one Newport left. It was on nights like this that the cravings really hit him hard. He wasn't only afraid of facing King if he fell off the wagon, but he had also made himself a promise.

In the dim darkness of the South Dallas dusk, DirtBag flickered his sterling silver Zippo lighter, and the bluish flame sprang free. He sat mesmerized by the glow, wondering how he had managed to lose so many of his precious years to the unforgiving blaze. The silver Zippo lighter was the only remnant of his once lucrative position as a prominent member of the upper echelon in Dallas' underworld. In all actuality, DirtBag wasn't the least bit interested in returning to the drug trade. He'd given King that speech because he knew that hustling was the only thing that the young man respected. Had he gone to him and told him that he wanted to get clean and live happily ever after, there was a good chance that King would've told him to beat it. So, he'd lied. He would use King's money to get as far away from Dallas and its temptations as possible.

DirtBag stepped out onto the balcony overlooking the parking lot of the motel and flicked his cigarette butt over the edge. He leaned over the railing to hopefully catch a glimpse of Trina. She stayed in Room 110, and she was perhaps the most beautiful woman that he'd ever laid eyes on. The irony of the situation with DirtBag was that the same thing that started him on his destructive path was now the very thing that motivated him to quit.

Trina wasn't like the many women that shuffled in and out of the flea-bag motel daily. The majority of them were dope users or hookers who used the hourly rate charged by the hotel to their advantage. Trina, however, was different. She was a single mother of a beautiful little boy named DeKovan. At nine years old, he was more intelligent than half of the people that DirtBag came in contact with on a daily basis. Trina had been kicked out of their apartment by DeKovan's father after he'd passed on syphilis to her. When she'd confronted him about it, he'd denied that he was responsible for her "burning," but she knew better. They'd argued and fought deep into the night, and when all was said and done, he had brazenly confessed and told her to pack her and DeKovan's things and get out.

Trina always talked to DirtBag, and they seemed to have more in common than either had been aware. She didn't treat him like a junky. She seemed to see past his drug use and talk to him on a more humane level. She was also a terrific cook. Almost every day, she would cook a hot meal and graciously walk up the two flights of stairs to bring him a plate. He was amazed at what Trina could create on a hot plate: collard greens with ham hocks, macaroni and cheese, and deep-fried hot water cornbread. During one of their conversations, after she'd put DeKovan to sleep, Trina had confided in him that she'd always been attracted to older men. Trina was pushing twenty-nine years old but didn't look a day over eighteen. She said that she'd be more than willing to give him a chance, but he had to leave the dope alone. He would not only have to get clean, but he would have to make a conscious effort to be a respectable man. And that was it. He wanted to please Trina; be the kind of man that she and DeKovan could be proud of.

He looked over the rail again, and this time he saw Trina appear with Dekovan through a breezeway. He whistled to draw her attention, and she looked up, smiled, and waved. Something was wrong, though. Trina's smile wasn't a smile at all. It was a tilted line on her face that spoke of some hidden pain that she had recently suffered.

She slid her key into the locked door of her room and disappeared inside with her head low. DirtBag went inside of his room and slipped a T-shirt over his thin frame. He reached for another Newport and lit it as he made his way downstairs to check on his adopted family. He tapped lightly on Trina's door and stepped back, waiting for her to answer. When Trina answered the door, it was obvious that she'd been crying.

"Come in, babe," she sniffled.

"What's wrong, baby? You don't look like yourself. Is there anything that I can do to help?"

"Man, I lost my job today. DeKovan's daddy came to my job with that bullshit, screaming about me putting him on child support, and got me fired. He brought that drama to my job! I wouldn't have to put his ass on child support if he would just help me. I don't know what I'm going to do now," she cried.

DirtBag hugged her. He could feel her pain and knew that in times like this, it was better to listen and let her vent.

She continued, "I just spent the majority of my check on groceries and clothes for DeKovan to go back to school. Man, this is bullshit."

"Why don't you and D move into my room? No stress, no strain. I mean, with you two being there, it'll actually keep me on the up and up. Plus, we can save some money by only paying rent on one room."

"That's so sweet, but that's your place, and I don't want to burden you with my problems, Reggie." She had never called him DirtBag, not once since they'd met, and he liked it.

"It wouldn't be a burden, honey. I actually want you guys with me, and I promise that if you take me up on this offer, not a day will go by that I don't work hard trying to make y'all proud of me and working toward making a better life for us all."

Chapter 11

Close Call

Just before dusk, Monica wheeled her new Chevy Camaro down a dusty road on the outskirts of Dallas. She'd told Bird of her meeting with Muldoon, and Bird had, in turn, planted the bug in Baby Face's ear that Monica had a hair appointment. As her vehicle approached the abandoned warehouse, she saw a quick flash of headlights ahead of her. She stopped her car in a cloud of dust and killed the lights. Muldoon exited his car and walked toward Monica's, and opened her door.

"Good to see you, Agent Dietrich. I was beginning to worry about you," he said, hugging the young undercover agent.

"No need to worry, sir. Everything is under control. I had a close call earlier today. King's lawyer informed him that there was a snitch in his camp, and since I'm the new kid on the block, he naturally assumed that it was me."

"So, what happened? I'm assuming nothing much, since you're still alive and breathing."

"When he pulled my record, he saw an assortment of criminal charges dating back to my teen years. So in his eyes, I'm a 'thorough bitch,' as he put it." Monica snickered.

"Now that you're in his organization, have you been able to gather any information that we can use to indict?"

"Not yet, at least nothing concrete that'll stick. The closest I've come was today at their money meeting."

"Money meeting? What's that?" Muldoon asked.

"It's a meeting that they have monthly, where all of King's captains get together and tally their earnings. He runs his drug operation like a corporate business. If we wanted to, we could get the whole organization with the RICO statute right now, but that would only be money laundering and tax evasion under RICO. They'd all be out in less than 48 months. I want his ass for life." Monica snorted.

She handed Muldoon her faux emerald earrings. With King's level of sophistication, she couldn't risk being caught with the surveillance equipment. Muldoon wanted her to keep the earrings, but he understood why she gave them back. Without the earrings, she was *truly* on her own.

"How's Jasmine, Agent Muldoon?"

"There has really been no change, unfortunately, Monica. If there is any change, you will be the first to know," Muldoon lied. He straightened his tie and wiped the beads of sweat from his brow.

Monica watched Muldoon through her rearview as she sped away into the night toward Bird's condo. She was meeting Bird for dinner before the whole organization went to Club Concise for the party that King had planned. He was making some sort of big announcement, and he wanted all of his people present, Monica included. As she drove toward her destination, she thought of her parents.

Before her parents' overdose, they had been the typical family living the American dream. Monica's father, Robert Dietrich, had taken a job as an auto mechanic at Harrison's Garage and had almost instantaneously fallen in love with the owner's daughter. Being a white man living in South Dallas was taboo enough, but to date a black woman would most certainly raise a concerned eyebrow or two. And so began the whirlwind romance between a poor white immigrant from Germany and the shop owner's daughter. Kendra Harrison was in heaven, and against her father's wishes, she had gone out with Robert and fallen madly in love with him. Although he'd been in the United States since he was thirteen years old, at twenty-two, he still held his German accent, and Kendra found it both sexy and cute the way the young man stumbled over his words in broken English, trying his best to find the right combination to express his love to her.

The elder Mr. Harrison had worked menial jobs his whole life, toiling, enduring countless hours, scrimping and saving until he had saved enough money to open his auto shop. He had built his business from the ground up and had managed to secure not one but two of the largest contracts in history for a small minority business. Harrison's Garage had been awarded contracts by both the Dallas Independent School District and the city of Dallas. He serviced their fleets of school buses and city work trucks, a task that kept him both busy and flush with cash. He'd always done right by Kendra's mother, Mildred, and up until her death, he'd made sure to give her the best of everything. Kendra was the only family that he had left, and he didn't want to lose her to a man, let alone a white man. It didn't matter to Mr. Harrison that the man was from Germany. He was white, and in Dallas, tension was still thick between the white and black populations.

Benjamin Harrison didn't feel like Robert Dietrich was good enough for his daughter. She was a college graduate, graduating from SMU with a degree in business, and he was a mechanic that had yet to prove himself in Benjamin Harrison's eyes. She had stepped right into his business, transforming his company from a shade tree mechanic's shop to a well-known staple of business in the Dallas metropolitan area. It was she who'd helped to secure those large contracts.

Against his wishes, Kendra and Robert married in a small ceremony at his shop. But much to Benjamin's astonishment, Robert actually made a wonderful husband for his daughter. He was a hard worker, and he seemed to live to make Kendra happy. Ben Harris had grown to love the young man as a son. He'd only wanted his daughter to be happy, and from the looks of it, Robert Dietrich was the perfect man for the job.

The birth of Benjamin's first grandchild, Monica, had brought him more joy than he could have possibly hoped for. She had given him back the love that he'd lost when Mildred died, and he showered her with lavish gifts. Six years later, the birth of his second granddaughter, Jasmine, was just as special, but life was beginning to change. Robert and Kendra were less concerned with being parents and more concerned with running the streets.

Robert had his first taste of cocaine working late nights at the shop. He'd initially used the drug to stay awake while working on cars late into the night, but the powdery substance had lost its effectiveness over time, so Robert promptly graduated to crack and crystal meth. When Kendra found out about her husband's drug use, she was understandably shaken and upset, but he'd convinced her to try it in pure peer pressure fashion.

"This is nothing, baby. I control the dope. It does not control me!" he explained.

Kendra loved her husband, so when Robert whispered sweetly in her ear, "Try it, baby. You might like it," she took the crack pipe and put it to her lips while Robert cheered her on, holding the lighter. Smoke swirled through the glass cylinder, passing through her parted lips, and euphoria registered in her college-educated brain. Kendra had a heightened sense of clarity. The world seemed to speed up and then slow to a snail's pace.

From that moment forward, they were both chasing bliss in search of that first hit, and Benjamin Harrison grew to hate them both for what they'd allowed to happen to their family. When they overdosed, he'd sat Monica down and explained that drug use was a disease; not a disease in the physical sense, but a disease of the mind. He'd candidly recounted tales of her parents doing just about anything for a high. He spoke of how her father had pimped her mother out for drugs.

Benjamin looked her in her eyes and gently told her, "Monica, you're a product of your parents, but you aren't your parents. Always strive to stand apart from the crowd, honey, and if you ever need me, baby girl, don't you hesitate to call me."

Monica smiled to herself. She had always been able to count on Pop Pop to help her through any situation. She was indeed a product of her parents, and she would use it to her full advantage. Monica knew the streets, and the rule of thumb in the streets was that snitches got stitches. She had often heard her grandfather say, "If you can't take the heat, get your ass out of the kitchen." But she would not only stay in the kitchen; she would cook a full-course meal.

Chapter 12

The Squad

King dressed slowly in his full-length body mirror. He knew that his wardrobe brought plenty of envy, but that went with the territory. King's signature had always been his extremely long, perfectly braided cornrows, but tonight was different. Tonight, he would let his hair down—literally. His silky, curled, jet-black ringlets had been straightened to perfection. His bone-straight locks fell effortlessly past his shoulders. He looked down to see Noisy Boy sitting at attention at his feet.

"Tonight is the night, little man. Daddy is going to see if he can find you a mommy," he said affectionately to his puppy.

Club Plush would be his crew's destination, and he couldn't be more excited. He'd told everyone at the meeting that their soiree would be held at Club Concise, but King was smart. If, indeed, there was a snitch in his camp, then the Feds would focus their attention on that club. He would put out calls to his crew leaders at the last minute with the location change, leaving the Feds with no time to regroup.

He smiled to himself as Monica crossed his mind. He'd never given women much of a second thought because so far in his young life, they had all been the same, but Monica was different. King had always been attracted to a certain breed of woman, and although he wasn't a very spiritual person, he felt a connection with her. Maybe God had sent this perfect angel his way to cleanse him. He had no desire to get out of the game, but to have a woman that could match his hustle had to be a Godsend. His life had been anything but perfect, and King had no compunction when it came to letting Monica know that she was indeed on his radar. He completed his baby blue ensemble with an array of sapphires and diamonds.

"How do I look, baby boy?" he asked the dog. Noisy Boy gave a high-pitched yelp in King's direction.

Bird paced back and forth across his living room floor when Monica walked in. "Goddamn, Monica, where have you been?" Bird asked testily.

"I had a meeting with Muldoon. What's going on?"

"You weren't followed, were you?" Bird asked. He was visibly shaken, and it made Monica nervous.

"I very seriously doubt it. Why do you look so nervous?"

"Man, that nigga Drak just pulled up on me out of nowhere while I was pumping gas. The shit freaked me out because I had been looking in my rearview mirror, watching headlights, hitting corners, and trying to be extra careful, and this crazy-ass dude just pulls up on me out of nowhere."

"What did he say?"

"That's the crazy part is that the fool didn't say shit. He just watched me for a long time, and when I finished pumping gas, I was about to walk to his car and ask him why the fuck he was watching me, but he sped off. They know something, man. I can feel it."

"Calm your hyper ass down. Shit, I'm the one undercover, so I should be the one nervous. That's a tactic that we learned in the Feds. A guilty person always will show their guilt if you make them feel uncomfortable enough. You let me take care of Drak."

Chapter 13

Club Plush

Monica and Bird walked into Club Plush, and her jaw dropped. The club was exquisite. It was unlike anything that she'd ever seen. The club was dim but not dark, giving it an aura of intimacy. The waiters all wore form-fitting black pants with black bowties but no shirts. Each of them looked as though they had been hand-picked from a Chippendale's calendar. The female waitresses wore black catsuits with rips and tears strategically placed to accent their voluptuous bodies. Monica noticed that the waiters only catered to females and the waitresses only catered to the men, which she thought was a unique touch. Men and women co-mingled, talking amongst themselves as they waited their turn to make it into the unisex restrooms. She was so busy taking in the scenery that she didn't notice when King stepped up in front of her.

"You like what you see, Money?" King asked.

She looked into King's icy eyes and smiled. "Yes, this is nice. We don't have anything like this back home."

"Yeah, I bet you country niggas be having ho-downs in barns and shit." King laughed.

"We are country, but we're not hillbillies. I mean, we have nice clubs, but nothing even remotely close to this. We only have hole-in-the-wall clubs, really."

"I'm just fucking with you, sweets. What up, Bird? Y'all come on up. We have the whole VIP section upstairs."

Bird gave a quick *what's up* head nod in King's direction and made his way through the crowd toward the stairs. King stood blocking Monica's way and stared at her intensely. This was the second time that they had faced off, but this time was different. There was something in King's eyes that made her feel comfortable. His gaze was soft and inviting. It was confusing to Monica because since meeting King, he had always given off an arrogant and brash vibe. His demeanor was now relaxed and poised.

J. Cole's voice wafted through the massive speakers, drowning Monica in a relaxing bass riff. "She got me up all night constantly singing these love songs. She got me open all night, down and out with these love songs," he rapped. King leaned in and kissed Monica gently on her lips. Her first instinct was to pull away, but surprisingly, she welcomed his soft and eager tongue. His tongue explored the heat of her mouth, and the kiss was as close to perfect as she'd ever had. When he'd finished, he pulled her close and whispered in her ear, "I'm going to make you mine, Monica, or die trying."

Monica shivered from his cool breath on her ear. "I'm already yours, King, but be clear: I'm not like these other little thirsty hood rats that ride your dick and hope for a payday. I'm my own bitch. I get my own paper, and I'm not trying to have any kids until I'm married," Monica whispered into his ear.

"I guess a nigga better wife you then, huh?" he shot back.

"Whooooa. Hol' up, swole up. Not so fast. Let's take shit one day at a time!" Monica said.

She knew that she'd said the right thing because King smiled and winked at her. He stepped behind her and pressed his firm manhood against her body, leading her through the crowd of clubgoers. As they made their way through the club, King was greeted with hellos from other hustlers and side-eyed glances from those that hated his swag. Many of the women that they passed looked at King as if they were ready to drop their panties right then and there, but Monica was met with blank stares and heated glimpses, wondering where she'd come from and who she was.

King was a living legend, and many of the women present had either slept with him or were waiting their turn. This scene was a change because he never showed public displays of affection. None of the women in the room had been privy to the whereabouts of his residence, let alone being seen openly affectionate with him. When they got to the stairs, King moved to the side of Monica and held her hand as they ascended the royal blue carpet-clad staircase. They walked into the VIP area, and all eyes were on them. All of the men present stared at Monica as if she were a cold drink of water in the desert. The skin-tight red dress that she wore with red stiletto heels accentuated her every curve. The front of the dress barely covered her ample breasts, and her nipples pressed firmly against the silky fabric. The tips of her toes and fingers were painted the same ruby-red hue. Monica gave a quick look around and shed a sly grin. The one thing that she knew about human nature, especially men, was that if they liked you, then they would champion your cause. As long as the men in King's camp had lust in their eyes, she never had to worry about one of them trying to get information and expose her to King.

The VIP area was magnificent. Plush couches, lounge chairs, and tables were strategically placed to give the VIPs a sense of connection to one another. The walls were covered in Swarovski crystals, except for the front walls, which were made of softly smoked glass. Each table had one small candle in the center of it that flickered and danced seductively to the sound of muffled voices and whispers. The combination of candlelight and crystals cast an iridescent glow throughout the area.

King led Monica through his merry band of hustlers to a table nestled discreetly in the corner of the private area. He pulled a high-back bar stool out for her to have a seat and then sat across from her.

“Damn, Money. You got me being all gentlemanly and shit. This isn’t like me, but you make me want to do better.” King blushed.

“I like this side of you, Kochese. I mean, everyone knows that you’re a gangster, but if I’m going to be your one and only, then you’re going to have to learn to separate your hard side and soft side.”

“Nah, ain’t nothing soft about me, sweets,” he said, standing up quickly, then just as quickly sat back down. He smiled his huge, model-like smile. “I’m just bullshittin’. I understand where you’re coming from. So, tell me about *Monica*. I mean, what do you like to do for fun, what turns you on, stuff like that?”

Monica gave King a glimpse into her make-believe world. She made up stories that included both her and Bird so that King kept it on his mind that her “play cousin” was not to be touched. She reached across the table and stroked his hand gently. “There are a lot of things that turn me on, and you’re one of them. Tell you a little secret? I went to your Facebook page and stole this picture.” She pulled her iPhone from her clutch and showed King a picture of himself. He was shirtless and sweating. His abs and muscles seemed exaggerated by the sheen added by his perspiration. In the background, Bird and Baby Face stood holding a basketball.

"Oh, shit. I remember this day! I smashed your cousin on the court," King said.

"Yeah, well, when I'm alone, I look at this picture and play with myself," she said seductively.

For the first time in his life, King opened his mouth to speak but couldn't form the words. He stared at Monica like a shy child.

"Cat got your tongue, Kochese?" she teased.

He still didn't speak, but got up, leaned across the table, and kissed her softly. "Nah, Money got my tongue."

"Can I ask you something?"

"You can ask me anything you want to, Pretty Red."

"Do you ever get tired of being feared? I mean, do you ever see yourself getting out of the game?"

"I think about it all the time, but look at me, Monica. I barely have an education and I've been selling drugs since I was ten years old. I'm an unemployable ninth-grade dropout. I've made more money in my twentysomething years than a muhfucka twice my age working on a nine-to-five could ever dream of making."

"I understand that, and that's sad, but you could always get a trade or go back to school."

"Listen, man, you've been my girl all of twenty minutes and you're already trying to change a nigga. But understand me when I tell you, Monica: I didn't choose this shit. I was thrown into this shit!"

"Calm down, baby. I didn't mean to upset you. I'm just trying to get to know you, that's all."

"I feel you, but that shit brings back really bad memories, you know?" King said somberly.

The look in his eyes told Monica everything that she needed to know. Kochese Mills did have morals and principles. He was a young man trapped in a world of reputation and expectations. He was in deep and had no idea how to get out. Monica's heart went out to him. She was just learning about the man in her file, but she could see that he had been damaged beyond repair.

"Look around, Money. Look at these people's faces. This is our family. They have families, and they depend on me to feed those families. If I did choose to get out of the game, do you have any idea how many kids would go hungry? How many kids would wake up on Christmas to absolutely nothing under the tree?"

Monica looked around. It was true. The men and women in his squad looked happy. They laughed and joked amongst each other in moods of joviality. King had made sure to have an assortment of liquor ranging from Hennessy all the way to Louis XIII. He stood up and moved to the center of his workers.

"Listen up. I have a very special announcement to make. Bird, close that door over there, my nigga. All right, listen up. Like I said, I have a very special announcement to make." There were hushed whispers among the hustlers, but no one dared speak above a whisper after King had instructed them to quiet down. "I want to congratulate each of you captains and your squads. We literally made a killing this month, and I'm beyond excited."

Loud applause erupted, and King raised his hand to quiet them once more.

"I know everybody eatin', 'cause some of you muhfuckas are getting fat. On the real, though, I really appreciate y'all hustlin' and keeping this thing alive."

"We love you, dawg, and we couldn't see this shit any other way, mane. To King Kochese!" Baby Face shouted.

The other hustlers followed suit and echoed the young gangster's sentiment. "To King Kochese," they all said in unison, raising their glasses.

Again, King raised his hand, but this time he motioned for Monica to join him among his minions. "We've welcomed Money into the fold, and she's a hustlin' muhfucka, right? Well, I'm King Ko-muhfuckin'-chese, and every King needs a queen. So, I'm here to tell y'all that Money is that queen! All hail the queen!" He raised Monica's hand.

Bird and Drak exchanged glances. Neither man had ever witnessed King serious about any woman, so they were indeed perplexed. Still, both raised their glasses.

"All hail the muhfuckin' queen," they said.

Monica turned to King and kissed him deeply, letting her hand brush his cheek gently. She turned to the crowd, who waited to hear her speak.

"I'm not sure how the last queen did shit, but I'm not here to make waves. I'm here to serve my man and help grow his business. I'm not a hard person to get along with, but I need each of you to understand that if any one of you gets out of line with me, I will not hesitate to put a bullet in your head and pay for your funeral," Monica said calmly.

Throughout the room, the quaint smiles turned to worried faces.

"All right, hustlers, next month, if we repeat these numbers, I'ma take all of y'all down to Miami," King shouted. "Now, let's party like a muhfucka and get twisted."

Chapter 14

A Bullet and a Dream

Kochese and Monica stepped out of Club Plush hand in hand. Both were a little tipsy, but neither was drunk.

Monica saw the black unmarked van sitting in the distance moments before the black sedan raced down the street and headed in their direction. The automobile's lights were out, and Monica's adrenaline began to rush. It all happened so fast, but Monica was faster. She shoved King toward the crowd just as the barrel of the TEC-9 began to fire. Screams from the club patrons erupted as round after round struck innocent bystanders and inanimate objects. As the car sped past, Monica reached underneath her dress to her thigh holster and removed her .380. She raced to the center of the street and emptied her clip in the direction of the speeding car. The back window of the sedan exploded in shards of glass as the car made a sharp left turn out of eyesight. She had made certain to take note of the license plate number: Q10-2RU. She looked back at the van just as it sped away in the opposite direction. The license plate had been covered with a piece of cardboard.

Monica ran back to the crowd, where Bird and Drak had both covered King to shield him from the barrage of bullets.

"Are you hit, baby? Are you okay?" Monica asked King.

He stood up and brushed himself off, looking around. "Yeah, I'm straight," King said, obviously flustered.

"What the fuck was that shit?" Drak asked.

People eager to catch a glimpse of the negativity had started to regroup in front of the club.

"We need to get you out of here before the police come, bro!" Bird said heatedly.

"Now you two niggas concerned?" King spat. "Get the fuck away from me, mane. Where the fuck were you two punk-ass muhfuckas when them niggas tried to blow my fuckin' head off? Maybe y'all set this shit up!"

"Hold up, King. I been with you too long for you to come at me with this bullshit, nigga," Drak said. "You need to go home, get some rest, and holla at me tomorrow."

"So you're giving me orders now, Drak? Don't get it twisted, my nigga. I'm still the same dude. I don't bar that bullshit you talking, playa."

Drak made a move toward King, but Monica blocked his way with her .380 pointed at his stomach. "I like you, Drak, so don't make me gut you like a fish," she said, cocking her pistol.

"You know what, Money? You're right, baby girl. Tensions are high, and I love my little nigga too much to snap his neck. King, you got a good one with this one, but you need to learn the difference between someone who's with you because they wanna be and somebody who's scared of yo' ass, partner!" he said, turning to Bird. "You think you can run me to the crib, bruh?"

Bird looked at Drak and then at King. He had never witnessed the two men so much as having a disagreement, let alone a full-blown argument with witnesses.

King's eyes burned holes in Bird, but just as quickly softened. "Take that old nigga home, Bird, before I bang his ass up. Straight up, Drak, that's my bad, my nigga. This shit just caught me off guard," King said jokingly, trying to lighten the mood.

Drak looked back and mumbled some barely audible curses in King's direction as he made his way to Bird's car.

King palmed Monica's firm butt. "I guess since you saved my life, you think I owe you now, huh?"

"You don't owe me anything, babe. I don't play about my man. Now, if you wanna hook a bitch up with a little something something, then you know," Monica said, winking at King.

He felt his groin twitch. He wanted Monica, but he also didn't want to ruin it with her.

"Since you rode with Bird and Drak rode with me, I guess that means I can either take you to Bird's or take you home."

"Take me home? I stay with Bird, silly."

"Yeah, that shit sounds good, but no woman of mine is staying with another man. I don't give a damn if he is your cousin."

"What if I don't want to come and stay with you, Kochese?"

"Then Noisy Boy is going to be really disappointed, because I already told him I was going to bring him a new mommy, and you know you're the only mommy he's going to accept," King said, laughing at the same time.

"Okay, for mama's Noisy Boy, I'll come. But King?"

"Yeah, Pretty Red?" he replied.

"If you cross me, especially with another bitch, I will cut your dick off and feed it to Noisy Boy. Do you understand?"

King studied her face for a hint of a joke, but the joke never came. She was gravely serious, and the way that he felt about her was real, so there was definitely no need for her to worry.

"Girl, you don't ever have to worry about that. Shit, like Biggie Smalls said: if the head right, King there e'ry night. Just keep it real with me and never leave me, and I'm good, babe. Trust me."

He tossed Monica the keys to his Range Rover and opened the driver's side door so that she could get in.

"Don't spoil me, King, because the same way you start this is how you need to end it," Monica warned.

"And who said that I wanted it to end, shorty?" King closed the door and walked around to the passenger's side to climb in. They pulled away from the curb lining the front of Club Plush and headed toward King's palatial estate. King let the seat on the passenger's side recline and closed his eyes as Trey Songz sang over his melodic beats.

Monica looked over at the man whose life she had managed to infiltrate. He was so trusting, so very naïve, and for the first time since she had taken the case, a small twinge of guilt crept into her mind. She needed to get King home and do some thinking, but tomorrow Muldoon would have to explain what went wrong. They came too close to killing her for her comfort.

Chapter 15

Who Shot Ya

The soles of Monica's pink and gray Air Jordan sneakers squeaked loudly against the tile floor. "Is Muldoon in his office?" she asked the skinny brunette sitting behind the semi-circular receptionist's desk.

"Yes, but you can't go in. He's with someone," she said, but Monica ignored the woman and walked through the large wooden doors that led to his office.

Muldoon sat in his office with Bird, laughing and talking as if nothing had ever happened. Bird sat with his back to the door, and he seemed to be explaining something to the elder agent because his moves were exaggerated and animated. Muldoon looked up and saw Monica and stood quickly, drawing Bird's attention.

"Agent Dietrich, I'm so happy to see you this morning," Muldoon said.

"We have to stop disappearing at the same time, Monica, or King is going to get suspicious," Bird said.

"First of all, don't worry about King," she said, then turned her attention to Muldoon. "What the fuck was that last night? Your boys almost shot me while they were gunning for King. So, basically, I'm expendable?"

"Mind your manners, agent," Muldoon said. "Those shooters were not agents. They didn't belong to us, but truthfully, it couldn't have happened at a better time. I'm sure that your fast act last night more than sealed King's trust for you."

"If it wasn't you, then who was it?" Monica asked. She didn't believe Muldoon. King was a feared man in Dallas, and she was intelligent enough to realize that envy bred hatred, but the streets often talked, and a botched hit on King would bring a lot of bloodshed.

Muldoon reached into his desk and removed a file. Inside was the picture of a man that she'd never seen before. "Who is this?" Monica asked.

"That's Shawt Dawg. He used to work for King briefly, but according to Bird, he is, well, no longer with us."

"He owed King money and tried to duck and dodge until he was finally caught," Bird said. "That cold-hearted bastard had the man fed to his bullmastiff, Beast."

"According to Mr. Bircher here, the men that tried to kill King last night were friends and family of Mr. Short Dog. It was in retaliation for his murder."

Monica laughed uncontrollably. Her guffaw was loud and shrill, much like borderline hysteria. Bird and Muldoon exchanged worried glances. Monica wasn't acting like herself, but they had both learned that there was always a method to her madness.

"What is so funny, Miss Dietrich?" Muldoon asked.

"The proper way that you say Short Dog. It's Shawt Dawg!"

All three laughed at the inside joke. The seriousness of the situation, however, wasn't lost on any one of them. With someone gunning for King, it would most definitely add an element of danger to Monica's job.

"King thinks I went to Bird's house to grab a few things," she continued. "He asked me to move in with him last night, so I guess you could say I'm really in now," Monica said. She had a faraway but reflective look in her eyes. King had a hold on her, and she didn't like it.

Muldoon noticed but decided against accusing her. Instead, he generalized his statement. "Monica, I know you may have noticed parts of Kochese that seem *human,* but remember that he's a cold-blooded killer, and he needs to be brought to justice," he said.

Monica didn't utter a word, but her cold green eyes told a story that had already been written: Monica Dietrich was in too deep.

Bird turned in his chair to watch her exit before speaking. The sway of her voluptuous hips moving from side to side lulled him into a rhythmic trance. "You think she can handle this shit, Muldoon?"

"I hope so. Lord knows I hope so, because if not, I will have to bury *both* of you."

The duality of that statement wasn't lost on Bird. Either Monica held up on her end of the bargain, or they were dead, whether literally or figuratively. If King didn't kill them, then Muldoon would make certain that they both rotted in prison.

Chapter 16

The Judas Kiss

Drak sat on the top floor of the lavish penthouse loft that he called home. He had his guns spread out on the table with all of the necessary tools needed to clean each one. He still fumed over the argument that he'd had the previous night. King had never tried him like that before. He had always been as loyal as possible to King, but Kochese had let a woman come between them. He would get his soon enough, but for now, he would bide his time.

His cell phone vibrated against the glass coffee table, reverberating from wall to wall in the spacious apartment. He picked it up and looked at it. It was King. He thought about not answering it, but King had no drawbacks about coming to Drak's home and pounding on the door until he opened up. King was like that, almost childlike in his approach to certain situations, but he was also extremely calculating, manipulative, and dangerous.

"What up, King?" Drak said angrily into the receiver.

"You sound like you're still heated, bruh. I apologized last night, so you need to let this shit go, mane."

"Nah, I ain't heated, dawg. I just got a lot of shit to do. What's going on?"

"I just wanted to let you know that there are some changes coming. Baby is moving in with me and Noisy Boy. It's some more shit, but I don't want to talk about it on the phone. How long will it take you to get out here?"

"Give me an hour, and I'll be out there. Have you heard from Bond on that little snitch situation?"

"Not yet, but as soon as I know something, you'll know something."

"A'ight, bet," Drak said, hanging up the phone. He tossed the phone to the table and walked to the shower. It was almost impossible for Drak to remain angry with King. He had been in King's organization so long that it was a wonder that he even got angry at the man anymore. He knew King, and his intentions were rarely ever evil if he liked you. If he didn't like you, well, that was another matter altogether.

There was trouble brewing; Drak could feel it. He stepped into the shower and stepped back out just as fast. He ran to the living room of his loft and dialed a number. When the phone was answered, Drak spoke two words into his phone.

"Baby Face."

He hung up the phone. He walked naked back to his shower, leaving watery footprints in his wake. He had set a plan of detrimental proportions into motion, and he would pit bishops against pawns and pawns against kings.

King wasn't accustomed to waiting, but he was too happy and excited to be angry. The previous night had been spectacular, with the exception of someone trying to gun him down. Monica was a different breed of woman than what King was used to. She was sassy and gorgeous, not to mention a hustler. She had really shown him a different side of herself the night before when she'd come to his aid. Monica was down for him, he could feel it, and he was very seldom wrong.

They'd slept together the night before, and King was surprised at his behavior because they'd done just that, *sleep*. No sex, just a little kissing and touching, but no penetration. He hadn't minded at all. He wanted to respect her and give her the world, and that's exactly what he would do. When she'd said that she was going to Bird's to get her things, he'd felt an instant disconnect. He missed her face, her walk, her scent, her smile. She had come into his life and completely mesmerized him, and King had no compunction in admitting that he was sprung even though they hadn't even slept together yet.

"You want Monica to be your new mommy, Boy, huh?"

Noisy Boy looked up at his master with soft, pleading eyes and gave a sharp yelp, showing his approval. King curled up on his oversized white couch and turned on the television. Maury Povich read the results of some hopeful mother's DNA test, but rather than laugh as he'd done so many times in the past about the women running off stage in tears, *knowing* that the accused man wasn't the father, it caused him to reflect on his own pedigree.

King had been born to a mother that was both a drug user and a whore. His earliest recollection of his mother was finding her in bed with two men sharing her body and a crack pipe. From a very early age, he'd learned to take care of his mother out of both necessity and guilt. When things were good, they were good, but when they were bad, all hell usually broke loose.

He could remember asking his mother on many occasions who his father was, only to have his mother look him in the eyes and tell him flatly, "I don't know. He was just a trick, Kochese. Find a horny white man that likes black pussy, and then take your pick." Although the brashness of her words had cut deep into his soul, they gave him clarity. He was a nobody, a bastard child with no roots and no purpose.

During one of his mother's blackouts, Kochese had rifled and rambled through all of his mother's papers and pictures and happened to run across a picture that looked as though it had been cut out of a magazine. It was of a handsome, fair-haired white man with ice-blue eyes. According the write-up in the article, he was Hayden Cross, a successful businessman in the Dallas tech world. He owned a computer component distribution firm called Cross-Tech, and according to the article, he had been recently named among *Forbes* magazine's twenty richest men in the United States. Underneath the article were bundles of letters wrapped in rubber bands. Kochese went through the letters, and each one bore the same stamp in bold red letters: RETURN TO SENDER. They were addressed to Hayden Cross, and the man had never so much as opened one of them. Kochese was an exact replica of the man, down to his ice-blue eyes.

Kochese sat on the floor of his mother's bedroom crying, not understanding how his father, his sperm donor, could deny him his birthright. Kochese walked to the kitchen of their home and filled a large cake bowl with ice-cold water. He walked to the couch and stood over his mother, Evelyn Mills, seething with rage. He stared down at the woman who had given birth to him but had never really been a mother. He took the water and doused her violently.

She awoke with a startle, struggling and gasping for air. "What the fuck is your problem, little nigga?" she spat between gasps.

At fourteen years old, King stood a menacing five-foot-ten; not a giant by any means, but he towered over his mother's five-foot-one frame. His chest swelled with anger, and his temple throbbed uncontrollably. Kochese clenched and unclenched his fist, noticeably agitated, and it wasn't lost on her. Her demeanor and attitude changed upon seeing his mood. "Why are you so upset, baby? Tell mama what's wrong."

Kochese looked at his mother. *Evelyn.* He knew her manipulative ways as well as he knew his own. She would, by habit, make him feel guilty about being in pain. She had a knack for turning the situation around to make herself seem like the victim, but not this time.

"Why would you tell me that my father was just a trick and that you didn't know who he was, Ma?" he asked.

Evelyn sucked her teeth. She had no desire to answer questions coming from a teenager. She had taken care of her son independently with no help from Kochese's sperm donor. He had chosen to forego being a part of his son's life, and in Evelyn's eyes, it was his loss. Why should she explain her actions to her only son?

"I told you that to protect you, Kochese. I might not be perfect, but I'll be damned if I let anyone hurt you."

"That wasn't your choice, Ma. You robbed me of a childhood. While you're out running the streets, I'm here. While you're turning tricks with these dudes, I'm here. I wear bullshit to school, I'm teased on a regular basis because everybody in my fucking school knows that my mom is a two-dollar crack ho, but that's okay, right? Well, I'm leaving!"

Kochese left the house, slamming the door behind him. He walked to the bus stop on the corner of Oakland and Grand Avenue and sat for a long while. He had stormed out of his mother's home in anger, but in all actuality, he didn't have a plan. It was late, and the temperature had begun to drop. The thin white T-shirt that he wore did little to shield him from the rigid Texas fall wind.

The smell of grilled onions and deep-fried chicken filled Kochese's nostrils. His stomach growled, almost doubling him over in pain. He looked toward where the sweet smell of nourishment came from. It was the Good Luck burger place on the corner.

"What's going on, youngsta?" a voice said from beyond the shadows of the bus stop.

Kochese looked around but didn't see anyone. He stood and scanned the street. Near the back of the bus stop, parked at the edge of the driveway leading to Good Luck, sat a snow-white Cadillac Eldorado. Even in the darkness, the chrome on the Cadillac gleamed from the streetlights. The dome light of the Cadillac lit up the interior of the car, revealing the mystery man behind the voice. It was Michael Ross, the neighborhood drug dealer whose name seemed to be on the lips of every hustler in Dallas. He was a legend in his own right. His name alone carried with it the weight of the world, and he could be Kochese's savior if willing to give him a chance.

"Nothing much. I'm hungry as hell, man," Kochese said.

"Get in, young nigga. Let me put a bug in your ear," Mike said.

Kochese got into the vehicle, leery of what might happen, but he *needed* to trust someone. He wanted to trust Michael Ross, and he also needed money.

"Fuck you doing out here on these streets, little nigga?" Mike said. "You too fuckin' pretty to be runnin' these streets, boy."

"Ain't nothing pretty about me, playboy. Don't let these blue eyes fool you," Kochese said, revealing a blade that he had hidden in his pants.

Michael Ross threw up his hands in mock surprise. "Hold up, little dawg. No harm intended, my nigga. Let me put you down with something, though. Never bring a knife to a gunfight, fool." Mike reached down between his car seat and pulled out a nickel-plated 9 mm.

The blood drained from Kochese's face. He knew that he had no chance for escape. It wasn't much of a surprise to the young man. His life had been one disappointment after another, and God had long since abandoned him.

He dropped his head and waited for the inevitable to happen, but it never came. Instead, the drug dealer gave him something that he'd longed for and searched for his whole life.

"What's your name, playa?" Mike asked.

"Kochese, mane."

"I'm going to put you down with me, Kochese. Instead of hiring you and putting you on the block to scramble, I'm gonna train you personally. I'ma ask you something, and I want you to be totally honest with me. Can you do that?"

"Yeah, I can do that. What's up?"

"If I put you down, my nigga, what's your ultimate goal? What do you want out of this shit?"

"I wanna be the king of Dallas, man. I want niggas to respect my name. I want muhfuckas to tremble in fear when I walk into the room."

"I know you always hear people say that respect is earned and shit, but on the real, respect is taken at the end of the barrel of a muhfuckin' gun. Yeah, you can run this shit, and I'm gonna show you how, but understand this: If you cross me, I'ma do you, my nigga, and no matter what you think, it's only two ways out of the game, fool. The only two options are death or a life sentence." Mike waited for his young predecessor to say something, but Kochese seemed to have retreated into his thoughts. "Stay loyal to me, youngsta, and I'll show you how to get money, bitches, and riches. From now on, I'm gonna call you King Kochese."

Michael took King to each one of his haunts, introducing him as his protégé and touting him as the youngster who would one day rule the streets of Dallas with an iron fist. King had smiled it off, almost blushing at the vote of confidence but never really believing that he could be any more than a mid-level drug dealer. At the time, King had no idea how very wrong he had been.

Although Michael Ross had afforded him the opportunity to become the most powerful teenager to ever walk the streets of South Dallas, that power had come with a price. One day, during his senior year of high school, he'd whipped his Jaguar into Mike's afterschool spot called The Pit. It was a hangout that was frequented by high school kids, many of whom were responsible for King's torment in his younger years, *and* was the unofficial base of operations for Mike Ross. As Kochese had grown, so had his legend, and being handpicked by Michael Ross had definitely had its perks. Kochese had walked into The Pit and into a full-fledged mob meeting. He'd heard rumors of a black mafia, but it was just that in his mind: a *rumor*. Each man present in the back office of The Pit looked like money, and there was no denying whose presence he had stepped into. They were called The Family, and they controlled not only Dallas, but the state of Texas as a whole.

"We have to expand. Texas is good money, but in order for us to really be in the positions that we've planned, we have to move now," Mike said. He beckoned for Kochese to join him at the round table. "This is the young man that is going to usher us into a new era."

The family members looked at one another, puzzled.

"I can't speak for these niggas, but I'm not trusting my organization to no young, wet-behind-the-ears-ass punk," a huge black man by the name of LA said. "This little nigga still got milk on his breath. Look at them blue eyes. Who the fuck's gonna fear this dude, man?"

With no hesitation, King whipped out his 9 mm Ruger and put it to LA's head.

"Muhfucka, you don't have to be scared to catch a goddamned slug," King said.

LA had a look of both confusion and fear, wondering how he had allowed the teenager to get the drop on him.

"Yeeeeeeah, nigga, I guess you answered your own question," Mike Ross teased. "I guess you're the one that's scared of this little nigga, huh?"

"Mike, call off ya fucking bulldog, man," LA said, raising his hands in defeat.

Mike motioned for King to lower his gun and winked at the young kid. King had grown to be everything that Mike Ross had hoped he'd be. He was a savvy businessman and a stone-cold killer. Michael Ross knew that he was on his way out, likely headed to prison for his crimes against the state, and King would be his successor.

That had been years earlier, and now King sat atop a vast criminal empire that reached from Dallas to Chicago and beyond. Through planning and diabolical calculation, King had been able to systematically eliminate all of The Family's former members. He sat staring at the TV thinking about the fate that had befallen Mike Ross. He had not only given King his nickname, but he had also given him his identity. It was unfortunate that after all Mike Ross had given him, the only thing King had been able to give him in return was a gunshot to his frontal lobe.

Monica walked into Kochese's house and was greeted by Noisy Boy at the door. His tail wagged ferociously underneath his shiny white coat.

"Hey, mama's baby. Where's daddy, huh? Where's daddy?" she said to the puppy.

"I'm in here, Money," King yelled from the other room. She walked into the sitting room to find Kochese and Drak sitting across from one another as if hatching some sort of master plan. There was a bottle of Hennessey sitting on the table with two half-finished glasses of the potent cognac.

"You're just in time baby," Kochese said, motioning for Monica to join their conversation.

"I'm happy to see that you've been able to settle this nigga down, baby girl!" Drak said. "I've been kicking it with him for years, and you're the first woman that has seen daylight hit this house, let alone move in. Just promise me that you'll take care of my boy."

Monica smiled at Drak. She wasn't too fond of him because she felt like he was using Kochese and was only out for himself. But if King liked it, she would love it.

"I got him, Drak. As long as he keeps it real with me, I will do the same. Hey, baby." She walked over and kissed King softly on the lips.

"I'm glad you're both here. Besides Noisy Boy, you two are the only people that I can really tolerate," King said.

Drak and Monica both looked at each other, bewildered. As far as they knew, King didn't trust anybody *but* Noisy Boy.

"What's going on, playboy?" Drak asked. "I've never heard you say anything remotely close to you trusting anybody."

"Yeah, well, there is a first time for everything. I've fallen in love with this lady, and although some people may call me foolish, I want to share everything with her. That's why I'm making her my pickup and delivery girl for the northern sector of Dallas over to Chicago. Bird will retain the southern sector down to Austin and over to New Orleans. By the first of the year, I want us to be leaving the drug trade and going into legitimate business," King said triumphantly.

Although Monica was stunned, she realized that she still had a role to play. "Do you mean it, baby?" she shouted, full of glee. "You're going to leave the business?"

"You're damn skippy, babe. That shit last night taught me something. Niggas want me dead. You can always utilize one-half of the poor to murder the other half of the poor, remember that."

"Fuck's that s'pose to mean, nigga?" Drak asked.

"It means that it's a dog-eat-dog world, and we're all vying for a position of power on this rock," King said. He walked to the bar and retrieved a note. On the piece of paper two names were scrawled: Baby Face and Shawt Dawg. He handed the scrap of paper to Monica, who read it and handed it to Drak.

"What's this, King? Shawt Dawg is dead," Drak said.

"I know that! It was his family that tried to murder me last night, but they fucked up, so I'ma deal with it my way," King said, smiling.

"So why is Face's name on this paper?" Monica asked.

"Bond called me a few minutes before y'all came and gave me this info. That little snitch problem that we've been having? Yeah, that pussy-ass nigga Baby Face is responsible for it. I got something real special in mind for that little weasel-ass nigga."

Drak hadn't known that his planted seed would take root so quickly. "I don't know about that, my nigga. Baby Face is a pretty thorough cat," Drak said reflectively.

"Man, listen. I don't put shit past nobody. That's probably why that little nigga is always smiling and shit. I don't want to talk about that. Monica, where the fuck is your cousin? Shit, as far as I know, that nigga Bird could be snitching."

"Kochese, I am growing to love you one day at a time, but you're paranoid as fuck," Monica said. "I believe that there are people who are praying for your downfall, but Baby Face doesn't strike me as a snitch, and my fucking cousin is certainly no snitch."

Either she is extremely fearless or extremely stupid for talking to me like this, King thought. He brushed it off. Monica's love had him blind to any and everything.

Besides, there were more pressing issues. He wasn't sure how Shawt Dawg's family had found out about his murder, but they would have to be dealt with. They were small-time hoods and thugs with no structure. King would hit them swift and hard before they realized what was going on.

He walked to the window and stared out into the summer sun. Waves of heat swept across the lawn of his palatial estate. He enjoyed the money, but he was tired of the lavish lifestyle. He'd done what he'd set out to do from the very beginning. He'd gotten rich, he'd made the underworld respect him, and he'd found the woman of his dreams.

He turned and looked at Monica. She was indeed a gorgeous woman. Her green eyes beamed with excitement at the thought of starting a life with him. It was written all over her face. He didn't feel deserving of a woman of her caliber, but love would have to wait. He had some regulating to do *in blood.*

Chapter 17

DirtBag Gets a Grip

DirtBag walked to the corner store with his head held low. He had his hands sunk deep into his pockets. He had a lot on his mind, and things had to change. Trina and DeKovan were depending on him to come through, and he would come through by hook or crook. He had been having the urge to backslide and smoke crack, but every time he made a motion toward one of the many crack dens that the motel housed, he saw Trina's face and felt the warmth of her embrace. The brutal Texas sun sizzled on DirtBag's weathered skin. He could feel the heat rising from the asphalt beneath him. There were so many things running through his mind, like how school would be starting soon and DeKovan would need new school clothes. Plus, they couldn't live in a motel forever. Trina tried very hard not to pressure DirtBag, and he knew that, but he was a man, and as a man, he had to make something—anything—happen. He walked into the corner store and was greeted by the raspy-voiced store owner, who seemed to be sweeping in the exact same place every time he came into the store.

"S'up, Dirty?"

"S'up, Nate? Lemme get a pack of Kool filter kings, man?" DirtBag said.

"All right. How's that cute little thang you done copped?"

"She's good. Say, Nate, you wouldn't happen to need a sweep-up man around here, would you?"

"Shit, word is, you're supposed to be working for King, so why in the hell would you want to come and work for me making peanuts?" Nate asked.

Before DirtBag could answer, Nate began to cough violently. Too many years of smoking cheap cigarettes had finally caught up to him. "Damn, excuse me, Dirty, this goddamn cancer has me by my nuts."

"It's all right, man. Just let me get those squares so I can get back to the motel," DirtBag said. He walked out of the store feeling worse than he had when he'd entered. Of course, he'd gotten a position with King, but truth be told, King would never let him make enough money to really sustain a way of living. King saw him as a dopefiend. Nothing more, nothing less. DirtBag didn't notice the black sedan that had pulled up and parked near the store entrance.

"Excuse me. Are you DirtBag?"

"Who wants to know?" he replied.

"Get in the car, and you'll find out," Silk said, flashing his gun.

He hadn't worked for King long enough for the Feds to have been watching him. For that matter, he wasn't involved enough with King's business for them to even care about him, so he had no worries, but he was curious.

He hopped into the back seat next to Silk and stared at the man as if he'd lost his mind. "So, what's this all about? I'm trying to get back to my family."

"I'm aware of that, and this won't take long. How would you like to make twenty-five thousand dollars?" Silk asked.

DirtBag's breath caught in his throat. That wasn't a lot of money, but it would most certainly give them a nice start to a new life. Hell, at this point, DirtBag was almost willing to sell his soul to ensure that he never lost Trina.

"So, what exactly would I have to do?" he asked.

"Listen, man. King killed my little cousin on a fucking whim, so you're gonna help me get that son of a bitch, or I can kill that fine little girl you keep hidden in that fleabag motel. Or you can get this money and put your new family into a decent home."

"Like I said, what do I have to do?"

Silk knew that he had the man by the balls. He'd been watching DirtBag for a few days, and the man hadn't so much as smoked a joint. His new addiction seemed to be this woman that looked too young to be his girlfriend and her son. On the surface, they seemed to be a happy family, but he knew that DirtBag had demons. Silk noticed the faraway look in his eyes.

"What's wrong, fella? You need a hit?"

"Hell naw! I don't smoke that shit no more man, I'm clean!" DirtBag shouted. "I'm just trying to figure out what the fuck I could possibly do to make you want to give me twenty-five grand?"

"Hold up, playboy. Lower your fucking voice, first of all. This is the way that it's going to go: you're going to put a bullet in King's temple."

"And how do you propose that I do that? I'm a lookout, that's all. He pays me a measly three hundred a week to stand on the corner and watch out for the police. I don't know that man's movements."

"I tell you what. If you take this number and give me a call when you see that faggot, I'll give you ten grand. If you can find enough nuts to do it yourself, I will give you the whole twenty-five, deal?"

DirtBag nodded his head slowly. He knew that he could potentially be signing his death warrant, but if he played his cards right, he and his new family could soon be on easy street.

"I see your wheels over there turning, DirtBag. So let me put your mind at ease. If you cross me, you can die with that nigga, but if you're down, then you can get this paper. What the fuck has this nigga ever done for you besides murder your best friend? This is what I'm prepared to do for you. As a show of good faith, I'm going to put some bread in your pocket, but you owe me. Say it. Say, 'I owe you, Silk.'"

"I owe you, Silk."

"Good man, good man," Silk said, reaching into the pocket behind the driver's seat and handing DirtBag a wad of money.

"What's this for?"

"It's just a little pocket money. I think it's five bands. That should keep you happy for a little while. Take this." He handed DirtBag a small handgun and a cell phone. "Remember, if you do it, I'll give you twenty thousand more, but if you can't, then call me from this phone and let me know that he's around, and I'll do the rest."

DirtBag nodded and got out of the car. For his brief time in the plush sedan, the air conditioning had spoiled him. It seemed as though it had gotten a hundred degrees hotter as he exited. He watched the sedan as they pulled away. He scurried away hastily once they were out of sight. DirtBag was careful, looking over his shoulder nervously as he made his way toward the motel.

Maybe this shit is a setup, he thought. If it was a setup, then it was King's own fault for testing him with money, he reasoned. He made it to the motel with no bullet wounds in his body, so DirtBag assumed that Silk had been on the up and up. He walked through the breezeway into the courtyard of the motel. The smoldering sun made the rank odor of urine and garbage more pronounced. He started walking toward Trina's door and stopped in his tracks, smiling to himself, remembering that she no longer stayed in that room and that she had moved in with him.

His smile quickly dissolved when he saw King, Drak, Bird, and Monica talking to Trina in the hallway in front of his room. Drak held DeKovan in his arms much like a father would, but that didn't mean much. He'd witnessed King murder a grown man, all the while maintaining a smile. DirtBag couldn't breathe. His heart thumped angrily against his frail chest. He took the steps leading to his room two at a time. By the time he'd made it to Trina and the rest, he was panting and out of breath.

"What . . . are you . . . guys . . . doing here?" he asked between gasps.

"You have very nice friends, boo. They want to take us out to dinner," Trina said excitedly.

"What up, Dirty Dirt? Yo' girl Trina says that you been clean," King said. "She said you haven't so much as smoked a joint, mane. I think we need to celebrate."

"King, we need to talk. It's urgent, bruh," DirtBag said.

"Why don't I take Trina and DeKovan to the store so that you fellas can talk?" Monica asked.

King nodded at Monica, giving her the go-ahead to carry out her plan. Without hesitation, Monica and Trina both took DeKovan's hands and started to descend the stairs.

"A'ight, Dirty, let's go inside and talk. You seem shook. What's going on?" King asked.

DirtBag was flustered, knowing that it could backfire in his face if he told King that someone had paid him to set him up. King was volatile like nitroglycerine. The wrong thing could set the kingpin off with potentially fatal consequences.

They walked into the small hotel room, and the three men stared at DirtBag, anxiously waiting for him to reveal what he had been so eager to share with King secretly. His hand shook uncontrollably as he reached into his pocket and removed a Newport cigarette. The flame from his lighter danced and flickered violently as he tried feverishly to steady his hand to light his cigarette.

Noticing his uneasiness, Bird reached into his pocket and produced his own lighter to help the old fiend out.

"Why you so muhfuckin' nervous, DirtBag?" Bird asked.

DirtBag looked up at Bird and then King.

"Kochese man, you been knowing me since you was a kid, man. When I was out there running shit for Michael Ross, you knew I was a stand-up dude, little brother." Between drags of his cigarette, DirtBag continued, "Mike was my best friend, man, and you took him from me. Me and that nigga came up together, man, played on the same basketball team at Lincoln High and everything, and you killed him, man." DirtBag looked up at King meekly.

"Nigga, choose your words carefully," King said heatedly. "And fuck your trip down memory lane. What the fuck you need to tell me?"

The harshness of King's tone caused DirtBag to unknowingly shiver with fear. "W-w-well, I know anything that you do, man, you have reason," DirtBag said as he pressed the cigarette butt into the ashtray and lit another.

"Are you high, nigga? Didn't I tell you not to be smoking that shit, fool?" King huffed.

"I'm clean, man. I'm trying to tell you what happened today, my nigga. I went to the store to get a pack of smokes, and when I came out, some nigga named Silk jammed me up and put money in my pocket to set you up. He said he was Shawt Dawg's people. I ain't never been no snitch, man, and as much as I get mad thinking about how you gunned down my playa partner, I still try to be a standup guy."

DirtBag began to cry, and it caught each man off guard. His tears were years of built-up repressed feelings coming to a head. He'd watched King execute Michael Ross in the name of the almighty dollar, and DirtBag hadn't lifted a finger to stop him.

"So, if what I did to Mike bothers you so fuckin' much, why not take the money, set me up, and run?" King asked.

Honestly, DirtBag didn't have an answer. He'd wished King dead on many occasions, and although he owed King no loyalty and was a crackhead, he still considered himself a man of honor. "Shit, I don't know. I guess because although I may not be your biggest fan, I at least *know* you. I don't know them niggas from Adam." DirtBag shrugged.

"I can respect that, playboy, and trust me, it is more than appreciated," King said. "I want you to disappear. I don't care where you go, just get the fuck out of Dallas and don't come back. Shit is finna get real hot around here, and I don't want your name popping up in shit."

Truth of the matter was that King didn't want to run the risk of DirtBag being interrogated by the police once his murder spree started. King would deal with Silk and his people with swift retribution.

"Drak, give this nigga some bread," King said. He put his hand on DirtBag's shoulder. "You did good, Dirty. You did real good. We will handle it from here. Take your new family and disappear, bruh."

DirtBag had been in the game a long time, and King's words weren't a request but a warning. Drak passed DirtBag two wads of money and made his way to the door. Before he could open the door, Monica, Trina, and DeKovan entered the room. Trina had no idea how dangerous the people in the motel room were, but DeKovan sensed it. He went to DirtBag and put his small fragile arm around the man's neck. As they exited, King stopped at the door and looked back at DirtBag. The men held each other's gaze for what seemed like an eternity before King broke the tension and smiled at the crackhead. His smile gave DirtBag the chills. He'd seen firsthand what King's smile *really* meant.

DirtBag looked at Trina lovingly. She trusted him wholeheartedly and unconditionally. He'd told her after King and his cronies had left exactly who they were and what they were capable of. Drak had given him a little over $8,000, and with the $5,000 that Silk had given him, DirtBag, DeKovan, and Trina had a nice nest egg to start over with.

He held her and hugged her tightly as they boarded the Greyhound bus headed to Chicago. The windy city would be a nice change for DirtBag. He felt as though the South had always been his downfall, and he welcomed the change that the Midwest would bring. He stared intently out of the smoked glass window of the bus while Trina snuggled up close to him. The bus driver's voice crackled over the loudspeaker,

"Welcome aboard Greyhound bus lines, ladies and gentlemen. Sit back and relax. Our next scheduled stop is Sherman, Texas."

Chapter 18

Murder was the Case

Monica eyed Kochese curiously. He was indeed an enigma to the young agent. Not so much a problem as he was a mystery. In her time with King, she had yet to see the brutality that Bird had spoken so openly about in their briefings. She watched him intently as he whipped his Range Rover from lane to lane, not seeming to notice the other cars present on the street.

"Is everything okay, King?" she asked.

Without turning to face her, he mumbled and nodded. Monica took it as a sign that he was not in the mood to converse. She turned toward the window and stared out onto the blackened asphalt racing by.

"You know what bothers me more than anything, Monica?" King asked.

"What's that, babe?" she replied, turning to face him.

"I hate when muhfuckas play with my intelligence. I mean, don't get me wrong, I'm not the smartest nigga in the world, but I ain't no dumbass either."

For a split-second, Monica felt panic set in, which just as quickly dissipated. There was no need for nervousness on her end. Muldoon had made sure to insulate her identity from the outside world. The way that he'd stated it, though, made Monica uneasy.

"Who's playing with your intelligence baby?" Monica said, fingering the small .25 semi-automatic pistol strapped to her inner thigh, just underneath the hemline of her mini skirt. She didn't think that it would be necessary, but if the need presented itself, she would spill King's blood to protect herself.

"Nobody in particular—well, everyone in particular, actually. DirtBag shooting me that information about the dudes that tried to hit me at the club really opened my eyes. I'm not getting any younger, and this bullshit is getting old. The old cats in my hood used to tell me that the only way out of the game was either death or prison, and lately, I've been feeling like death is on me." He pulled the car into the immense circular driveway in front of his palatial estate and put his truck into park. Kochese sighed heavily, as if he had the weight of the world on his shoulders. "Do you love me, Monica?"

Monica nodded. It was somewhat true. She had been spending so much time with him that she'd begun to feel something. She couldn't be sure what that *something* was because she'd never felt it before, but there was most certainly *something* there.

"I mean do you really love me? Can I trust you? Would you die for me, Monica?" King's eyes burned into Monica, searching and waiting for an answer.

Monica looked into his eyes and watched with astonishment as tears welled in his ice-blue orbs. Her answer had to be clear and concise, almost razor-sharp to convince King of her sincerity.

"Baby, I love you like no other. Never in my life have I ever felt this way for any man. You can trust me with all that you have, your life included, and before I'd let someone harm you, I'd take the bullet myself."

She leaned across the armrest of the Range and kissed King deeply. Their tongues touched, and she could feel

King's lips tremble. She felt a warm sensation rush from her brain to the tip of her feet and back up to her groin, where it seemed to settle. The kiss lasted an eternity, and the longer it lasted, the moister her panties became. She bit King's bottom lip gently, sucking on it, teasing him. She let her hands explore the stiffness of his manhood and her labored breath caught in her throat. She felt it again. There had to be a mistake. She had only been with two men her entire life, and neither had had half the dick that Kochese Mills had hidden beneath his trousers. His penis was now fully erect and stretched the length of his thigh, the tip stopping just short of reaching his knee.

King gently moved her hand away from his erection and pulled away from their osculation.

"What if I told you that I wanted out? What if I told you that I wanted to spend the rest of my life with you, Monica?"

Monica didn't answer, caught off guard and at a loss for words.

King reached over and nervously played with a lock of her hair.

"Did you hear me, baby? I said I love you and I want to be with you. I just need to step away from this lifestyle. I don't want to bring a child into the world with me doing wrong, constantly looking over my shoulder, afraid of dying in these D-Town streets."

The silence inside the car was deafening, and uncertainty loomed heavily in the air.

"What are you trying to say, Kochese? Don't write a check that your ass can't cash."

King huffed from frustration. "Monica, I don't play games, baby girl. If I'm with you, I'm with you. I ain't never loved nobody but Noisy Boy, so this is serious. I want you to be my wife."

"Man, you don't even know me, Kochese," she said somberly. For a split second, she forgot that she was an undercover DEA agent. She wanted—hell, she needed—to believe that this gorgeous hunk of a man loved her the way that he said he did.

"I know your ass well enough to know that I don't know you! Shit, for that matter you don't know me either, but I'm willing to learn you. Fuck these drugs, fuck these niggas, and fuck this lifestyle. I'm gonna hit one last big lick and I'm out, baby! It's gonna be me and you."

"If you mean it—if you really mean it—then I'm with you one hundred percent."

A wide, boyish smile spread across King's face. He lifted the armrest and produced a black velvet box. Kochese opened the box and exposed a two-carat princess-cut diamond. Even in the vehicle, the lights that illuminated King's manor danced merrily from the many facets of the brilliant stone.

"Will you marry me, Monica? Will you be Mrs. Mills?" King placed the engagement ring on her finger.

"Yes, baby. Yes, I'll marry you!" she exclaimed. They embraced in a long, passionate kiss.

Monica had every intention of consummating their engagement. She would seal the love that King had for her by giving him her most precious gift, her body. She wasn't sure if she was going overboard by sleeping with King, but Muldoon had given her the go-ahead from the first time they'd met.

"*I don't care if you have to suck his dick in the back of a crowded theater!*" he'd said.

"Baby, will you make love to me?" Monica asked.

"Nothing would make me happier, Money, but before we do this, I need to tell you *who* I am."

This was it. King would incriminate himself to Monica, the details of which she would use against him in court.

King took a deep breath. He was about to clean his closet of all of his skeletons, and it would either bring them closer together or frighten her to the point of losing her.

"Monica, I am not a good person, and truth be told, I've never loved anyone or anything except Noisy Boy, not even my own mother. I don't know what you've done to me, but I love you, and I want you to know me and love me for who I am. So, I'm going to tell you everything, and if you no longer want me when I'm done, then I will completely understand."

King exited the car and stepped around to the passenger's side, opening the door for Monica. She stepped out of the car and looked King in his eyes.

"Baby, before we go inside, I need you to know something," she said. "No matter what you tell me, it won't lessen my love for you. Just know that."

Chapter 19

To Catch a Killer

"Did you hear that? I don't know if that was fine work for the agency or if she's falling for this knucklehead!" Muldoon said to the young agent next to him. They sat in the Dallas field office of the DEA listening to every word that had been spoken of King and Monica's conversation.

"I thought she gave the wired earrings back to you. How did we manage to get a wiretap on them?" the agent asked.

"This is the Fed, boy. We manage to do whatever we want," Muldoon said, laughing heartily.

Muldoon knew that they would miss the really juicy details of King's confessions, but if Monica was half the agent that he thought she was, then they would have no problem making their case.

"I think that this calls for a celebration," Muldoon said. He walked to the wet bar in the rear of his office and poured two stiff shots of cognac. He downed his glass quickly and poured another. He handed the agent a glass of the potent liquor and watched him wince as the warm liquid slid past his palate and down to his empty stomach. Muldoon laughed and slapped the agent on the back. "Yes, my young friend. King's black ass is going down! If Agent Dietrich pulls this off, there is most definitely a promotion waiting for her at the other end of this case."

***

Kochese and Monica stepped into their home and were greeted by Noisy Boy. He wagged his tail ferociously upon seeing his master enter the house. Kochese kneeled and stroked his puppy's back.

"You happy to see us, boy? Guess what? Monica's going to be your mommy. Would you like that boy, huh?" Kochese asked affectionately. Noisy Boy let out a brisk yelp, signaling his approval.

"So, baby, I want to talk about these things that you are afraid may make me no longer love you," Monica said, trying not to lose the momentum that they'd held in the car.

"I really don't know where to begin, Monica. I guess at the beginning is best, huh?"

"That's the best place, I suppose, baby."

Kochese inhaled deeply. He had never bared his soul to anyone, let alone shared all of his inner demons. He'd done things that warranted the death penalty, or at the very least earn him a life sentence.

"I haven't always been this way, Monica. My upbringing was typical, you know? It was always me and my mom. Kind of like us against the world. I was a trick baby. My father was a rich white boy that had a taste for the flesh of young black women. The only problem with that is that he had no desire to have a child with a leisurely crack user. I would've never known who he was if not for the fact that my mom had kept a log of their contact. Plus, she'd kept all of his accomplishments through newspaper articles," he began.

King choked back tears as he told his story. He continued, "I went to dude's house to explain to him who I was, and he slammed the door in my face. For a few days, I watched him, and it became apparent that he had no plans to claim me as his child. That would've have tarnished his lily-white lifestyle. I watched this muhfucka toss the football around with his son while his soccer mom wife and prissy-ass daughter watched them in awe. There was nowhere for me to fit in with these people. The son appeared to be a few years older than me, so I'm assuming that this piece of shit was cheating on his wife with my mother.

"Man, I left there feeling so defeated, so empty. I mean, for the most part, my life had been somewhat acceptable, but after seeing that shit, it totally deflated me. I went home that night, and me and my mom got into it big time. I asked her why she'd kept my father's identity away from me, and she laughed and told me that she didn't owe me an explanation. In my mind, I wanted her dead—and I honestly think that I could have killed her—but a small part of me wanted to succeed to show them both that I could be something greater than a trick baby."

Kochese stopped talking and looked at Monica to gauge her reaction to the things that he'd said. If his words had somehow swayed her opinion of him, she hid it extremely well. Her face was stoic, and her features emotionless. Noisy Boy, sensing his master's anguish, circled aimlessly before coming to rest at his feet.

"Anyway, during that time, I met a cat named Michael Ross. He took me up under his wing and taught me how to sell drugs. He filled a void, you know? Like that father figure that I'd never known. I was too blind to see that this nigga was using me. Yeah, he taught me the game, and I made money, but he made way more money than he paid me. He exploited the fact that he was the only positive in my life, and he loved it. I committed my first murder at age fifteen in the name of loyalty. And this dude never let me forget that he held my freedom in his hands. While I'm out killing niggas for coming up short with his money, this son of a bitch was helping my mother feed her addiction. I wanted to believe that he was just giving her the dope thinking that if she was happy, then I would be happy, but that wasn't the case."

King bit his nails, and Monica put her hand on his to subside his nervousness. "How do you know that it wasn't the case?"

"Because I went to the nigga about it, and he laughed in my muhfuckin' face, man. I asked him why he would feed my mom drugs knowing the situation with her, and he laughed and told me that it didn't have shit to do with me. He said that he was a drug dealer, and that's what drug dealers do—sell drugs. I was furious, but I was scared of him, man, so I left. I walked home with every intention of giving my mother an ultimatum—either stop using drugs, or I was out of her life forever. When I walked in the door, she looked so pitiful."

Kochese looked down at the ground as if ashamed to make eye contact with the woman to whom was baring his soul.

Monica could hear the pain in his voice and silently wished that she could ease his anguish. She caressed his cheek softly.

"I walked over and stood in front of my mother and stared down at her. The strong and stern mother that I'd once known had become a fragile shell of a woman. She was crawling around on her hands and knees, searching our dirty-ass carpet for crack. She crawled around, picking up anything and everything on that carpet that happened to be white and examining it, hoping that it was her precious drug. She didn't even notice that I'd come into the room. She loved them fucking drugs more than her own damn son."

Kochese shook his head. He stood and walked to the mahogany bar against the far wall in his spacious sitting room, then looked back at Monica and turned away quickly when he realized that tears flowed freely from his eyes. He removed a bottle of VSOP from the bar and cracked the seal on the container. Rather than pour himself a glass, he took a long gulp from the bottle and walked back to the couch where Monica waited.

"I screamed at her, Monica. I screamed at her, and she looked up at me with this sick and pathetic look in her eyes. It was almost as if she wanted to tell me something, but that look disappeared quickly, and she got mad. She jumped up and ran at me, and I grabbed her. She spat in my face, Monica. I backed up and just stared at her, not believing that my mother had just treated me like some random nigga on the street. It was the drugs, though.

"I asked her why she treated me so bad, you know, why she hated me so much. She just shrugged and looked at me like she was disgusted with a nigga. Then she said she should've just aborted me. She said that I was the worst thing that ever happened to her and that she never loved me, not even as a baby. My heart sank to my stomach, Monica. Like, did I really deserve this? You know, she hated me so much, Monica. She hated me so much that this selfish lady killed herself." King choked back tears.

"What?" Monica gasped.

"Yeah, she sat there looking at me like she wanted to kill me and then pulled a knife out and slit her wrists," King said in a faraway tone. "Before I could make it across the room to help her, she cut her own throat. The last thing that my mother told me with her dying breath was that she hated me and that I would never amount to shit, and then she was gone. I was sixteen years old with a dead crackhead mother and a father that didn't want to have shit to do with me."

King cried, unable to contain his sadness any longer.

Monica embraced Kochese and kissed him gently as he wept into her bosom. Her heart ached for him.

He was a broken man beyond repair, and she knew it. There was no redemption for Kochese Mills. His soul had been tortured and beat down, but Monica had a feeling that there was much more to King than he'd shared, but she wouldn't push. She would let Kochese reveal more at his own pace.

As if sensing Kochese's pain, Noisy Boy stood and whimpered. He laid his head across King's lap. Without hesitation, King's hand went to Noisy Boy's head and began to pet him gently. Kochese looked from his puppy to his woman, and he smiled.

"Thank you for listening, baby. You're a good woman, Monica, and I am lucky to have you in my life. You and Noisy Boy are the only good things that I have in my life, and I don't know what I would do without you."

Monica was conflicted. She was an agent of the law who had allowed herself to fall for an accused drug dealer and murderer, but she couldn't shake the feeling of sympathy that loomed in her heart for King. He had lived his life in torment, craving a love that was neither present nor possible. Crack cocaine had destroyed many families, hers included, so she knew the pain that he endured . . . but justice had to be served, and King's transgressions had to be rectified.

Chapter 20

Stop Snitching

Bird reclined on his plush sofa, staring intently at his television. There was no volume, only movement on the monumental screen. Bird had long since muted the TV in favor of letting his thoughts run rampant. The sooner Monica worked her magic, the better. Bird wanted out, and the thought of it made him antsy. With Shawt Dawg's family *and* the Feds after King, it would be only a matter of time before all hell broke loose, and Bird didn't want to be anywhere near the drama.

He lustfully fingered the trigger of his 9 mm pistol. Bird contemplated driving the 40-plus miles to King's house and putting a bullet in his forehead as soon as he answered the door, but instead of avoiding prison, he'd be locked away for life. Besides, Bird didn't consider himself a killer. He was nobody's bitch, but he wasn't a murderer either.

He'd been a good boy growing up and had come from an astute and rather influential family, but it was a dictatorship not a democracy. His father's strictness caused him to turn to the streets, much to his mother's dismay. He'd always maintained his grades and even managed to make honor roll a few times, but the street life had called him, and he'd answered with no compunction. Bird had been a playground legend and a high school superstar known for his prowess with a basketball, but unless he got a scholarship to college and got drafted into the NBA, basketball wouldn't pay the bills. While he was in school being the consummate student, the world was passing him by.

At age fifteen, a chance encounter with Kochese had changed his life forever. Bird had been on the basketball court in the projects when he'd first met King. Back then, Kochese was only a fledgling kingpin who'd yet to solidify his place in urban lore. He sat nearby on the hood of his old school Monte Carlo, watching Bird and the rest of the ballers play a game of twenty-one. Bird made the game-winning shot and walked to the water fountain nearby, careful to keep his eyes on Kochese. There was something spooky about the kid that made Bird feel uneasy. He couldn't have been more than a few years older than Bird, but his eyes spoke of too many years of heartache and strife.

"Aye, who's that right there?" Bird asked a kid anxiously scurrying past him on his way to a nearby restroom.

"Who, him? Oh, that's Kochese, mane. That nigga got that fetti."

Bird understood how profound that statement was. He was also fully aware of how legends were built, whether they were completely true or not. His mom had always held to the standard of "act as if . . ." Even if you didn't have anything, act as if you had it all. Maybe Kochese had it, and maybe he didn't. Whatever the case, Bird intended to find out. Kochese could be his ticket into a life that he longed for. He wanted the popularity and quick money that the street life brought with it.

His parents had always stressed the importance of hard work and sacrifice. They had not only preached it, but they'd been able to show it through their diligence. It had, however, taken them most of their adult lives to show their children the fruits of their labor. Bird's older brothers and his younger sister had fallen into step with their parents' example. They were polar opposites from Bird, and couldn't have been more different. Where Bird had wanted the street life, his two older brothers were at college. His little sister was intelligent enough to realize that beauty alone wouldn't land her that knight, so she consumed books, which not only served to further her intellect, but had also served as her escape into worlds away from the strict universe that their parents had created.

Bird walked to where Kochese sat, watching the spectacle taking place on the court.

"What's up, buddy?" Bird said, extending his hand in Kochese's direction. "My name is Calvin, but my friends call me Bird."

Kochese stared at Bird as if he had somehow lost his ever-loving mind.

Noticing that Kochese had no intention of shaking his hand, Bird continued his conversation. "Anyway, I was coming over to see if you wanted to run a game of twenty-one with us?"

"First of all, little nigga, 'buddy' eats shit and barks at the moon. Do I look like a dog to you? And second of all, have you ever heard the term, 'Never let them see you sweat'? Well, I take that shit literally," Kochese replied. "The extent of my physical labor is counting money, my nigga. I quit school because they had recess, so that ought to tell you that I don't play no goddamn games. Get your young ass on somewhere."

Kochese turned away from Bird and let his gaze fall to a young, curvaceous girl that couldn't have been more than sixteen years old. She sat on the bleachers nearby, reading a book, and seemed to be more into her novel than the basketball games taking place around her.

Bird noticed that Kochese's attention had been drawn, and followed his line of sight. He realized that it had come to rest on his kid sister, Kim. Inwardly, Bird smiled. He could use Kochese's obvious lust for his little sister as a catalyst to spearhead his own money-laden relationship with the drug dealer, or he could do what was right and protect his sister from Kochese's advances. Bird chose to protect his little sister. He stepped into Kochese's face, blocking his line of sight.

"Don't be looking at my sister like she no street ho, buddy," Bird said, intentionally disrespecting Kochese.

"Nigga, get the fuck outta my face before I beat yo' little ass."

"Stop looking at my sister, and I will get out of your face," Bird replied, standing firm.

Kochese stared at the young boy. He was either incredibly brave or incredibly stupid, but something in his eyes amused Kochese.

"Are you willing to die for your little sister, fool? Do you know who the fuck I am?" Kochese asked, brandishing his chrome 9 mm handgun.

They locked eyes, both refusing to avert their gaze until the sound of Kim's voice and a car horn drew both of their attention.

"Bird, mom is waiting for us," Kim said in her syrupy, child-like voice. She stopped just short of Bird and Kochese and stood firm, with one hand planted on her hip and the other hand holding her book. "Bird, I know you hear me talking to you!" she shouted.

"Man, I hear you. I'm coming, damn!" Bird said, turning back to Kochese. "Stay away from my sister."

Kochese laughed in Bird's face. He actually liked the kids' tenacity. Kochese had plans of building an empire, and if it was going to happen, he would need to build a young, strong, loyal team . . . and Bird could be his first recruit.

Bird turned slowly and walked toward where his mother and sister waited. He sank his hands deep into his shorts pockets and lowered his head. He felt as if he'd failed. Kochese seemed to be someone that could have changed his life, and he'd blown it with his attitude. As he approached his mother's car, Kochese came up from behind him and put his arm around Bird's shoulder.

"Look out, playboy. I want to talk to you when you get a chance—call me later," Kochese said, handing Bird a cell phone.

Bird looked at the phone briefly before shoving it deep into his pocket. He loved his mother, but she could be beyond nosey sometimes, and the last thing that Bird wanted to do was answer a barrage of questions concerning his business. If she'd noticed Kochese giving him the cell phone, there would be a full inquest by not only her, but his father as well. He nodded at Kochese and quickened his pace.

Bird climbed into the back seat and waited for the questions to begin, but they never came. His mother and sister were too busy gawking at the skinny kid with fair skin, long hair, and ice-blue eyes.

Bird wanted to call Kochese, and it was hard not to. He wanted in on the lifestyle that Kochese lived, but he didn't want to seem overly anxious, either. Bird reluctantly dialed the number that had been stored in the prepaid cell phone.

"Hello," a deep baritone voice said from the other end of the phone.

"Yo, what up? This is Bird."

"Yeah, what's up, player? You ready to get paid?" Kochese asked.

"Hell yeah. What I gotta do?"

"First thing you gotta do is not talk about business on the phone. Meet me at Lagow Park at noon, and we can talk," Kochese said.

Bird hit the END button on the cell phone and tossed the phone to the bed. He felt larger than life. If the meeting went well, then there was a possibility that Kochese would put him in the mix of things and show him how to get money. He showered and dressed in basketball gear. His parents never questioned him about playing basketball, but if he left home in street clothes, there were always questions. Bird left his house a little earlier than necessary because the three miles that he had to walk to Lagow Park would be a hike.

When he arrived, Bird approached the park apprehensively. He walked slowly, dribbling his basketball and contemplating what he would say to the drug dealer. He wanted everything that the streets had to offer, but he had no earthly idea how to get it. As he approached the park, he could see Kochese's Monte Carlo in the distance.

"Yo!" Bird yelled in Kochese's direction.

The kingpin looked up toward Bird with a scowl on his face. His facial expression and silence said what words could not. He was silently telling Bird to be quiet, that he was too loud, and that King wasn't one for drawing attention to himself. Still dribbling his basketball, Bird made his way to Kochese's car. Kochese was sitting sideways in the driver's seat, smoking a blunt. Underneath Kochese, just at the base of his feet on the asphalt, were the remnants of the innards of his cigar. Bird eyed the interior of the Monte Carlo admiringly. The seats looked and smelled like the finest Italian leather.

"You like this shit, junior?" Kochese asked, smiling.

Bird stepped back and scrutinized the entire car. Its royal blue candy paint shimmered under the Texas sun. Bird could see his reflection in not only the paint, but in the chrome rims as well. The tires gleamed brightly from the silicon tire shine that Kochese had used to brighten them.

"This baby is clean, bro!" Bird said excitedly.

"This baby is clean, huh? You talk like that all the time?"

"Like what?" Bird asked.

"Like a character from *Leave it to Beaver*, with that 'gee golly wow' bullshit," Kochese said, laughing uncontrollably.

Bird had no rebuttal. He'd never known that there was anything wrong with the way that he talked. He was well aware of the fact that he wasn't a street dude, though. The majority of his life had been spent sheltered from the ills of ghetto life. His parents had chosen to raise their children in the church versus the streets. They'd opted to shuttle their children to schools outside of the inner city of Dallas. Plano, Texas, was a well-to-do suburban community, where children could thrive and parents could rest easy knowing that their hard work was rewarded with safe streets and good schools.

Kochese noticed that his statement had made Bird uneasy, so he changed the subject. "Anyway, I want to talk to you about getting some paper, playboy. You do like money, right? Well, if you fuck with me, you're going to get more paper and more pussy than you ever could've imagined."

Bird's eyes lit up much like a child's would on Christmas morning. This had been easier than he'd anticipated. He'd been certain that he would have to beg Kochese to take him into his organization, but as Bird learned, there was no organization. He would be the first of Kochese's recruits in his quest for dominance over the narcotic-laced underground of Dallas.

"Hell yeah, I like money. Man, I'm loyal, too! If you give me a chance, I promise I will always have your money right!"

"Yeah, that's all well and good, but it's deeper than that. If you can answer three questions for me, then I will make you a rich man. As a sign of good faith, I'm going to give you a thousand today, but you have to answer these questions. Are you ready?"

Bird nodded. He wasn't sure what the questions were, but if it would help him get his hands on a thousand dollars with the promise of more to come, then he would answer any question that Kochese could think of.

"First question: If I put you on with me, what are you willing to do to ensure that we take this organization to the next level?" Kochese asked.

Bird thought for a long while. He hadn't known what to expect as far as the questions went, but he decided to be honest. He'd been raised to believe that honesty was the best policy, and what better time to exercise that philosophy?

"I'm willing to do anything that you need me to do to make sure that this organization grows. I don't know much, but if you're willing to teach me what I need to know, then I know that I can be a good soldier."

"Okay, good answer. Question two: Would you lie to protect me and our organization, Bird?"

With a straight face, Bird answered, "Yes." There was no hesitation in his voice.

Kochese studied his young friend closely. If Bird was as dedicated as he appeared to be, then he would have no problem building his empire.

"Okay, Bird. Last question: Would you die for this organization?"

"We all have to die sometime, right?" Bird blurted out. The thought of dying had never crossed his mind. He was only sixteen years old, and up until that point in time, death had always been thought of in Bird's mind as something that he would inevitably face in his golden years. He had envisioned dying of old age after a lengthy life. Here he was now, having a conversation about death with his new boss.

"Yeah, we all have to die sometime, but the question is, will you die for me and this organization?" Kochese mocked.

"Yes."

Kochese reached into the glove box and removed a wad of hundred-dollar bills. He watched as Bird visibly salivated at the sight of the easy money. He extended the knot of money toward Bird, but when Bird took hold of it, Kochese maintained his grip.

"One last question before I hand you this money, playboy. Would you kill for me?"

Bird had never once considered such a nefarious act. "Thou shalt not kill" is what he had been taught in Sunday school. This, however, was not Sunday school. This was real life, and the money that he held between his fingers was the proof.

"Hell yeah!" Bird said.

Kochese laughed. He was almost certain that if it came down to it and Bird was backed into a corner, then maybe—just maybe—he could kill a man, but Bird wasn't a natural killer.

"You think you can kill a man, huh?" Kochese asked.

"If the need presented itself, I'm sure that I could."

"Okay, let's see. Get in the car, nigga!" Kochese said, releasing his grip on the money.

As they drove around Dallas, Kochese explained his plan of rising to prominence in the drug world. He said that there was only one thing that stood in his way. He worked for a very disrespectful man by the name of Michael Ross who refused to let him grow and prosper. Michael Ross, according to Kochese, had been part of the reason that his mother hadn't been able to get clean, and Kochese meant to get even. He'd also explained that Michael Ross didn't believe in security because, as he'd put it, as long as you were a good person there was no need for security.

"This nigga thinks that he's all that, but he ain't shit. If we get rid of this fool, we will own Dallas, my nigga! Are you with me?" Kochese asked.

"I'm with you until the casket drops, bro!"

Kochese had never had a brother. If Bird was truly sincere about making him his brother, then he would do his part to make Bird a rich man. He wheeled his Monte Carlo onto I-30 and fired up another blunt. The pungent odor filled the small space of the car as Kochese popped a CD into the deck of his stereo system. A huge, sinister smile creased his lips as he passed the blunt to Bird, who reluctantly took it and inhaled deeply. He settled back on the passenger's side, absorbing the thump of the bass from the fifteen-inch woofers in the trunk and the snap of the tweeters in the dash. Eminem's nasal but melodic voice blared through the speakers with rhythmic syncopation. He rapped unapologetically:

I'm sorry, Momma!
I never meant to hurt you!
I never meant to make you cry; but tonight
I'm cleaning out my closet. I said I'm sorry, Momma!

They had been riding for hours by the time they pulled into an unpretentious neighborhood in Rockwall, Texas. Michael Ross believed in keeping a low profile, and in doing so, he'd settled for accommodations well below his financial means. The small, unassuming house was well-lit and inviting. Before they left the car, Kochese reached under his seat and removed a 9 mm pistol and handed it to Bird. He then reached underneath the passenger's seat and removed a .45 caliber pistol.

Bird watched in dazed confusion. Although they had driven a long time to get there, he was still high from the blunt. He tried to shake the feeling of depersonalization, but there was no use. He felt as though the whole scenario was playing out in his head like some twisted scene in a movie with D-list actors and a bad plot.

"Listen, Bird. I'm about to deal with this nigga my way! If it's anybody in there, just hold your gun on 'em. If they move, blast on the muhfucka, ya dig? Damn, this is going to be a hell of a birthday present to me!" Kochese said, laughing.

"Birthday?"

"Yeah, nigga, today is my eighteenth birthday," Kochese said proudly.

Bird just stared at Kochese. Whatever happened to cake and ice cream? Oh well, he had given Kochese his word that he would have his back no matter the situation, so he cocked the pistol to put a bullet in the chamber and exited the vehicle.

They reached the door, and Kochese knocked lightly. Michael Ross answered the door in a one-piece coverall. He looked more like a mechanic than a drug dealer.

"What up, birthday boy?" Michael Ross said excitedly, pulling Kochese close and hugging him much like a father would. "Who's your friend?"

"This is my nigga, Bird. He cool."

"What up, Bird? I'm Mike, and this is my podna Jappy."

He nodded toward the couch where Jappy sat. Jappy nodded a *what's up* in the two youngsters' direction and continued watching college football. He didn't look much like another drug dealer. Jappy looked like a dopefiend, but the gun on the table in front of him said that his position of importance with Michael Ross was deeper than that of a drug user.

"What you young niggas gonna get into tonight, players?" Ross asked in a jovial voice.

"Not shit. I'm showing Bird around the hood, around some of the spots. He might start working for us real soon," Kochese replied.

"Oh, yeah? And when did you start calling shots on who we hire and fire?"

"Man, you got all of these old-ass niggas working for us. Ain't nobody even remotely close to my age in the family. Shit, if it's that big of a deal, I will give the nigga half of my earnings until he can prove that he's down."

"Naw, don't worry about it. It's your birthday. It's time to celebrate!" Michael Ross said with the smile returning to his face. "I got something real special for you, baby boy."

He disappeared into a back room of his house. He returned a few minutes later holding a snow-white pit bull puppy with a pink nose and ice-blue eyes. The puppy wiggled in Mike's arms, yelping and whimpering, as if angry that he was being restrained. There was a huge royal blue bow attached to the puppy's collar, and Kochese's eyes twinkled with the wonderment of a child.

"What's his name?" Kochese asked.

"I don't know, nigga. Shit, he's yours. He doesn't have a name until you give him one!" Mike said as he handed the dog to Kochese.

Kochese held the puppy up in front of his face, examining him carefully. The dog couldn't have been more than a couple of weeks old. He barked relentlessly with his tiny puppy voice at Kochese. The bark was so high pitched and feverish that it caused Kochese to smile.

"I got the perfect name for you! I'm going to call you Noisy Boy. You like that, boy? Huh, you like that?" Kochese said to the dog lovingly.

Bird watched the scene unfold in astonished silence. He knew that Kochese had plans of *dealing* with Michael Ross; he just wasn't sure when. He stood by, fidgeting nervously as Kochese and Mike continued to converse.

Jappy watched Bird curiously. "Why are you so jumpy, youngster?" Jappy asked.

“Man, I gave that nigga some of that pineapple kush, and he don’t smoke weed!” Kochese said, laughing.

Jappy joined the laughter and excused himself to use the bathroom. Kochese caught Bird’s attention and motioned in the direction of Jappy’s gun with his eyes. He sat Noisy Boy on the couch and made his way to the bathroom, where an unsuspecting Jappy had gone. Kochese knew that if he burst into the bathroom, it would give him the element of surprise. He braced himself, drew his .45 caliber, and kicked the door to the bathroom wide open.

Startled, Jappy jumped and sprayed urine all over the back of the toilet. “What the fuck you doing, young nigga?” Jappy shouted.

Kochese slapped the man across the bridge of his nose with the butt of his pistol. Blood squirted from the wound, spraying its fine red mist across the mirror and wall.

“Shut the fuck up, nigga, and put your little shriveled-ass dick up.”

In the front room, Noisy Boy barked in excitement as Michael Ross made a movement toward Jappy’s gun. Before he could make it to the pistol, Bird had drawn the 9 mm and pointed it at his head.

“I don’t want to hurt you, but I will if you move again, so chill out,” Bird said as he scooped up the pistol from the coffee table.

Moments later, Kochese reappeared with Jappy at gunpoint. “Both of you old muhfuckas take a seat,” Kochese barked.

“Kochese, you know you’re fucking up, right? Nigga, I took you in and treated you like a son, and this is how you repay me? You’s a disloyal little bitch-ass nigga!” Michael Ross spat.

Kochese’s laugh bellowed throughout the small house. “Mike, I don’t know if you’ve paid attention to the man that I've become, but I don't particularly give a fuck about that shit. You've chumped me long enough, playboy. If my own mama and daddy didn't give a fuck about me, then why should I believe that you do? You see, I know I ain't shit. I'm cursed, nigga. I'm the devil. Now shut the fuck up before you piss me off."

Kochese's demeanor was so calm that it made Mike nervous. Mike tried his hardest to sink into his couch and disappear.

"Bird, go into Mike's room, lift his mattress, and get all of the money and dope that you can find," Kochese demanded.

Bird did as he was told. The only time he'd seen that much money was on television, but this was real life. There, hidden in a recessed bed frame underneath the mattress, were stacks upon stacks of hundred-dollar bills wrapped in ten thousand bands. Bird ripped the sheet from the bed and placed it on the floor. He tossed the money onto the sheet until the last stack was loaded. He turned the room upside down looking for drugs, but there were none. Bird tied the sheet together by its four corners and slung it over his shoulder. He walked into the living room and dropped the money on the floor.

"You get the money and the drugs?" Kochese asked.

"I found money, man, but no drugs. It's a lot of money, though."

"Where the fuck the dope at, nigga?" Kochese asked calmly.

"Go fuck yourself, Kochese. I don't talk to dead men."

"Man, all the dope is in the deep freezer in the basement, man. Please don't kill me, Kochese," Jappy pleaded. "Man, I always told this nigga Mike to let you do your thing, man. Please, Kochese! I will work for you for free, man. Just don't kill me, young blood. I got two daughters, man. I got a wife and a baby mama. I'm begging you, please don't kill me!"

The man sniveled like a frightened child as snot dripped from his cowardly nose. He opened his mouth to speak again, but Kochese smacked him in the mouth with the barrel of his gun.

"Stop begging, coward! You know what trips me out? Muhfuckas are tough when they hold the cards, but ain't no fun when the rabbit got the gun, huh? Bird, go down in the basement and get that dope, player."

Bird disappeared into the basement and returned shortly with five perfectly wrapped bundles of cocaine. Kochese smiled and winked at Bird.

"Happy birthday to me, happy birthday to me, happy birthday King Kochese, happy birthday to me," Kochese sang to no one in particular.

Kochese pulled a chair from the dining room into the living room, where Bird still had his gun aimed at the men. He sat in front of them and stared with a knowing smirk on his face. Murder was in his eyes, and malice coursed through his veins. He tapped the barrel of his .45 caliber against his forehead lightly as he stared at them, smiling.

"Kill me and get it over with, little nigga," Mike barked.

"Your days of giving orders are over, homeboy. I want to know why you did it. I mean, I've watched you fuck over people, and I kept my mouth shut. Hell, even when you kept giving my mother drugs, knowing that I wanted her to get clean, I didn't do shit. But for you, this piece of shit Jappy, and DirtBag to rape a little girl was too much. That was somebody's child, nigga! That could've been my little sister, muhfucka, and for that, you gotta go."

"You catching feelings behind a little piece of ass, Kochese? Her sorry-ass daddy and junky-ass mammy brought her to me so that they could get high. What the fuck was I supposed to do?"

"How about just keeping her until they brought you your money? How about not sticking your dick in her?

Y'all nasty-ass niggas gang raped a seven-year-old girl, man. That's just sick, and for that, your ass is gonna die today."

Jappy began to cry uncontrollably. He knew without a doubt that he would die. The only question was whether it would be before or after Michael Ross.

"Since you nasty niggas like to fuck so much, me and Bird gonna watch y'all fuck each other. Stand up and take your muhfuckin' clothes off," Kochese ordered.

Both men stood up and did as they were told. They both stood stark naked in front of each other.

"Now, you two bitches kiss! Kiss him, nigga, before I blow your goddamn head off."

Michael Ross leaned in and pecked Jappy on the lips. Jappy's manhood twitched and jumped erect.

"Well, I'll be damned, Bird! This bitch-ass nigga just got a chubby from being kissed by another dude. Jappy, since you getting off by kissing this nigga, get down and suck his dick," Kochese said.

Jappy looked at the man with tears flowing down his cheeks. "This is some bullshit, Kochese, I ain't no fag, man. I just wanna go home."

"I'm going to let you go home as soon as you suck that nigga's dick. Now get down on your goddamn knees!" Kochese shouted.

Jappy dropped to his knees and took Michael Ross's penis in his hands. He opened his mouth and took the man's now erect member into his mouth.

"Ewwww, you a nasty son of a bitch! I didn't think that you would do it. And this nasty nigga got a woody from another man sucking his dick." Kochese laughed. "Bird, turn on some mood music for these two love birds."

Bird did as he was told and turned the stereo on and cranked up the volume. Jappy had his eyes closed as Michael Ross thrust vigorously in and out of his mouth. Jappy never saw Kochese point his pistol at his head and pull the trigger. As he fell to the couch and slid into darkness, Michael Ross came, spewing his seed onto the dead man's body.

Michael Ross opened his eyes to see Jappy lying dead across his couch. His eyes were still open, and blood oozed slowly from the gaping bullet hole in his temple. He began to tremble. Up until this point, he had known that there was a possibility that Kochese would kill him, but now he was certain. Kochese was sick. He *enjoyed* torturing them.

"Why are you doing this, Kochese? What did I ever do to you? Man, I don't want to die," Mike pleaded.

Kochese did not reply. He had grown tired of talking, and play time was over. He rose from his perch and walked into the kitchen. Moments later, he returned with a gallon jug of vegetable oil.

"Bird, gimme your gun," Kochese said.

Bird handed Kochese his gun, and he soaked the barrel with the oil. He handed the gun back to Bird.

"Bend your bitch ass over, Mike. Spread your ass like the fag you are," Kochese said angrily.

Slowly, Michael Ross put his hands on the back of the couch and bent over, exposing his asshole.

"Bird, fuck this punk with the barrel of that heater, nigga!"

Bird hesitated. This wasn't the life that he had envisioned. Silently, he wondered if shoving the gun into the man's anus made him a homosexual. The sheer pleasure that Kochese seemed to be getting from it also made Bird uncomfortable. Still, Bird had given his word to Kochese that he would do his best to hold him down, so he obeyed. He eased the tip of his gun into Michael Ross's rectum, and the older man squirmed. Whether by reflex or by ecstasy, the feeling of the cold steel caused his penis to stiffen. Bird thrust the barrel in deeper, causing

Michael Ross to tremble. The fear of what was to come triggered an involuntary bowel movement, and he began to defecate.

"Pull the trigger, Bird! Kill that muhfucka while his dick is hard!" Kochese said excitingly. He was giddy as if he were a child finding a shiny new nickel on the ground in front of a candy store.

Michael Ross tried to remove the gun from his cavity, but it was too late. Bird pulled the trigger, and blood and fecal matter leaped from the hole as the bullet exited his stomach.

Kochese walked to where Michael Ross lay dead and put another slug into the top of his skull. Noisy Boy barked from excitement. Kochese picked the puppy up from the floor and removed the bow from his neck. He tossed it to the ground, where it came to rest in the puddle of blood that Mike and Jappy's wounds had formed.

"You see that shit, Bird? The man with the gold gets the power, but the man with the gun gets the gold, playboy. I will be the king of these streets, so from now on call me King Kochese."

Since then, Bird had witnessed Kochese kill more men than he cared to remember. His frustration mounted as he thought of Monica spending so much time with Kochese. He could never tell her that Muldoon shared with him where her passion had come from. He could never tell her that Kochese had eliminated one of the men responsible for the rape and torture of her baby sister, and that he had unknowingly eliminated the second man. They had both, however, allowed the third man in the trifecta to walk away years later with a clear conscience. DirtBag had escaped with his life intact, courtesy of the most coldhearted kingpin that Dallas had ever known.

Chapter 21

Give Me a Reason

"What!" Kochese screamed into his cell phone. The anger in his voice was apparent, and it caused Monica to awaken with a start. "Hold that muhfucka. I'll be right there, mane."

Monica stretched and looked at Kochese. She was trying to read his demeanor, but just as quickly as his anger had risen, it had dissipated.

"Well, good morning, sleepy head," he said, lying back down next to Monica and kissing her on the lips.

"Good morning, daddy. Is everything okay?"

"I love it when you call me daddy! Yeah, everything is straight. We just have a lot to handle today."

"You sounded really upset a minute ago. You actually scared me, baby."

"No need to be alarmed, baby. Just some shit we need to handle a little later, that's all."

Kochese stood, and Monica noticed his early morning erection pressing violently against the material of his underwear. She was in awe of King Kochese. They had been living together, but he had yet to make any advances toward sexual intercourse with Monica, and it left her confused and horny. The more that he held out, the more her wanton sexual desires began to manifest. Never before had a man stirred her sexuality so deeply, and she felt her panties moisten. She had come into this case with the intention of making Kochese want her, but his nonchalant disposition caused just the opposite.

"King, can I ask you a question?" Monica asked. Her eyes were still aimed at Kochese's crotch.

"You can ask me anything that you want, baby. What's up?"

"We've been together for a little while now, and you've yet to try anything with me. Don't you find me attractive?" Monica said, removing the covers to expose her ripe body, clad in only red panties and a Hello Kitty wife beater. Her nipples pressed against the fabric, jutting forward.

Kochese smiled. Truthfully, he wanted nothing more than to make love to the woman that he knew would become his wife, but he was afraid. He was afraid that he wasn't man enough, afraid that if they made love, his feelings for Monica might change. Rather than attempt to explain his thoughts, though, Kochese stepped out of his boxers and let his magnificent erection hang. Every muscle in his body rippled as the full magnitude of his manhood lay bare. His hair hung past his shoulders, and his blue eyes burned through Monica with desire. He stepped to the side of the bed, his rock-solid penis swaying left to right with every step. He stood regally at her bedside, and the tip of his phallus throbbed and pulsated with every breath that he took. He kneeled in front of her and took a deep breath.

"Money, I find you incredibly attractive, and if you wish for me to make love to you, then I will. I need you to understand that I bring with me certain baggage. I am a murderer, a thief, and a drug dealer. If these are things that you can accept, then we are meant to be."

"I love you, Kochese Mills, and every man deserves a queen," she said as she kissed him deeply and passionately.

Kochese pulled Monica to a seated position. He removed her wife beater and felt his breath catch in his throat from the sight of her firm and perky breasts. Her skin was smooth and blemish-free, and her nipples sat at the tip of them like pencil erasers. Monica looked up into Kochese's eyes with the full weight of her innocence. Her green eyes were filled with silent promises of lust and love. She took Kochese's stiff member into her hand and caressed it gently. Monica cupped his testicles; they felt heavy and full. She kissed the tip of Kochese's dick, and he shivered. She took the length of it into her mouth and twirled around the tip with her tongue. He had his eyes closed and his head back as a feeling of euphoric ecstasy washed over his body.

"Baby, I need to lay down," he said huskily.

Monica was by far nobody's freak, but she was beyond attracted to Kochese. For a split second, she wanted to give him her life. She wanted to devote herself to him fully and unequivocally. She needed Kochese. He had filled an emptiness in her that had been present since the death of her grandfather. Muldoon wanted his head on a silver platter, but they didn't know Kochese the way that she did. He had bared his soul to her, sharing with her his darkest secrets and most intimate aspirations. She bobbed and slurped on his cock until she felt his body go rigid. He thrust faster until Monica stopped.

"Not yet," she whispered.

Kochese was dizzy with desire, and he tried hard to regain his composure. A tiny bit of cum dripped from the tip of his manhood, which Monica gladly licked away. She was *his* freak; nobody else's, only *his* freak, and she relished in the thought of it. She needed to be everything that he wanted in a woman, and from the look on his face, she was most certainly doing her job. Kochese lifted her and placed her on her back and kissed her deeply. He kissed down the length of her body, circling her erect nipples with the tip of his tongue. He continued his trail of delicious kisses down to her navel while tweaking her nipples with the tips of his fingers. Kochese expertly navigated his way back to Monica's lips and kissed her fervently. He slid his fingers inside her panties and removed them in one motion.

Monica could feel her heartbeat between her legs. She wanted Kochese inside of her desperately. When he dropped down and buried his face between her legs, she screamed out in pleasured bliss. Monica arched her back, trying futilely to control herself, but Kochese moved his tongue to the rhythm of her body. He sucked her clit gently, sending waves of pleasure rushing through every nerve ending in her body. She thrashed and bucked insanely, grinding and gyrating against the flicker of Kochese's tongue. He inserted his finger up to the second knuckle and massaged her urethral sponge, still sucking her clit gently until Monica felt as though she had to urinate.

"I gotta pee! Babe, stop, please!" she begged.

"You don't have to pee. You're about to cum! Relax, baby. Let it come."

Kochese massaged it more vigorously, now knowing that Monica was at her climactic edge. She gripped the sheets and squealed in delight as torrent after torrent of wetness escaped her body. Her passion-filled juices soaked the sheets underneath her body. Her body jerked uncontrollably as she squirted on the thousand-count Egyptian cotton sheets.

"Oh my God, Kochese, you really are my king," she said.

"You ain't seen nothing yet, baby," he replied.

Kochese positioned himself over Monica and entered her slowly. She was tight, but her wetness felt good against his skin. Monica could not breathe. She tried to form her words, but with every thrust, she slipped deeper and deeper into the throes of passion until she felt as though she'd pass out.

"Kochese, Kochese, please don't cum in me. I'm not ready to have a baby," she said, but Kochese did not respond. He kept pumping, burying his shaft inside of her up to the hilt. He wanted to make sure that she would always remember their first time. There was no music, no rose petals on the bed, no romantic mood, just early morning, knuckle-biting sex. Kochese had often heard how good early morning sex was, but he'd never experienced it. He'd always been careful to not let women spend the night, and if they did spend the night, he'd usually have Drak waiting to take them home before the sun came up. This was different, though. Monica was his to do with as he pleased.

He pulled out of her warm refuge and lay on the bed. Monica saw that he was still hard and attempted to get on top of Kochese, but he guided her to the head of the bed. He positioned her body so that he could once again pleasure her with cunnilingus. She swiveled her hips and bucked against his tongue buried deep inside of her. Her body had never before felt the sensations that King gave her. There were a million tiny shards of electricity swimming through her bloodstream.

Sexuality pulsed between them. She'd begun to cry from the torrents of sexual delight surging through her body. Kochese flipped her over to her back and entered her again; this time more forcefully, but still gentle enough to be pleasurable. He thrust in and out, fast and then slow. Kochese measured his depth with every stroke. He kissed her and dug into her soul with his manhood. With every stroke, he sent orgasmic ripples sailing through her body until they both came together. At the onset, Monica had been concerned about Kochese impregnating her, but now she was ready for whatever might come her way.

Chapter 22

The Bond Is Broken

Drak, Bird, and Lucky sat in a semi-circle, laughing and passing a blunt between the three of them.

"Man, I can't believe that fool is snitching!" Lucky said.

"Yeah, when King gets to this muhfucka, all hell is going to break," Bird added. "Man, you can't trust none of these bitch niggas nowadays."

Drak's demeanor was stoic. He was so used to people coming into King's organization and professing their loyalty, only to be exposed as a snitch later, that it was no longer a shock. It was ultimately King's decision what he wanted to do with the exposed snitch.

"Please, guys. I've never snitched," the tattletale pleaded. "I've never uttered one negative word about King or this organization, and once he gets here, you will all see that you're making a big mistake."

"Man, kill that shit or I will kill it for you! I guess it's by coincidence that your name came up as a snitch, huh?" Drak asked in his deep baritone voice.

He walked to the snitch and stood in front of him. They had hanged him by his wrists, and his feet barely touched the ground. Drak signaled to Lucky to lower the chains just a little so that he was able to look at the man eye-to-eye. Drak removed a hunting knife from a sheath on his hip and put the tip against the man's face.

"Do you have any idea what King is going to do to you, playa?" Drak asked.

The condemned chatterbox began to plead again, but Drak silenced him with a wave of his hand.

"Stick out your tongue, snitch!" Drak ordered, but the man clamped his mouth shut much like a child refusing to eat his vegetables.

Drak hit the man in the stomach with a crushing blow, knocking the wind out of him.

"Bird, come hold this muhfucka's head, mane!" Drak shouted.

Bird obeyed, grabbing the man by his throat and squeezing, consequently forcing him to open his mouth, gasping for air. Drak reached into the man's mouth and cut his tongue out. He squirmed and tried to scream, but Drak hit him again, silencing his cries.

Blood was still pouring from his mouth when Kochese, Monica, and Noisy Boy entered King's Kennel. The sight of his trusted counsel, Bond, hanging from chains in his warehouse didn't really surprise him. Ambition was a powerful drug, and many men had fallen prey to its allure. Monica, however, was another story. The sight of Bond's bloody body hanging from the rafters by chains caused Monica to hesitate. Noisy Boy stepped in front of Monica as if to shield her from the grisly spectacle.

"You okay, baby? You are more than welcome to wait in the car," King said upon noticing her hesitation.

"No, I'm good. I promised you that I would be with you regardless. So, let's do it."

"Okay, sweets." He turned his attention to the men before him. "My niggas, my niggas! So, what do we have here?" His demeanor had gone from the soft and caring tone that he'd displayed with Monica to all business. In his lifetime, King had killed more men than he cared to remember, but Bond's snitching cut him deep. There were certain people in his organization that he never expected to become informants, and Bond had been one of them. It had also been brought to his attention that Baby Face might be talking, but he needed time to deal with him. Baby Face had been with him a long time, and although he was a far cry from sentimental, Baby Face had grown on him. King didn't however, hold any allegiance to Bond. He was well aware that Bond's agenda was self-serving, and King was okay with that. What he wasn't okay with was someone using his operation to serve those purposes.

Drak approached King and embraced him. "What's up, dawg? I got a surprise for you."

"Yeah, and what's that?

Drak grabbed King's hand and turned it palm up. Locking eyes with King Kochese, he placed Bond's severed tongue in King's hand. Before he ever broke eye contact with Bond, King already knew what it was. Without missing a beat, King turned and walked to the kennel where the oversized bullmastiff Beast paced anxiously, and tossed Bond's tongue inside.

"Bird, Lucky, let's spread some plastic under this maggot. I'ma show my baby what we do to snitches!" King said excitedly.

King disappeared into his office and returned moments later with white coveralls, plastic covers over his shoes, and latex gloves on his hands. He'd also taken the time to don a hairnet and face mask. To Monica, he resembled a butcher going to surgery. She had no idea just how close to the truth she actually was. As if on cue, Drak disappeared into a room adjacent to King's office and reappeared pushing a stainless-steel cart with an assortment of knives and saws. King went through each utensil, carefully attempting to choose the perfect piece. He smiled his perfectly straight white smile. The glint of metal gleamed in his blue eyes. His happiness made Monica's flesh crawl because only hours earlier, they had made love. They had shared their bodies and their souls with one another, but now they were at King's Kennel, and she was about to witness her lover murder a man. Of course, it would be good for her case, but she had feelings for King Kochese. She wasn't sure what those feelings were exactly, but they were there.

I need to stop him, she thought, but just as quickly dismissed the notion. If she tried to stop King, he could grow to resent her. Worse, he could grow suspicious.

"Bond, you fucked up, boy. You should've kept your mouth shut about my business. I see from the looks of things, my boy Drak already silenced your ass, but I'm gonna make it permanent. Drak, how long would it take that walk-in freezer in the back to freeze this muhfucka if you turned it all the way down?"

"Shit, if I turn it all the way down, this piece of shit will be dead in a half hour!" Drak said.

"A'ight. Bird, Lucky, y'all don't worry about the plastic. Lower this snitch-ass white boy and hang his pussy ass on that meat hook in the freezer," King said.

Bird and Lucky exchanged wary glances at one another. Neither was innocent in anything that they had ever done, but hanging a man on a meat hook was a totally different ball game. The look that King gave them said that it wasn't up for discussion. In King's organization, there was never room for discussion, not even for Bird. So reluctantly, both men did as they were told. Even from the center of the kennel, the sound of Bond's flesh being ripped by the massive meat hook could be heard until his muffled screams drowned out that sound.

Bird and Lucky emerged from the subzero temperatures of the freezer, both rubbing themselves vigorously. Bird put his hands up to his mouth, trying desperately to blow heat into his hands.

"Okay, boss, what's next?" he said to King.

King hated when Bird called him boss because it always seemed as though he was being sarcastic when he said it. He knew that Bird was just biding his time and that he really wanted out of the game. If things went according to his plans, then Bird would get exactly what he wanted.

"Yo, I need to see you, Drak, and Money in my office. Lucky, go get that chainsaw out of the storage closet and gas it up."

Moments later, Monica, Bird, and Drak sauntered into King's office. He lounged in a high-back, plush leather office chair, swiveling from right to left. Monica went around to King's side of the desk and sat on the arm of his chair. King stared at Bird and Drak for what seemed like an eternity. He eyed them curiously as if lost in some distant trance before finally speaking.

"I wanted to speak to you all to give you a heads up of things to come. I'm done, mane. Monica and I are cashing out, dawg. Bird, I know that you've been wanting out for quite some time, and soon you're going to be a free man. Drak, I'm not sure what you want to do when this shit is over, but I hope you've been stacking your paper."

"Man, why the sudden change of heart?" Bird asked.

"Yeah, dawg, no disrespect, but you're fucking with my paper, my nigga," added Drak.

Monica saw the look of exasperation in King's face. King wanted to cash out, and according to him, *nothing* and *nobody* would stop him.

"Listen, fellas, it's no secret that the only way out of this shit is either death or jail, and I'm not trying to lose my husband to these streets," Monica said. "Bird, you've been wanting out, so it works out for you, and Drak, from the looks of it, you're not getting any younger, so retirement should be on your menu as well."

There was a cold silence in the room. King had never let a woman sit in on a meeting, let alone speak for him. Monica had managed to tame the beast, and Bird smiled inwardly to himself. A small twinge of jealousy crept into his heart, though. He had been attracted to Monica from the first day he'd met her, but he understood that she had a job to do, and the last thing that he wanted to do was distract her with his own issues. But Monica was either an incredible actress, or she had actually fallen for King.

"Listen, I'm not complaining," he said, "but it's a lot of niggas that depend on you. And it's still a lot of muhfuckas out there with unpaid balances. What are we gonna do about that paper?"

King actually didn't care. His only concern was taking his money and his woman and getting the hell out of dodge. He was intelligent enough to know that his luck would eventually run out. King should have been killed a long time ago, but karma had been good to him because he'd always tried to be a good person. Of course he'd killed people, but only if they'd deserved it. To his credit, he'd never hurt a child or an elder, and for that, King was proud. He had far more money than he could've ever hoped for, and Monica had filled a void in his life. With Noisy Boy and Monica by his side, he felt like he could conquer the world.

King reached into his desk drawer and removed a cigar box full of black widow dro. It was the most potent brand of marijuana that King had ever smoked, and he needed everyone on his level for what he was about to say. He sprinkled the potent herb into the Garcia y Vega. He had his eyes trained on Monica as he twisted it and licked it, twirling his tongue expertly around the blunt. They locked gazes, and Monica smiled seductively. She felt a shiver run through her body from the sight of it, remembering King's tongue buried deep within her soul. King held the lighter to the tip of his blunt and inhaled deeply.

"Man, we are going to collect that money. Don't worry about that," King said. "We will set aside one day to collect that bread. I have a list, though."

"What kind of list?" Drak asked.

"A list of muhfuckas that's gotta be dealt with before we leave the game. I'm not leaving behind any loose ends to come up to bite me in my ass later—and don't worry about getting y'all hands dirty. I'ma take care of all of those fools myself."

King passed the blunt to Monica. She stared at it a long while, Muldoon's words echoing in her head. *If it takes selling drugs to do so, so be it. If you have to kill to prove that you're down for him so, be it. If you have to smoke a joint, snort coke, or suck his dick in the back of a crowded theater, I expect you to do your job with no hesitation*. His words played over and over in her head as if he were there in the room with her.

Monica put the blunt to her lips and inhaled deeply. She had lived her whole life drug-free. She was not only afraid of drugs but despised them. Drugs were for weak losers. Time and time again, she'd been witness to countless drug users who, even after the death of her parents, had come to her grandfather with their sob stories in hopes that he could somehow help them. "My phone is off; I need help with my rent; someone stole all of my groceries," they would say. She'd heard it all, and she'd grown despondent with dopefiends, realizing that once a drug user, *always* a drug user.

She inhaled deeply again, and this time, she held it. First came the intense, almost violent fit of coughing, then came the feeling of lightheaded euphoria, and last came the uncontrollable giggles that racked Monica's body. There was nothing funny, but still, Monica's giggles persisted. She apologized only to break out into hysterical laughter again.

"Fuck wrong with you, babe?" King asked, confused.

Bird stood and took the herb from Monica. "She don't smoke, my nigga. I ain't seen her hit no weed since we were in junior high."

"Oooooh, shit, my bad. I was wondering what the hell she was giggling about. Anyway, that nigga Junior gotta go, Corey gotta go, Baby Face gotta go, and that nigga Silk? Yeah, I'm saving him for last," King said in a matter-of-fact manner.

Bird knew that King was true to his word, and before all was said and done, each man on his list would be murdered by his hand. If there was anything that Bird respected about King, it was the fact that he had no reservations about putting in his own work. Most men with incredible amounts of money never wanted to get their hands dirty, but King was convinced that no one could take care of business like he could take of business.

"What about that fool DirtBag? You gonna just let him make it?" Bird asked.

"What do you mean, just let him make it? That cat is a non sequitur, Bird. Why should we concern ourselves with a fiend?"

Bird just shook his head; if King didn't get it, then who was he to bring it to his attention? DirtBag was a loose end in the greater scheme of things. He was also a baby rapist, a pedophile, the lowest of the low, and King had let him walk. If King had known that the girl that Michael Ross, Jappy, and DirtBag had raped was Monica's sister, there would have never been a question. Bird, however, couldn't tell him—couldn't even tell Monica for fear of jeopardizing the case. He did, however, harbor a certain amount of guilt. Was Kochese evil? Yes. Was he an asshole at times? Yes. One thing was undeniable, though, and that was the fact that King had helped Bird make hundreds of thousands of dollars, and for that he was grateful.

King instructed each of them to follow him to the freezer where Bond's frozen body hung. His lifeless, rigid body had begun to frost over. Frozen blood and mucus hung from every one of his orifices like red and yellow icicles. The shock of being impaled on the meat hook had caused Bond to release his bowels, with the strong odor of cold urine and fecal matter permeating throughout the small, dank enclosure.

King pulled the string on the chainsaw, but nothing happened. He pulled it again. Nothing. The third time that King pulled the cord, the chain saw whirred to life. The sound of the saw grew shriller with every press of the trigger.

"Lucky, gimme that bucket over there!" King instructed.

King started just below Bond's knees; the saw barked a throaty grind as it began to slide through Bond's frigid skin. Piece by piece, King hacked and sawed Bond's body until only his torso remained, still hanging from the meat hook. He took the chainsaw and sliced the remaining portion of Bond's body to complete his task. The only remnant of Bond's existence was the bucket containing his body parts and a small amount of blood that remained on the tip of the hook.

King ordered Lucky and Drak to each grab a side of the bucket as he went from dog cage to dog cage, tossing in Bond's body parts. He knew that between his assortments of pedigreed bullmastiffs, rottweilers, and pit bulls, there would be no evidence of his crime. His two prized pooches aside from Noisy Boy were the twin bullmastiffs, Beast and Psycho. They were more than capable of consuming Bond's entire body, but he would allow the other canines in the kennel the pleasure of tasting the snitch.

After leaving the kennel, King and Monica drove south on I-35, headed toward South Dallas. Silk would be the first on his list of people to eliminate. If he and Monica were going to live a normal life, it would be mandatory that he eliminated any form of danger that threatened the love that they'd found. He looked over at Monica, who stared intently out of the window.

Her mind was racing a million miles a minute. *How could he be so sweet to me and murder a man in the same breath*? she wondered. He had no problem with murder and was actually playing right into the hand that she'd dealt to him. He trusted her implicitly, and her case had been built. Even if the Feds arrested him now, he would face life in prison without the possibility of parole. Knowing the Feds like she did, though, they wouldn't stop until King faced the death penalty for his crimes against the state. Everyone in King's organization would fall with him—*everyone*, from the lowest-paid runner to the highest-paid lieutenant. They would all be charged under the RICO statute.

Although Monica understood the need to eradicate drug dealing on the streets of the inner city, it wasn't lost on her that the bulk of the young men being corralled into the system through the RICO Act were young black males. When she'd first explained to her grandfather that she had plans of going into the DEA, his instructions had been clear: *Make a difference*. He'd broken it down so clearly to her that there had been no room for confusion.

According to her grandfather, young black men had been targeted not by coincidence, but by design. It had started many years ago, almost as early as when the Africans arrived on the land that is now United States. They'd used divide and conquer to create separation between the slaves, ultimately making the "house niggers" look down on the "field niggers," and vice versa. It had always worked and had spread into modern times. The system made black men believe in hopelessness, and out of desperation, they were willing to do almost anything to ensure that their families were cared for.

He'd also explained that the government had played an integral part in dividing the black family by making the black woman feel as if she didn't need her husband to head her household. They removed the black man from the family largely due to his own stupidity, but the government had made it easier for the black woman to live without their husbands by making welfare and food stamps so easily accessible that the women no longer needed a man. Those who didn't receive government assistance carried with them the notion that, because they were successful in their own right, they didn't *need* a man. By design, the government and the powers that controlled the majority of the nation's wealth had been successful in their endeavor to divide the black family. And now here she was, playing into their hands. She was part of the same system, doing her part to hide her brothers, her people, in an unforgiving system.

Monica turned to King. "Baby, maybe we should go to another country where there are no extradition treaties."

"What do you mean, no extradition treaties?"

"I mean going to a country where, even if the United States decided to pursue a case against you later, they wouldn't be able to touch you, because they don't allow the U.S. to take people back home," Monica said. "With the amount of money that you have and the money that I've been able to save, another country would welcome us."

"How do you know all of this, Monica? You sound a lot like the police right now."

"I'm not the police, baby. I just happen to not be a dumbass," she snorted.

"So now I'm a dumbass, huh? Damn, that's cold-blooded."

The sound of sirens drew both King and Monica's attention before an argument could erupt. King instinctively looked down at his speedometer and cursed under his breath. He'd been so enthralled in his own thoughts that he hadn't noticed that he was speeding. He pulled over to the shoulder of the freeway and removed his driver's license, insurance, and registration. Kochese had always made sure that the paperwork on his cars was straight. That way he never had to worry about allowing the police the pleasure of defiling his vehicles.

The young cop walked to the driver's side of the vehicle and bent over to make eye contact with Kochese. "Do you know why I stopped you, sir?" he asked.

"I think I was going a little bit over the speed limit, officer."

"At least you know. License, insurance, and registration, please."

"No problem, officer. How is your day going so far?" King asked, trying to make small talk to put the officer at ease. His question went unanswered as the officer went back to his car to run Kochese's information. "Just be cool, baby. This shit should be over soon."

The officer returned to the car only to return Kochese's paperwork and ask Monica for hers. She had no worries because she knew that she was insulated. After she gave him her license, he returned moments later with his gun drawn. "Miss Bircher, I'm going to have to ask you to step out of the car, please."

"What's the problem, officer?" Monica asked.

"It seems as though you have an outstanding warrant from Raleigh-Durham, North Carolina, from a couple of years ago," he said more firmly. "Step out of the car, please."

Monica did as she was told, and in that instant, she realized that this was Muldoon's doing. He undoubtedly needed to get inside of her head, and he'd staged this arrest to get her away from King. She stepped out of the car and made her way to the front of the police cruiser. The officer put handcuffs on her and seated her in the back of the cruiser. Kochese stepped out of his vehicle and stood in the doorway.

"Officer, you think I can holla at my fiancée right quick?"

The officer nodded and waved Kochese to the back of the cruiser, where he'd let the window down to allow him access to Monica.

"Baby, you know I used to let Bond handle the bail bond shit, so it's going to take me a few hours to get you out. Hold on, okay? I love you," he said tenderly.

"I love you too, daddy. You need to hurry up and get me out, babe. I'm not with this jail shit."

Monica sat in a cold, damp interrogation room shackled to a stainless steel table. Muldoon entered the room, with the cop that had arrested her in tow.

"Greetings, Agent Dietrich. Long time no see," Muldoon said sarcastically.

Monica looked at Muldoon and then at the police officer.

"Oh, him?" Muldoon asked. "Yeah, you haven't had the privilege of meeting Special Agent Kilpatrick."

Agent Kilpatrick nodded, smiled at Monica, and placed a handheld tape recorder on the table. He pushed play, and every conversation that she and King had shared inside of his vehicles sprang to life.

She listened intently, not really realizing the extent of her feelings for King until she heard her own words.

"So, you've been spying on me?" she asked.

"Spying on you? No, Agent, I've been doing my job, which is what I thought that you were doing until I heard your conversation today."

"What do you mean, until today?"

"I mean, what the hell are you thinking giving King information and putting ideas of fleeing the country in his head?"

"I didn't give King shit, and I *am* doing my job, sir."

"Actually, you're in too deep, Agent. We talked about this shit before you even went undercover, and you told me that you could handle it. Did you not?"

"Yes, I did, but—" she started, but Muldoon cut her off.

"Are you in love with this piece of shit, Monica?" he asked. She hesitated, and Muldoon spoke again. "You're going to do your fucking job, or I will have your ass brought up on federal charges. Answer this question for me, Agent Dietrich. How do you think your little *boyfriend* would react if someone mysteriously mailed him a care package with these contents?"

Agent Kilpatrick tossed a manila folder in front of Monica. The contents made her blood run cold and her heart drop to the pit of her stomach. There was an array of pictures ranging from her time in recruitment to photos of Monica and Bird sitting in the head office of the DEA. She thumbed through the remaining pictures and saw images of her and King in various states of undress. There were pictures of them as they'd made love that morning, immediately turning her worry into anger.

"What the fuck is this shit?" she asked.

"This, my dear, is insurance. You will do your goddamned job, or you and King can both room together in Club Fed. I'm not fucking around with you. We are too close to a breakthrough on this case for you to drop the ball with this lovey-dovey bullshit now."

"This lovey-dovey bullshit, as you call it, is what's going to blow this case wide open. King Kochese is not only a drug kingpin, but he's a serial killer. Did you know that? Did you know that he's planning on killing anybody that can expose him for who he is? So don't tell me about doing my job, Senior Agent. I'm doing my goddamned job, and I'm doing it well. I hope your old perverted ass enjoyed seeing me suck his big black dick! Geesh, what the fuck is wrong with you people?"

Muldoon had no words, for he had truly believed that Monica had somehow slipped in too deep. He could have sworn that she had fallen for Kochese's charms and forsaken her post as an officer of the federal government, but he was wrong. Kochese hadn't turned Monica. On the contrary, it was the other way around. She had infiltrated King's soul and tainted his psyche.

Chapter 23

Realer than Fiction

"Monica Bircher, your bail has been paid. You're free to go," the elderly white correctional officer said.

Monica walked out of Lew Sterritt Justice Center and took a deep breath of fresh air. She inhaled deeply and exhaled a sigh of relief that she was on the right side of the law. The few hours that she'd spent inside hadn't been sweet. Muldoon had intentionally allowed Monica to be booked on her bogus charges and sent to holding. She'd tried to pay attention to her own business, but that was next to impossible. She was literally surrounded by the worst of the worst. It had reeked of hot urine and fresh sex in the cramped holding tank. Prostitutes and drug users milled about aimlessly, awaiting their judicial fate. Some of the women were there for serious crimes, and although Monica was a member of law enforcement, she couldn't help but feel sorry for some of them.

One woman in particular had captured Monica's attention. Her name was Gladys, and she was 47 years old. She had been arrested for murdering her husband. Gladys was a timid and soft-spoken woman who had seen better days. Her husband, according to her, had been beating her since they were first married. They'd gotten married under duress when she was just 16 years old, at a literal shotgun wedding in the backwoods of Alabama.

He'd gotten her pregnant, and her father had gotten his shotgun. Monica shivered at the thought. She couldn't imagine living in a violent marriage for over three decades. Gladys, however, had endured the agonizing pain of birthing seven children, and the unforgettable torture at the hands of the man that had sworn to love and protect her. The beatings persisted even after she'd gone to the police countless times, only to be told that there was nothing that they could do. The truth was that Gladys' husband had been a member of the Dallas Police Department's narcotics task force for twenty-five years. They'd known of her beatings and had swept it under the rug. The DPD was notorious for the good ol' boy mentality. They believed in caring for their own, and the fact that she'd killed one of theirs had made her public enemy number one.

She had dedicated her life to her husband only to have him decimate her self-esteem by pulverizing her. She'd taken the abuse for the sake of their children, but the abuse had spread to them. He had not only resorted to beating them, but he'd started trying to feed his sick deviant sexual desires with their eldest daughter. When Gladys had caught him trying to sneak into her room while she was asleep, he'd grown angry and beat her with a golf club, and then, according to Gladys, she snapped.

She went into his gun cabinet, removed and loaded his 12-gauge Mossberg shotgun, and headed to their bedroom. When she entered the room, he was sitting in bed with his back against the headboard, watching television, and Gladys knew that if she didn't get into bed immediately that he would come after her. She stood in the doorway with the shotgun behind her back and stared at him. Like clockwork, he jumped off of the bed and stumbled toward her, screaming slurred expletives. She'd raised the rifle and fired all six rounds into his chest. And that was that. She'd eliminated her problem, but the state of Texas was gearing up to crucify her for the death of the officer. They'd totally forgotten that he was her husband—her physically abusive husband—before he was an officer of the state.

Monica smiled as she made her way toward Kochese. He was leaning against his Range Rover with Noisy Boy at his feet, who, upon seeing Monica, ran full speed in her direction. She kneeled to greet the colorless puppy,

"Hey, honey snacks, how's momma's boy?" she asked.

Noisy Boy wagged his tail playfully as Monica stood and continued her stride toward Kochese. The closer she got, the more she realized how insanely beautiful Kochese Mills was. His physical appearance masked a sinister soul that had no drawbacks about killing. Monica silently wondered if he actually loved her or simply loved the *idea* of loving her. She hugged his neck tightly as she made her way to him. Her body trembled from a mixture of fear and excitement, partly from the fear of the unknown and partly from the excitement of harboring a dangerous secret. She was in too deep and she knew it, but she was in it nonetheless.

"I can feel you trembling, baby. Are you okay?" Kochese asked.

"Everything is fine, baby. I'm just happy to see my favorite boys."

Kochese held Monica at arm's length and studied her carefully. Her jade green eyes held pools of unfallen tears, swimming in lucid despair.

"You don't look all right, baby girl. Do you want to talk about it?" he asked.

"Just thinking about my grandfather on my mother's side, you know? He would be real disappointed in me if he knew that I'd been to jail," Monica lied.

Truth be told, it wasn't a complete falsity. Her grandfather had always held Monica to a higher standard. When Jasmine had been sent away to the Buckner Home, he sat Monica down day after day, picking her brain and preparing her for some invisible battle that had yet to take place.

"In my day, black folk knew the importance of education, and we fought for it," he once said. "Nowadays, kids fight to not go to school. What's more important than an education, Monica?"

"I don't know, Pop Pop. What is more important?"

"Enough common sense to know that there is nothing more important than education," he had replied, triumphantly.

That was the way that her teenage years had gone. Monica's grandfather had been there when the world had turned its back on her and Jasmine. His strength had given her a deep affinity for family and loyalty, etched deep in her soul She could hear his words as plain as day: "Never make a promise that you can't or aren't willing to keep." She'd broken her promise to Kochese, and she couldn't decide whether she was willing to keep her promise to the Fed. Her grandfather was her rock, her source of strength, and a beacon of what was good in the world when her parents had overdosed. He reassured her daily that although life was unfair, God made no mistakes. Her life hadn't ended when her parents died, and instead of blaming the drug dealers, it was her duty as a victim to help bring about change.

It had been no great surprise to Pop Pop when Monica had announced to him that she would pursue a career in law enforcement. He'd hugged her tightly and proclaimed his undying pride for his eldest granddaughter. Jasmine, however, had been a totally different story for the loving grandfather. He'd felt as if he was somehow to blame for her ordeal. The "what if's" and "I should haves" had all but consumed the aging Pop Pop, and the unwavering guilt ravaged him. He would ramble on and on about how he should've just taken the girls from their parents when he'd learned that their parents were on drugs. He'd sworn that if Jasmine didn't recover, he would surely die of guilt. As strong as her grandfather had been, she realized in that instance that she and Jasmine had always been his weakness. One day he had been in her life, bestowing upon her all of his quirky wisdom, and the next day he was gone. Monica hadn't taken his death well at all. The realization that she had to somehow remain strong for the sake of her little sister was the medicine that she'd used to help her bounce back.

The sound of fingers snapping brought Monica out of her reminiscing.

"Where you at, baby? Come back. You know what? I'm tired of waiting, baby. Let's just do it! Let's get married now!" King exclaimed.

Monica found his excitement to be amusing. His eyes sparkled like an excited child going on a rollercoaster for the first time. The prospect of marriage had overtaken King, and he wanted to move full steam ahead.

"Why the sudden rush, babe?" Monica asked, the excitement clearly showing in her voice.

"No rush, really. I'm just smart. I realize that I will never find a woman that loves me the way that you do, and I don't want to lose that."

"I feel the same way, baby. So when and how do you want to do it?" Monica asked.

"Well, I was thinking me, you, Bird, Drak, and Baby Face can fly down to Florida, and while we get our marriage license we can have the triplets rent us a yacht and find us a preacher. If you wanna invite your family from North Carolina, we will fly them down, too. Let's do this shit balla style!"

"I don't really fuck with my family like that, but I'm with it! Married on a yacht? Yeah, that's going to be hot," Monica said.

"You like that idea?"

"I love that idea, but baby, why are you bringing Baby Face? I thought you had a problem with him."

"I do have a problem with his snitching ass, but I'm going to take care of Face my way. You just watch big daddy work," Kochese said.

"I've been watching you work since day one, baby. You're a beast."

"You haven't seen the half of it. I want to show you something." Kochese wheeled his Range Rover expertly through traffic, heading toward King's Kennel. He pulled into the parking lot and circled a couple of times. His eyes darted curiously from shop to shop as if searching for something. He brought the SUV to rest in front of a small shop with a sign that read: EVELYN'S DRESS EMPORIUM.

"What's this, baby?" Monica asked.

"You'll see. Follow me."

Kochese unlocked the door to the dress shop and stepped inside. Monica followed closely behind him. He glanced out of the front window nervously once more and turned on the overhead lights. Monica gasped at the assortment of beautiful wedding gowns and prom dresses. One wall held hats and shoes of all colors.

"Is this where you want me to get my wedding dress, baby?"

Kochese's laughter reverberated throughout the enclosure. "Nobody works here, baby. It's a shell."

"A what?" Monica asked.

Without uttering a word, Kochese took her hand and led her to a back room that looked like a seamstress's work area. He walked to the countertop with an assortment of scissors, patterns, and measuring tapes on it and pushed it to the side. Underneath was a large trap door in the floor secured by a large master lock. Kochese removed the lock and pulled the large metal door open. The door creaked and crackled as it came to rest in the upright position.

"Noisy Boy, stay here. Holla if you need me!" Kochese said. Noisy Boy yelped as if he had understood his master's command.

"Nobody knows that this room exists, not even Bird, baby. By the time you leave this room, you'll either love me more for sharing my world, or you'll think I'm insane. Either way, I want you to know because I don't want to go into this marriage with lies or secrets."

Monica remained quiet. She was afraid that her words would reveal her disloyal plans for King's undoing.

He took her hand and descended the stairs slowly. A putrid stench invaded her nostrils and stuck to the back of her throat. Not until they reached the center of the room did Kochese flood the room with light. The first thing that caught Monica's eye was the graffiti on the far wall that read: KING'S KRYPT. Underneath the morbid words were bodies with their heads removed. Each one of them had been nailed to the wall with a large sixteen-penny nail. On each nail was a name tag and date.

"What—" Monica began, but before she could finish, King answered.

"These are the people I've killed, Monica, but just so you know, I ain't never intentionally fucked over nobody, and I never killed a man that didn't need killin'."

He stood behind her with his arms wrapped firmly around her waist. Monica was afraid to turn and look at him. He whispered softly in her ear.

"See this one right here? He was my first. I bodied his ass when I was only fourteen years old. The more I did it, the easier it became."

"But why?"

"'Cause sometimes people do the world a bigger favor by not being here." He shrugged.

The nonchalant manner with which Kochese spoke of murder caused Monica to shiver. She counted the bodies mounted on the wall. There were twenty-seven total. Monica scanned the rest of the room, and in a dimly lit corner, she thought that she could make out the silhouette of a seated figure. She squinted her eyes to get a better view, but it was no use.

Kochese, sensing her curiosity, moved forward and pulled the string to an overhead light, illuminating the small dark corner.

"Monica, meet my mother. Mama, meet Monica," he said, smiling proudly.

Monica shrieked in horror. There in the pale darkness sat his mother's mummified corpse.

"I know she didn't love me, but I tried to show her that I'm worth loving. See, look!" He rushed to a nearby closet to reveal an assortment of beautiful gowns. "Any dress she could've ever possibly wanted, I've had made."

Kochese's mother sat staring at Monica with lifeless eyes, her face contorted into a ghostly mask of shock and terror. Someone had tried unsuccessfully to sew the jagged cut that spread from ear to ear on her neck. He'd attempted to fashion a crude suture from something that appeared to be a long, thin strip of leather. Monica couldn't believe her eyes. Kochese, it seemed, was more disturbed mentally than she'd originally believed.

He unlocked the door to an adjoining room and stepped inside. "I call this the Green Room, right here!" He excitedly flicked the light switch, and the 100-square-foot room was flooded with green translucent light. There were three rows of wooden pallets with four pallets in each row stacked with money. There had to be literally hundreds of thousands, if not millions of dollars, in that room.

"We have more than enough money to disa-fucking-ppear forever. All we have to do is find one of those countries that you were talking about."

Monica stood in the room, staring. She had never seen so much money in one place in her life.

"Why don't you have this money in a bank, baby? This is a lot of money to just have out in the open."

"Yeah, I'm gonna just roll up to the bank and deposit a hundred racks at a time? Nah, you know what would happen? Some slick-ass banker would try to clip me for my bread, and I'll end up killing his ass. So no, thank you, I'll keep my shit," Kochese huffed.

They stepped out of the room, and Kochese locked the door. He stopped in front of the mummy and kneeled. "Mama, me and Monica are getting married. She loves me for me, and we want to be together." He paused, and there was an awkward silence as if he were waiting on a response from his maternal Crypt-Keeper. He leaned in closer, and let his ear touch his mother's mummified lips. What started as a smirk blossomed into a full smile.

Chapter 24

Leave No Trace

Bird sat at a table in Baby Face's small apartment, sipping a glass of Hennessy. Baby Face paced the room nervously. He'd received a call from one of his runners saying that Silk had put a bounty on his head for running with Kochese. It was common knowledge that Face was a top lieutenant in Kochese's underworld army, but Face had grown up with Silk and Shawt Dawg. They had all come into the game together, and when Face decided to do business with Kochese instead of the people that he grew up with, Silk had taken it as a personal affront to his person. In his eyes, Face had somehow violated the hustler's code. The truth of the matter was that *everyone* wanted to get down with Kochese, because his wages were far above average, plus, once a man was down with King, he was considered family. Silk's organization was a gang of ragtag misfits who'd either been to prison or weren't far from going, and Face hadn't wanted any part of it. And now Bird and Face were both waiting on Drak to show up. They needed to handle Silk before someone got hurt. Silk was a loose cannon, and if it took too long for someone to carry out the hit, he would do it himself.

"Fuck you pacing for, nigga?" Bird asked.

"Man, listen, don't judge me, nigga!" Baby Face shouted nervously. "It ain't your life on the line. Besides, have you seen them ugly-ass niggas that run with Silk? All of them look like they were born with guns! Where the fuck is Drak, man?"

As soon as the words had escaped his lips, there was a thunderous knock at the door. Without waiting for a response, Drak entered. "You must not be too worried about that nigga Silk, 'cause you're sitting here with the doors unlocked. What up, Bird?"

"Sup, Drak?"

"Not shit. Goddamn, Face. You sweating like a whore in church. That nigga Silk got you shook, huh?" Drak asked.

"Man, fuck all that. How are we gonna get this nigga up off of me?"

"Comfort," Drak said bluntly.

Bird and Face exchanged fretful glances.

"Comfort?" Bird echoed.

"Yeah, comfort," Drak said. "This nigga Silk and his little squad have the same routine every Friday. They head to the strip club, get drunk, and trick on bitches. They lack imagination, and that will be his downfall. Tomorrow we will hit those fools so hard that they'd rather sack groceries at the Piggly Wiggly than be in these goddamn streets."

"How are we gonna do that?" Face asked.

"I swear, sometimes you're slow, boy. Between you and Bird, I want y'all to assemble every soldier we got. Last I counted, between lookouts, runners, and cookers, we had close to eighty people. I don't want any captains or lieutenants—just soldiers. This will be the perfect opportunity for us to see who's really down."

"Yeah, it all sounds good, but how are we gonna do the shit?" Face asked.

"You ask a lot of goddamn questions, nigga! Just make sure that your squad is here tomorrow at eight o'clock at night. I will have everything in place by then. Tell them all to wear baby blue T-shirts so that we can tell who's who. You got me?" Drak said, making his way to the door.

Bird followed Drak closely. "All right, Face. I'll see you tomorrow, my dude. Aye, Drak, hold up. Let me holla at you, mane."

They walked out into the dimly lit apartment complex toward the parking lot.

"So, what up, B?" Drak asked, taking a drag from his Newport cigarette.

"Yo, first of all, don't you think that nigga King gonna flip out about taking all of these soldiers off of the street? And second, you know how that fool is about killing. If you have these little gangsters kill Silk, he is gonna be heated."

"I can dig your concern, Bird, but with Kochese, you know as well as I do that he'd rather have Silk's life than money," Drak said. "We are gonna shut down Silk's entire operation and deliver him to King Kochese in the process. Now go and get some sleep, because it's about to go down tomorrow, playboy."

Bird nodded and walked to his car. He had never really been a smoker, but he needed a cigarette, a blunt, something. "Yo, Drak, let me get one of your squares, man," he said, running to Drak's car as he backed out of his parking space.

"Here, nigga. Don't make it a habit. I ain't tryna support your little addiction."

"Whatever, nigga," Bird said. He sat in his Dodge Charger and looked in the back seat. It was an old habit that was hard to break. The streets had a way of making a man paranoid, and Bird was straddling a thin line between paranoia and reality. He hadn't been home in days because he wasn't sure if his plush condo was safe. He had instead been holed up at the Loews Anatole. He pushed the lighter in until the tip glowed a bright pumpkin orange. He lit the cigarette and inhaled deeply. It dawned on Bird that he was still sitting in his car, so he stepped out and sat on the hood. Smoking a cigarette every once in a blue moon was his guilty pleasure, but not so much that he wanted his car smelling like cigarette smoke. He puffed again and inhaled deeply, tilting his head back to blow dull gray smoke rings from his mouth. Soon, he would be away from the very thing that he'd wished for so long as a child: the street life. He still had his head raised to the sky, admiring how the stars twinkled and danced across the dense black sky, when he heard a familiar voice.

"What's up now, Bird?" the voice said.

Bird looked up to see Corey's sister, Markeisha, standing not twenty feet away. Her clothes were tattered and dirty, and she reeked of musk and urine. Her eyes looked wild as if she hadn't slept in days, and she had foam spittle in the corners of her mouth, resembling a rabid dog. There was something in Markeisha's hand, but Bird could not make out what it was. His first thought was that it was a gun, but Markeisha had surpassed common dopefiend status, so had she possessed a gun, the local drug dealer would have surely owned it now in exchange for drugs. Markeisha stared at Bird, but she looked lost and confused. Her eyes were soulless pits of strife and despair. He met Markeisha's gaze, and her eyes followed his eyes to her hand. She brought her hand up into full view as if to give Bird a better look to appease his curiosity. She held a butcher's knife. The shiny metal glinted dangerously in the moonlight.

"Sup, Markeisha? Fuck you gonna do with that knife, bitch?"

Markeisha didn't answer. Her eyes remained stoic as she moved toward Bird slowly. Her trance-like state not only angered Bird, but scared him as well. He'd heard tales of dopefiends that seemed to have superhuman strength when they got angry or afraid, and Markeisha looked to be both.

"Look, ho, I ain't gonna say this shit but once. Put the goddamned knife down."

Still, Markeisha inched toward him like a cheetah stalking its prey. Bird slipped his hand into his pocket slowly and removed his car fob. He hit a button, and the trunk sprang open. King had been telling him for years not to keep his pistol in the trunk but close, and now his disobedience had put him in this dilemma. Bird moved swiftly toward his trunk, but he wasn't quite fast enough. Markeisha moved with catlike quickness, burying the knife deep into Bird's stomach. His abdomen burned as she yanked the blade from his belly. Bird's hand instinctively went to his gut where he'd been stabbed. Blood poured from the gaping, three-inch incision that the blade had made. He stumbled but caught himself, closing the trunk in the process. Bird wanted to scream, but the pain radiating from his paunch was too great. Markeisha lunged toward him, swinging the knife wildly. Bird raised his hands in defense and felt the sting of the cold metal slicing through his skin.

"You didn't have to kill my little brother, Bird!" Markeisha shouted.

Bird flipped over onto his stomach and pressed his hands against the warm asphalt. He steadied himself and attempted to stand. Thoughts of his family flooded his mind. Everyone in his family, with the exception of Bird, had fared well. He was the proverbial black sheep of the family. And then his mind flashed to Monica, whom he felt that he had somehow let down.

He then felt the knife sink deep into the fleshiness of his back and scrape the bones of his scapula. Bird yelped from the agony of the wound. He had never felt so much pain in his life, and the shock caused him to collapse and lay on his stomach. His head was twisted in an unnatural position, but he was unable to move.

I'm about to fucking die at the hands of a dopefiend, he thought. Bird watched the blood spill from his hands, and he could feel the blood from his stomach pooling underneath his body.

As her last act of defiance, Markeisha sat on Bird's back, pulled his head back by his forehead, and slit Bird's throat. Markeisha stood, towering over Bird, laughing insanely.

"I told you, nigga. I told you. You didn't have to kill my little bro—" But before she could finish her sentence, Baby Face pulled the trigger of his .45 caliber Desert Eagle, pointed at the base of Markeisha's skull. Her body slumped to the ground next to Bird into a pool of blood and brain matter. Bird and Markeisha stared blankly at one another, clinging to hope, trying their best to fight the pain.

Chapter 25

Be Easy

The shrill sound of Kochese's house phone shocked him out of his slumber. It had been quite some time since someone had been brazen enough to ring King's phone before the sun had risen. King glanced at the clock on his nightstand and cursed under his breath. It read 3:13 A.M.

"Hello, and this had better be damn good," he barked. King sat straight up in bed. "What?" He screamed into his phone.

"What's wrong, baby? Is everything okay?" Monica asked.

Kochese didn't answer her. He sprang from the bed and began pacing the hardwood floors, still talking to the person on the other end of the phone. "Is he okay? Aw, hell naw. Fuck, man! Yo, meet me at the kennel. All right, peace." He hung up. "Baby, we have to hit the kennel and meet up with Drak. That nigga Bird got stabbed up last night. Drak said Baby Face killed the bitch that stabbed him, so Face is being detained. He also said that my dude has a punctured lung. The doctors aren't sure if he's going to make it, and they have him on breathing machines and shit. Get dressed so that we can dip."

Monica couldn't believe her ears. Bird had grown on her, and a small part of her felt connected to him. He had been her guide into the street life and would become her ticket into the DEA hall of fame.

"What? Who? How did this happen, Kochese? How am I supposed to explain this to my family?"

She stared at Kochese with open contempt and hatred dripping from her eyes. Everything that he touched went sour.

An hour later, they were pulling into the parking lot of King's Kennel, where Drak was parked, sitting in his car on the phone, smoking a cigarette and listening to the radio. Drak stepped out of his car with the receiver still pressed firmly to his ear. He nodded a *what's up* in Monica and King's direction. They both waited somewhat impatiently for him to get off the phone. Noticing their impatience, he covered the phone with his hand.

"They got me on hold. They are calling it a 'justifiable homicide,' so Face is straight. The fool had a nice-sized sack of weed in his pocket, though, so his bond is low—hold on. Hello? Yes, ma'am. Yes, ma'am, no problem. I will be down shortly. Thank you. You too," Drak said, ending the call. He turned to King and Monica. "Okay, this is the deal: his bond is only fifteen hundred, so I will go and get him in a minute. Man, Bird is in critical condition, y'all."

"What happened, Drak? How did this shit happen?" Monica asked.

"Remember the cat named Corey that Bird had put down? Well, Corey's sister caught him slipping and got some get back. The shit must've happened right after I left," Drak said, shaking his head.

"Right after *you* left?" Kochese asked.

"Yeah, it was supposed to be a surprise for you. Silk put a hit out on Face. Little pussy-ass nigga got in his feelings because Face was getting down on our side instead of his little flop squad. So, me and Bird went over to his crib to calm Face down because he was shook. We were supposed to get a bunch of our little soldiers together today and go handle the shit, but looks like that's a no go now."

"Nah, I got something special for that fool," Kochese said. "Let me handle his ass. As far as Face goes, I will deal with him later. All right, you go and get Face before the little crybaby turns rat. Me and Monica are gonna go and see Bird."

Monica and Kochese entered Bird's hospital room and were immediately seized by the smell of sanitary cleaning solutions and solvents. It almost smelled *too* clean. Everything in the room was stark white, except for the colorful bouquet of flowers that they'd brought. Bird lay completely still with tubes in his nose and mouth. He had white gauze wrapped around his throat, and through the gauze, there were traces of blood and the outline of stitches. His left hand had gauze also, but it was no longer white. The blood had seeped through, turning the once-white bandage a crimson red. Monica took Bird's right hand and clutched it hard.

"Damn, cuz," she said, weeping softly.

"Damn, playboy. You shoulda killed that nigga's whole family," Kochese scolded. "You wouldn't be laying in this bitch looking like a mummy."

His words cut into Monica and stung like alcohol poured on an open wound. Here was a man that had, up until recently, dedicated his entire life to King's organization, and King was speaking to him as if he were nobody. He continued his verbal tirade until Monica exploded.

"Not that you give a fuck, but you do realize that he is still my cousin, right? You're talking really reckless right now, and I don't like it."

"Bird been my nigga, my little brother, for a long time. He knows how I am, babe!" Kochese said. He wasn't used to being challenged, especially by a woman, but he loved Monica too much to offer much resistance.

"Newsflash, Einstein, he's not responding," Monica snapped.

"You know what? I'm gonna go and handle this Silk situation before I say something that I'll regret. You stay and enjoy your cousin," he said, bending to kiss Monica on the top of her head. He walked toward the door but stopped short of leaving. "I love you, Monica."

"I know you do," she said.

Kochese parked across the street from the small, nondescript brick building. He watched patiently as individuals disappeared into the building, slipping in carefully so as to not to bring attention to themselves. His excitement was piqued as he watched a couple stroll toward the building, hand in hand. Kochese hopped out of his car and crossed the street at a brisk pace.

"Excuse me, yo, excuse me," he said as he approached the couple.

Chapter 26

Here Comes the Bride

Monica stood in the window of Bird's hospital room and looked out onto the parking lot. She nervously dialed Muldoon's number. "Hello, Gramps, it's Money."

"Hello, Monica, how are things?"

"They aren't good. Bird was stabbed really badly last night. I am at the hospital with him right now, but it's not looking good."

"Are you okay? I mean, are you going to be able to close the case soon?"

"Wow, you guys are all the same," Monica said. "A man is lying on his death bed, and everyone is caught up in their own selfishness."

"Excuse me, Ms. Bleeding Heart, if I'm not boohooing about a drug dealer getting his just desserts. I need you to get your head out of your ass and get it in the game. This is bullshit. First, it was the lovey-dovey crap with Kochese, and now it's some emotional shit with Bircher. I'm starting to wonder if I made a mistake by trusting you with this case! Either do your fucking job or so help me God, I will have you brought up on charges. By the time I'm done with you, you won't be able to get a job flipping burgers at McDonald's!"

The call was disconnected before Monica could respond. She didn't like his tone, and she most definitely didn't like not having the chance to respond, but she knew that he was right. She needed to end the case so that she could get Jasmine out of the Buckner Home. She had been there for much too long, and Monica missed her terribly. She remembered the good days when her parents, along with her grandparents, would have a game night with her and Jasmine. Every Saturday night, they would order pizza or Chinese food and play Monopoly. It had been Jasmine's favorite game, and she'd gotten so good that she'd usually end up with the majority of the property and all of the money. She contemplated calling Kochese and telling him that she was going to call a cab to go to the mall or something so that she could sneak away to see Jasmine, but it would be just her luck that he would say that he was on his way back and that he would be glad to take her. She took a deep breath and dialed his number.

"Hey, baby, where are you?" she asked.

"I'm on the south side. What's up?"

"I'm bored, babe," she pouted, whining in her most babyish voice.

"Okay, I should be done in an hour or so, and then I will come and get you."

"Nah, don't worry about it. I'm going to catch a cab to the mall, and then I will come to the house, okay?"

"Okay, baby, have fun. You gonna buy me something?"

"Yep, and I'm going to make you work for it if you want it," she teased.

"How am I going to do that?"

"You think about it while I'm at the mall. Just be ready when I get home," she said, ending her call. Kochese was intelligent enough to realize that a woman shopping could potentially take hours, so Monica had plenty of time to visit with Jasmine.

***

Monica sat in the visitation area of the Buckner Home, waiting patiently for the orderlies to bring in Jasmine. Months had passed since she'd seen her little sister, and there was much to discuss. Not that she would respond, but Monica needed to vent.

Jasmine walked into the room, and Monica's breath caught. Her hands flew to her mouth to cover her approaching cries of joy. Jasmine moved with the grace of a gazelle. Her lithe body seemed to glide toward Monica. Her skin glowed, and her smile was radiant. During Monica's previous visits, Jasmine had always seemed to be heavily medicated and withdrawn, but now she was alert and lucid.

"Hey, Monica! Oh my God, I've missed you," Jasmine said.

Monica hadn't heard Jasmine use a complete sentence in years, and she was at a loss for words. She stood, looking at her younger sister in dazed amazement, wondering where the sudden change had come from.

"What's the matter, Monica? Cat got your tongue?" Jasmine teased.

"I'm just really surprised, that's all. I mean, the last time I saw you, you could barely complete a sentence. I come back today, and you're chatty Cathy."

"I understand, but honestly, you know what it was? I've been visiting with your boss, and he really reminds me of Pop Pop. He is so blunt and so forward." She laughed. "He told me that I needed to stop playing the victim and pick myself up. After he said it so many times, it started to sink in, and I stopped swallowing those pills that they were giving me. And then, like a miracle late one night, it dawned on me that he was right. For too long, I had been feeling sorry for myself and playing the victim. Not being doped up finally allowed me to wake the hell up."

"Whatever made you better, I'm glad, and I will forever be in Muldoon's debt for helping to bring you back to me," Monica said. She embraced her sister tightly. She breathed in Jasmine's essence. A mixture of lavender and baby powder rushed through her nostrils. It reminded her of the day that her mother brought Jasmine home from the hospital. It had been one of the happiest days of her life. She had vehemently campaigned against having a little brother, and like most parents, her mother and father had entertained her whim by telling her that she had to pray really hard to God if she wanted a little sister. She had prayed laboriously, even going as far as to write letters addressed to Jesus himself. Finally, when her parents had come home, they'd presented her with Jasmine. Her father had kneeled down to her with Jasmine in his arms so that she could get a better look at her and had whispered in her ear, "You see, Monica? Prayer works." And just like that, her faith was born, believing wholeheartedly that God took care of his own.

Monica and Jasmine were as close as sisters separated in age could be, but Monica loved her sister. She harbored the guilt of needing space from Jasmine and felt partly responsible for the bad things that had happened to her little sister. Jasmine must've sensed Monica's guilt creeping up to ruin her mood, because she hugged her tighter. She took her hand and led Monica to a nearby couch on a patio overlooking the wooded area to the rear of the Buckner Home.

"I want to tell you some things about myself, Monica, and I don't want you to say anything, I just want you to listen, okay?" Jasmine said.

Monica didn't utter a word. She nodded, still in awe of the transformation that Jasmine had gone through. Although to the untrained eye they could've passed for twins, they most definitely had distinct differences in appearance. Monica's hair was jet black and bone straight, and Jasmine's was jet black but hung in large, curly ringlets. They both held a set of jade green eyes and the same silky olive-colored skin, but Jasmine's was characterized by a beauty mark just above her left eyebrow.

Jasmine smiled at Monica's admiration. She could feel her sister's love, and it warmed her heart, but there were things that Monica needed to know.

"Monica, I remember so clearly the night that those men raped me. You were away at camp, and I'd cried myself to sleep every night, wishing that I was with you. I know I must've gotten on Mom and Dad's nerves, because Daddy made the statement to Mommy that this was the reason that he got high—to deal with my constant sniveling and whining. They'd gotten into a heated argument because Daddy had sold our PlayStation and their wedding bands. Mom was pissed, because Daddy had taken her rings while she was in the shower, but by the time he'd gotten back home, whatever drugs he'd sold them for were already gone."

Jasmine stopped talking to catch her breath. She had never recounted the events of that horrific night to anyone, not even to her therapists, which was part of the reason that she hadn't talked in so many years. She choked back her tears as she continued her horrid tale.

"Mommy was angry, angrier than I'd ever seen her before, and she swore that she would leave if Daddy didn't find a way to get her some dope. He called Pop Pop, but I think he must've cursed Daddy out because Mommy got on the phone begging and telling Pop Pop that he didn't understand.

"I remember walking down the street with both of them holding my hands. I think we went to a hotel, because there was a man behind the counter. Daddy went up and said something to the man, and he pointed down a long hallway.

"Some of the things that I saw that night, no child should ever have to see. People were sitting in the hallway doing drugs. I saw a lady sucking some guy's dick in the doorway to one of the hotel rooms. The lights were so dim in the hallway that it resembled a horror movie, but I had no idea just how close to a horror flick we actually were. As we walked down that long hall, men groped at me, touching my butt. Mom and Dad seemed to be oblivious to the obvious pedophilic activity taking place as they dragged me to my fate. Daddy knocked on the door, and we were ushered in by gunpoint. I remember being terrified because I wet my pants.

"Mommy approached a table where three men were sitting and asked if they could front her some dope. They told her hell no, to come back when she had money. Then she offered to fuck all of them for the dope, and they laughed in her face. Daddy offered to suck their dicks for the drugs, and they cursed him out. I didn't know what that meant at the time, but looking back on it now, those drugs must have really had a hold on them to make Daddy go out like that."

The two sisters were both crying. Monica couldn't believe her ears. While she was away at church camp learning basket weaving and archery, her little sister was caught in a living nightmare. She gripped Jasmine's hand tighter as her sister continued.

"The main guy told mom that her pussy no longer had value because she had been run through, but they might be willing to work out a deal if they were willing to leave me for a little while. I prayed in my head that they wouldn't leave me, but it was like they didn't even think about it. As soon as they put the idea on the table, Daddy nudged me forward like I was a herd of cattle."

The tears flowed freely from Jasmine's eyes as she lay her past on the table.

"They got their drugs and scurried away like two roaches. They left me there to deal with whatever torture and torment that those guys were about to give to me. The first man climbed on top of me and tried to put his tongue in my mouth, and I threw up on him. He hit me in my eye, and the more I cried, the more he beat me. He snatched my panties off and forced himself inside of me. As he thrust, it felt like my insides were being ripped to shreds. The other two men came into the room and had their turns with me, remarking how good it felt to have some 'tight stuff.' Over and over again they raped me, Monica, until I could no longer take it and blacked out. I had my eyes trained on the door the entire time, waiting for Mom and Dad to come and rescue me, but they never came. The next thing I knew, I was waking up in the hospital. I hated you after that, Monica. I hated you because I thought that you abandoned me."

Jasmine buried her head in her hands and sobbed heavily.

"Oh my God, Jasmine, I am so sorry," Monica pleaded.

"I realize now that it's not your fault. I used to think that I was a bad person, that I had done something to deserve it. Then it became clear to me that there are just some sick people in the world, and it wasn't my fault."

"I can't wait until you come home with me so that we can start over," Monica said.

"I'm so ready, Monica. Can I tell you something, though?"

"You can tell me anything, Jazzy Bell."

"Does it make me crazy that I have thoughts of hurting people?" Jasmine asked.

Monica thought for a while before answering. After all that Jasmine had gone through, there was no wonder that she had thoughts of hurting people.

"I think that it's natural to feel that way, sis. I mean, look at all of the things that you've gone through. I don't blame you one bit for the way that you feel. As long as you don't act on it, you're okay. Like Pop Pop used to say: It's not what you think that makes you a bad person, but rather, what you do."

"Yeah, I suppose you're right. As long as I don't act on my thoughts, the world is safe."

Chapter 27

Evil Is as Evil Does

On any other occasion, King would have gone in with guns blazing, but he wanted Silk to feel pain. Killing him would be too easy. He needed to humiliate Silk so that he would never forget who ruined his life. King Kochese sat in his Lexus LFA across the street from Hard Body's Gentlemen's Club and waited. Silk was so predictable that it was almost laughable. He and his merry band of misfits would pour out of the club and wait to see who could bed one of the strippers ending their shift. Eventually, Rufus, a surly, thick-necked bouncer, would come out to shoo them away so they couldn't harass the girls. Silk always parked his car behind the club, away from prying eyes, just in case one of his conquests happened to be less than stellar in appearance. *That* would be his downfall.

Like clockwork, Silk stumbled out of the back door of the club. He had a female with him who looked more like a fry cook than a stripper. Her choice of clothing left no doubt about what her chosen profession happened to be. She wore a fishnet body suit and black thong with black patent leather thigh-high boots. She put her hand down Silk's jeans and giggled coyly.

Silk handed her a few bills, and she kissed him on the cheek. He grinned like a horny teen flipping through porn and never noticed the black unmarked van that pulled alongside him. In his drunken, lustful stupor, Silk hadn't seen much of anything. He leaned against his Jaguar, trying desperately to focus on his car keys until he realized that his car was a push-to-start. *I really need to stop drinking*, he thought. He threw his head back and laughed heartily. The heavy clouds overhead made the night seem much darker and later than it actually was. A light mist began to blanket the small concrete parking lot, and Silk welcomed the cool droplets that sprinkled his face.

He dropped his head just in time to catch a glimpse of Damion coming toward him with a pillowcase in hand. He wanted and needed to resist, but the liquor wouldn't let him. Each of his appendages felt heavy, as if weighed down by lead. His stomach turned in nervous anticipation as Damion threw the pillowcase over his head and duct-taped the bottom around his neck. Kendrick violently hit him in the stomach, and he vomited a little bit inside the pillowcase. The sweet sickly stench of stomach bile and Patron Gold threatened the release of the entire contents of his stomach.

"What the fuck, man!" Silk screamed.

He had never been what most would call a badass. His reputation had been built on the backs of others. In all actuality, Silk was a coward, and his persona was about as real as a six-dollar bill. He surrounded himself with goons, men who had actually lived the lifestyle that he'd immersed himself in. There was no denying that he was a hustler, but that's what gave Silk his power. He'd always paid his henchmen well. Silk wasn't liked, he wasn't feared, and he wasn't respected—he was merely tolerated.

Kendrick slid the side door open, and Damion tossed Silk inside and climbed in behind him.

"Man, don't kill me. I got like four stacks in my pocket. You can have it if you don't kill me, man," Silk cried.

"Oh, we're not gonna kill you. We're going to make you wish you were dead." Damion laughed as he bound Silk's hands with duct tape.

"Where to, daddy?" Kendrick asked.

"Drive to the south side. Let's hit Rochester Park."

Kochese followed the van at a safe distance. If the van was pulled over, he didn't want to be anywhere near the fallout. Kochese felt his manhood stiffen. The prospect of death had always caused sexual arousal in him. His foot felt heavy, and he noticed that he was closing in on the van rather fast and eased off of the gas. His anxiousness resulted in carelessness, and Kochese couldn't afford any mistakes. The van pulled into a deserted field just shy of the woodline bordering Rochester Park, and the lights went out. Kochese watched from a distance of about two hundred feet. He parked in front of an abandoned house at the end of the dead-end street running adjacent to the woodline. Kochese leaned his seat back to an almost parallel position, but was lifted up just enough to keep his eyes on the van. It would be a long night, but he was prepared. He smiled a dastardly smile as Tupac's sinister baritone gave him eargasms:

Got some static with some niggas from the other side of town

Let my little cousin K roll; he's a rider now

What you want from us muhfuckin' thug niggas

I used to love niggas; now I slug niggas and plug niggas

Kochese settled into his plush Italian leather seats and sparked a blunt. As the potent herb smoke began to fill the car, a ruthless and narcissistic thought crossed Kochese's mind: *I kill niggas for sport, and I ain't even gotta touch 'em.*

***

Damion took a large hunting knife and cut the pillowcase from Silk's face. Kendrick sprang into action, covering his eyes and mouth with duct tape to silence his impending cries. Damion began to unbuckle Silk's belt. He fought and squirmed, trying to free himself from the large gay man's clutches.

"Stop moving before I gut you like a fish!" Damion barked.

"Well, he is a fish, and we are about to gut him, sooooooo . . ." Kendrick said, letting the words linger for emphasis. He removed Silk's shoes so that Damion could pull down his pants. After he'd removed his pants and boxers, Damion snatched the tape from Silk's mouth. He stuck his finger in Silk's mouth. Silk quickly yanked his head away.

"Come on, man, don't do this shit," Silk pleaded.

"I like it when a man begs before I bust him out," Damion said. "You think I would pass up a chance to bust out a piece of sweet virgin ass? Now turn your bitch ass over."

He grabbed Silk and forcefully turned him over to his stomach. Kendrick reached into his man purse, removed a large tube of KY jelly, and emptied the contents onto Silk's exposed buttocks. At the sight of his victim's rear end glistening in the darkness, Damion's arousal was heightened. He ripped and clawed at his clothes, trying to undress as quickly as possible. He had a look of perverted anticipation in his eyes that made Kendrick uneasy. Although it made him uncomfortable, it also aroused him to see Damion being so forceful.

"Goddamn, man, I got a grip at my house in my safe, dawg. Let me go, and it's all yours," Silk cried.

Damion's laughter bellowed and shook the small van. He looked into Kendrick's eyes and said, "I love you so much that I'm going to let you have the first stab at that tight ass." He bent down until his mouth was even with Silk's ear. Spittle dripped from his wet mouth as he whispered, "After my wife finishes with you, I'm gonna show you the damage ten inches can do to your insides, bitch. Welcome to my world. Welcome to the disease that there is no cure for."

More than two hours later, Damion emerged from the back of the van, zipping his pants. Kochese smiled. By the crazed and satisfied look in Damion's eyes, Kochese knew that the deed had been done. Kochese stepped out of his car and stretched. He grabbed the two manila envelopes that lay on the passenger's side seat. He crossed the field slowly and met Damion midway. The sun rose in the distance, painting the dawn of a new morning a mixture of brilliant oranges and blues, but it was still dark enough to hide their heinous crime.

"So, it's done?" Kochese asked, handing Damion one of the envelopes.

"Yep, little pussy shitted on me, but he's going to remember me for a long time," Damion said with a devilish smirk.

"Both of y'all skeeted in the little bitch, right?" he asked, but there was no answer. There was only Damion's twisted sneer of self-satisfaction.

They crossed the field together and approached the van. When they opened the back door, Kendrick covered his naked body with his clothes, much like a woman who was ashamed of her body might. The overwhelming stench of fecal matter and sweat, coupled with lubricant and cheap cologne, assaulted Kochese's senses as he stared down at Silk's bloody nakedness. He chuckled to himself at the rape victim's rectal discomfort. He lay in a puddle of blood and excrement, unwilling to move for fear that his sexual ravaging might begin again. The more he'd resisted when the couple had begun, the more brutal his rape had become.

"Did you like it, nigga?" Kochese asked.

Silk turned his head toward the voice. For an instant, he thought he recognized it but dismissed it. He unknowingly nodded his head yes. He wasn't actually nodding his head to the question. He was nodding because it was the person's voice he thought it was. But to his psychotic onlooker, he seemed to be in agreement about enjoying his own brutality.

"I knew you were a little bitch. See, I was gonna put a bullet in your temple, but killing you quick is too good for your punk ass, so I let my new friends handle it for me."

"King Kochese?" Silk asked.

"Yeah, nigga, King Ko-muhfuckin'-chese. Every time you look in the mirror and see your emaciated face, you're gonna think about me. Every time you take a shit and remember the humiliation of these dudes dragging your insides out, you'll think about me. Every time you think about the fact that you have full-blown AIDS and it is slowly eating your insides away, you'll think about me. And when you're tired of suffering and can't take it anymore, you'll come to me on your knees begging for forgiveness, begging for me to put a slug in your dome to take you out of your miserable excuse for an existence."

King spat on him.

Chapter 28

Ass to Appetite

"What's good, playboy?" Drak said. "Get dressed. We need to meet King and Monica at the airport by nine."

Baby Face wiped the sleep from his eyes and smacked his lips. He was still in his boxers, happy to be home after spending most of the day in a holding cell.

"Meet King for what? I got company, dawg, if you know what I mean." Face moved to the side to give Drak a better view of his living room.

He'd made a larger-than-life pallet on the floor with blankets and pillows. Four young girls lay naked, sprawled out on the floor. The youngest was perhaps nineteen, the oldest maybe twenty-two. They were all different shades of brown but equally as gorgeous. Drak smiled to himself. If there was one thing that he could say about Face, it was that he kept a flock of beautiful women. He would never commit, and he was a known womanizer with commitment anxiety, but he loved having beautiful women at his disposal.

"Man, fuck all that!" Drak sneered. "You're more than welcome to call that ign'ant-ass dude and tell him that you're not going to his and Monica's wedding because you got a house full of pussy. Gone, be my guest."

"Oh, shit. Naw, let me get a shower and pack, then I'll be ready."

"Just take a shower, don't pack. We'll just buy clothes when we get there. Go wash your stinkin' ass. I'll keep these little freaks company while you're gone," Drak said with a smirk.

He sat in a nearby chair, staring at the nubile young women. Face looked back and smiled at Drak. *This old-ass nigga can't hang with these young-ass bitches*, Face thought as he made his way to the bathroom.

Baby Face started the shower and stepped in. He washed quickly but thoroughly. He was well aware that he didn't fit the typical drug dealer profile, and he liked that. He dressed like a preppy college kid, with his polo shirts and Jordans. He was known to crease his Levi 501 jeans so heavy that he could stand them up in a corner and leave them. Since joining King's organization, Baby Face had made a nice living for himself and had actually managed to save a nice nest egg. At twenty years old, he was pulling in enough money to pay his bills, have money in the bank, and help his mother and father. They thought that he was away at college and had been fortunate enough to get an internship. It wasn't entirely untrue. He *was* kind of in college—*the School of Hard Knocks*.

After twenty-seven years at Boeing Aircraft, they'd laid his father off, and he'd yet to find work. His mother had always been a stay-at-home mom, so their income was all but nonexistent. Baby Face felt like it was his duty to help out. He was his mother and father's only child, and they were all that each other had; no grandparents, no uncles or aunts, just the three of them against the world. King had always paid him decently, but he'd recently been given an opportunity to strike out and do a few side deals. No harm, no foul . . . or so he thought. King's organization sold any- and everything remotely close to narcotics, but Baby Face could boost a car in under a minute, and that lifestyle had started to net him a nice supplemental income. King wanted complete loyalty, but even after Baby Face shared with him the need for more money, he wasn't very receptive. Face did what he thought he needed to do and had kept it to himself.

He stepped out of the shower and dried off. He stopped the water and was surprised to hear the sound of jovial giggles coming from the living room. He heard Drak's deep voice, but he couldn't make out what was being said. As he entered the living room, he was taken aback by the sight he encountered. The four young women were entertaining Drak. He sat in the same position as when Face had left to get into the shower. The girls were dancing with one another, kissing and touching, while one of them sat on Drak's lap. She was facing him, and from the looks of it, she must have been stroking Drak's member. She looked back at Baby Face and smiled sheepishly.

"I was just keeping your friend company, Face. Damn, he got a big dick," she said.

"I don't wanna hear 'bout no other nigga's dick, mane. Y'all need to put some clothes on and dip. I'm about to skate out for a few days," Face said.

There was no argument, only pouting faces as they dressed quickly in preparation to leave. Face had never considered pimping, but the thought crossed his mind as he watched his beautiful harem. After the girls had gone, Baby Face seized the opportunity to speak privately with Drak.

"Man, check this out. I've been doing something that I think that nigga King needs to know about, but I don't know how he is going to react," Face said.

"What you do, my dude? Have you been doing side deals?" Drak asked, giving Baby Face the side eye.

"Naw, man. I've been boosting cars to make a little side bread. I just hope dude understands."

"Dawg, I'ma give you some advice. Don't ask, don't tell, my nigga. You ain't hurting nobody by getting you some paper. King don't know about it, and it's best you keep it that way."

They exited Face's apartment and walked out into the morning brightness. There wasn't a cloud in the sky, which only seemed to increase the heat. They drove to the airport in silence, both consumed by their own thoughts—one of greed, the other of murder.

King and Monica waited in front of DFW International Airport for Drak and Baby Face to arrive. Monica was still angry with King for staying out all night and not calling. He'd come home overly excited about Silk's demise, explaining to Monica how he'd made it happen. She thought it was sick, but it was actually good for her case. When King went to trial, he would not only be charged with countless murders but for rape, solicitation of rape, and attempted murder, as well for knowingly having Silk infected with AIDS.

Monica was so conflicted in her thoughts that it showed in her features, and as much as she tried to hide it, she could not contain her emotions. The sooner Monica could end the case, the better. She was about to marry Kochese in less than 24 hours, and although it was part of her job, she had somehow managed to fall in love with him. Monica was a classic woman. She knew that Kochese was sick, she knew that he was a murderer, she knew that he needed help, but she also knew the *man* inside of him. King Kochese Mills absolutely adored her, was enamored by her beauty, and was captivated by her wit. She had come into his life and helped him see the pot of gold at the end of the rainbow, and she knew this. She sat on her Louis Vuitton luggage, looking straight ahead.

"Are you okay, Monica?" King asked." You look stressed out. You're not having second thoughts, are you?"

"No, I'm just worried about Bird. I talked to my grandfather yesterday while you were taking care of your business, and he tried to imply that it was somehow my fault."

"Damn, that's fucked up. What did he say?"

Monica hadn't expected King to dive into it, and she was at a loss for words. She was, however, a pro at improvisation. She didn't know where the skill had come from, but she used it whenever necessary. She had been watching and learning from Kochese since the first day she'd met him. She was learning how to read people, about what made them tick and what made them do the things they did. She knew Kochese almost better than he knew himself. He wanted her love and her approval. After all that he'd been through with his mother, he only wanted the love of a woman, a sincere love that he could call his own, and he was willing to do whatever it took to keep it. Monica would use these findings against King.

"I don't want to talk about him, baby. You're the only man that matters to me. Later today, we will be on a yacht and getting married, and that's where my mind is. I love you, and I don't want to think about anything that has the potential to make me sad."

There was nothing left to discuss. King towered over her and smiled down. Just like that, Monica had ended the entire inquiry, and she smiled up at King.

"Y'all looking like y'all can't wait to get married and start the honeymoon," Drak said as he approached the couple. Baby Face followed closely behind, not making eye contact with anyone.

"Hey, Baby Face. How are you?" Monica asked.

"I'm straight. Y'all excited?"

King's eyes flashed brightly in Baby Face's direction. He had no trust left in the young man. According to his source, Baby Face was a snitch, and King had too much to lose to tolerate a snitch. Once he and Monica were away and out of the country permanently, the snitches could have a field day, but until then, he would silence *all* snitches.

"Now boarding Flight 1372 from Dallas/Fort Worth to Fort Lauderdale," came the call over the loudspeaker.

Three hours later, their plane landed in the sunny state of Florida. Laughter and lighthearted jokes floated in the air as they exited the plane. The triplets waited outside close to a Hummer limousine and smiled broadly as King approached.

"Hey. King. Hey, Monica," they said in sing-song unison, as if they had rehearsed it.

Monica silently wondered if they were jealous. Bird had offhandedly let her know that the triplets had wanted to bed King, believing that the thought of sleeping with triplets would somehow hold weight with him. He had, however, politely but firmly declined. He was intelligent enough to realize that business and pleasure never mixed well, not to mention that his whole Florida operation hinged on their continuing loyalty. Their connection with the Haitians, Jamaicans, and Colombians in south Florida was invaluable, and a night of sexual bliss wasn't worth losing those connections.

They rode to Ocean Boulevard in South Beach to shop for the wedding, and the mood among everyone was happy. Nobody in attendance ever thought King would take a steady woman, let alone a wife. They laughed and reminisced, speaking freely about trafficking and murder in front of Monica, as marrying King made her an immediate part of the family.

The triplets disappeared with Monica into the Chanel store on Ocean Boulevard while King and his men kept shopping. They'd agreed to meet at Prime One Twelve Steakhouse for lunch before heading to the yacht for the ceremony. Monica listened intently to the triplets as they continued to share King's exploits openly. It was almost as if they were trying to scare her away with the information, but it didn't work. What it did serve to do was ensure that when King was arrested, they would be swept up in the indictment as well. They'd inadvertently sealed their fate with their loose lips. Although King was the main focus of the federal investigation, anyone doing business with him was susceptible to the forthcoming charges. Under the RICO act, they were all considered part of the organization and would be dealt with accordingly.

When they arrived at the yacht, the crew greeted them and showed them to their quarters. King whispered something into the ear of one of the crew members and handed him a wad of cash.

"What was that all about, baby?" Monica asked.

"I told him to get me some chum, nothing major."

"Some what?" Monica asked, bewildered.

"Some chum. It's like bloody fish parts."

"What do you need that for?" Monica asked.

King didn't answer. Instead, he grabbed Monica, pulled her close, and kissed her deeply and passionately.

"You know, in less than an hour, you're going to be Mrs. Monica Mills—Mills being the key word—so you're gonna have to kill these questions," he said, laughing. He smacked Monica on her butt, and she giggled. Then he grabbed his bags and headed for the cabin door. "Now, get dressed. I'ma go and get dressed in Drak's room. A groom isn't supposed to see his bride before the ceremony, remember?" He winked at Monica and exited the room.

Monica stepped out of her clothes and stood naked in the middle of the room, admiring her body in the full-length mirror. She let her hands surf the contours of her curvaceous body. She felt her nipples stiffen under the pressure of her soft hands. She let her hand slide down her stomach to her heated moisture. She thought of King's manhood and felt her juices flow freely down her fingers. She stopped touching herself and walked to the nightstand, and clicked the remote to the radio. R. Kelly was playing, and her horniness started all over again. Monica cursed under her breath. She didn't like the fact that King had a hold on her body the way that he did. Their bodies fit together as if they were made for each other. Monica started the shower and stepped in. R. Kelly sang sweetly, as if talking directly to Monica until she couldn't help but to finish the job that she'd started.

Monica slid her finger into her wetness. She removed the head of the shower and set the stream to pulsate. Monica put one leg up on the edge of the tub and leaned back against the cold tile. She let the steady stream of warm pulsating water massage her clitoris. She slid her finger into her vagina up to her knuckle and applied gentle pressure in search of her G-spot. She found the bean-shaped erogenous zone and fingered it softly. Her knees quivered, and she moaned in delight. She closed her eyes and imagined King sliding his erect member inside of her. She inserted another finger and masturbated more vigorously.

"Oh my God, Kochese!" she screamed. She felt her legs shudder as the hot wetness of an intense orgasm coated the palm of her hand. Monica dropped the shower head and groped her breasts firmly, still sliding her fingers in and out of her now-sensitive vagina. She finished by using her soaking wet finger to make circular motions on her clitoris gently. When Monica stepped out of the shower, she steadied herself against the sink, determined not to fall. Her legs felt like Jell-O, but she felt reinvigorated and fresh.

Besides the crew, there was only one person on board the Lady Majestic yacht, and that was the reverend who would perform the ceremony. The triplets had arranged for a dinghy to take him back to shore after the ceremony so that they could party without the preacher feeling uncomfortable. The captain and the crew were willing to do anything that King and the squad wanted them to do. The triplets had paid them a flat fee of ten thousand dollars and a threat. The money was almost five times what they regularly charged, and the threat was that if anything that happened on the Lady Majestic made it off of that yacht, they would *all* be murdered. No ifs, ands, or buts about it. The captain had reluctantly agreed; after all, it wasn't his anyway. The owners of the yacht were Northerners from Connecticut who wouldn't be back until the beginning of winter. They were "snowbirds" who only came down to escape the harsh New England winters, and the captain and his four-person crew had used the yacht on many occasions to throw free parties. So, if some young drug dealers wanted to pay them to have a wedding a few miles off of the coast, and they were willing to pay that type of money, he was all for it. The reverend stood at the bow on the deck of the yacht. The deck had been decorated with white roses, and everyone was present except Monica.

"Excuse me, sir. We are about ten miles from shore. Would you like for me to anchor the boat?" the captain asked King.

"Is the water deep out here? Like, do people go swimming out here?"

The captain chuckled lightly. People that weren't familiar with water always amused him. Swimming in waters as deep as the ones off of the coast of Florida was asking for trouble. "Sir, the only people in the water out this far are deep sea divers. You wouldn't want to go swimming out here unless you want to be a shark's snack."

"Well, I guess we're in the perfect spot, so yeah, go ahead and drop that anchor, Cap," King said with an impish grin. He turned and continued his conversation with Drak and Baby Face. "So like I was saying, mane, this is it. After this ceremony, we get back to D-Town, and I'm done, players. I'm cashing in my player's card, and I'm finna live like Cliff Huxtable."

"Yeah, I'll believe it when I see it," Drak said half-jokingly. He nudged King slightly and nodded toward the entrance. Monica strolled toward them regally. She wore a stark white Chanel bathing suit with a long sheer train like a wedding dress would have, white and gold Chanel stilettos, a white wide-brimmed hat, and white-framed Chanel sunglasses. She looked as though she'd stepped out of the pages of a magazine, and every man there openly gawked at her, including the preacher.

"Shall we begin?" the reverend asked. Everyone stood as Monica approached, and King took his place in front of his sparse audience. Monica took her place next to King in front of the right Reverend Rutherford J. Ponds. The young star-crossed lovers faced each other and held hands. The reverend's voice boomed and echoed over the deep blue waters.

"We are gathered here today to join this man and this woman together in a holy union anointed in God's grace and wonderful mercy. They have written their own vows in an expression of their purest love for one another."

King removed a small card from the pocket of his white Sean John shorts. He cleared his throat and began to speak. “Monica, I promise to love you without condition, to honor you each and every day. I promise to laugh with you when you’re happy and to comfort you when you’re sad. I promise to guide you when you ask for direction and to challenge you to be a better person. And most importantly, I promise to allow you to do the same for me. I promise to be your biggest fan and your ever-present listening audience.”

Monica was momentarily speechless. King had never presented himself as a wordsmith. She felt tears welling in her eyes, threatening to undo the MAC makeup that she had taken care to apply.

“Kochese, I pledge to you to live together with mutual understanding, support, and trust; to accept our happiness and difficulties with cooperation and understanding. I promise to strive to lead a life as one soul and one being. I promise to share all of our fortunes. I will pray for healthy and loving children. I promise to consult each other in all major decisions, and I promise to remain true to you and to live together eternally.”

“Kochese Mills, do you promise to love and honor Monica Bircher and walk in the ways of the Lord until death do you part?” Reverend Ponds asked.

“I do.”

“Monica Bircher, do you promise to love and honor Kochese Mills and walk in the ways of the Lord until death do you part?”

“I do, always.”

“Kochese and Monica, these rings are a symbol of your unbreakable bond, a symbol of both of your pledge to hold each other in the highest regard, under the watchful eye of God’s mercy,” Reverend Lovejoy said. “By the power vested in me by the State of Florida and the anointed grace of our Lord and Savior Jesus Christ, I now pronounce you husband and wife. I present to you, Mr. and Mrs. Kochese Mills.”

Claps and whistles erupted as Kochese and Monica embraced and kissed deeply.

Kochese turned and handed the reverend a wad of bills. "Thanks, Rev, I really appreciate it."

"No problem, son. You two have a wonderful life together and remember to walk with the Lord."

"Yeah, I hear you. Be careful on your way off of the boat," Kochese said.

As soon as the preacher boarded the small dinghy, the party began. Everyone was handed a blunt of the finest sour mango kush that Miami had to offer. They toasted with rosé, and as soon as the bottle was gone, they started on the heavier liquors. They were a quarter of the way into a bottle of Patron when Kochese motioned to the deckhand to bring him the bucket of chum. He put on a pair of yellow rubber gloves and began to toss the chum in the water. Before the bucket of bloody fish parts was gone, it had started attracting the sharks. When he'd finished dropping the second bucket of fish guts into the water, the sharks were whipped into a frenzy. King beckoned for all of his people to meet him at the side of the boat.

He fingered the tip of a large butcher's knife as he began to speak. "Listen, man, I'm appreciative to everyone that's taken time out of their busy schedule to come out here to witness the nuptials between my baby and me. All y'all know me, and you know if it's one thing I can't stand, it's a snitch. It's been brought to my attention that somebody in the camp has been flapping their gums, but I'm not worried about that. I'm letting y'all have this bullshit. I'm out. I'ma promote somebody and give them all of my connects, and let them take over this shit."

"Man, if that promotion comes with a raise, I think I want that job!" Baby Face said with a huge grin on his face.

Kochese walked to him and put his hand on his shoulder. “You think you can handle my job, Face? You would have to learn how to keep your muhfuckin’ mouth shut first, playboy.”

“What you mean, dawg?” Face asked.

“What do I mean? I mean, you would have to learn how to shut the fuck up, snitch!” Kochese sneered.

He stuck the knife deep into Baby Face’s stomach and ripped it upwards. Baby Face let out a blood-curdling shriek as the blade sliced through his organs. He reached for King, trying his hardest to hold on to him before he slid down the boat’s deck. He looked up at King as if to ask *why*, but King kicked him away. Crimson-red blood began to cloud the white Akoo linen suit that Baby Face wore.

“Your services are no longer needed, muhfucka, and just so you know, I already knew about your little car-boosting thing, nigga, but snitching? Naw, not in my camp, homeboy. Drak, throw this piece of shit overboard to the sharks.”

Drak did as he was instructed, and as soon as Face’s body hit the water, the sharks ripped him to shreds.

“Now that’s how you kill a muhfuckin’ snitch. No body, no goddamned evidence,” King said as his baleful laughter filled the air of the approaching nightfall.

Monica was beyond herself with grief. She knew that King Kochese was a killer, but she had never been privy to this side of him. Although the wedding was a sham, it still bothered her that King had chosen to murder Baby Face on their wedding day. As the night settled in on them, Monica stood at the spot where Face’s body had been dumped and stared at the water.

The moonlight shimmered on the water. The radiant beams of light leaped from wave to wave, looking like diamonds against the black water. The sight was so beautiful that one would've never known that less than two hours previous, a man had been ripped to pieces by man-eating sharks while his soul had sunk into the abyss of the Atlantic Ocean. Monica looked up at the moon and wondered if Jasmine was seeing the same moon. She also thought about if Face had a relationship with his family. She wondered if Bird was feeling better, and then oddly enough, if the caretakers at the kennel were taking good care of Noisy Boy.

She looked into the moon and said a silent prayer, and then she began talking to Pop Pop, asking him to forgive her for not being a good girl. Throughout her life, Pop Pop was the only man to truly show her respect and teach her. Monica's mind was tormented because she had allowed herself to fall in love with a serial killer, a man with obvious mental problems, and if she didn't end the case soon, one of them would surely meet their demise at the hands of the other.

Chapter 29

I Am Who I Am

"Why are you looking at me like that, Moni?" Kochese asked.

"Looking at you like what, Kochese? Like, I'm wondering why you chose our wedding day to do that shit?"

"Babe, I got that nigga on the boat because they'll never find his body. I'm not trying to spend the rest of my life in a prison cell behind one of these lames. I told you what I was, who I am!"

"Yeah, you did, and I still chose to marry you, but damn, baby, you could've at least waited until the notion of marriage settled on me."

They hadn't talked much on the plane ride back to Texas. King hadn't wanted to intrude on Monica's private thoughts, and she hadn't wanted to argue with him on the plane. Instead, she'd put her headphones on, settled into her seat, and tried to sleep all the way home. She wasn't like most women that dreamed of horse-drawn carriages and snow-white wedding dresses. She hadn't sat as a little girl dreaming of the day she would meet Prince Charming, but she was there now. She was in a situation in which, on the day that should have been the happiest day of her life, she was living a lie. She was disgusted by Kochese and his reckless disregard for human life. His mentality terrified her, and she wanted out, but she needed his sex one last time.

"When are we gonna go and get Noisy Boy, King?" she asked.

"I was going to go and get him in the morning if that's cool. I'd like to have a night alone with my wife."

"Okay, babe. Let me call my granddaddy right quick so that he knows that we made it home safely," Monica said.

King nodded. She had already told him that her grandfather had all but accused her of getting Bird hurt, but if she wanted to call him and it made her happy, he didn't have a problem with it.

Monica dialed Muldoon's number and waited for him to answer. Moments later, Muldoon answered, and Monica said, "Hey, Grandpa, it's Monica. We are back from Florida. When do you think you can come down to meet my new husband?"

"I can put a strike team together as soon as the morning. Do you have enough to put his ass away for good?"

"Yes, I have enough, Grandpa. Thanks for asking."

"Good job, Agent Dietrich."

"I love you too, Granddaddy. See you soon."

"What did your granddaddy say, baby?"

"He said he's going to try and get down here soon to meet you and asked me if we needed anything."

They pulled into the driveway and could barely keep their hands off of one another. Kochese loved Monica, and her being his wife made him horny. By the time they made it inside the house, they were almost undressed. As soon as they entered the house, Monica ran toward the stairs, and Kochese chased. He caught her at the top of the stairs, threw her onto the carpet, and buried his face deep between her legs. He tried to rip her lace panties with his teeth, but Monica wiggled free, ran into the bathroom, and locked the door. King smiled as he went into the bathroom down the hall. He bathed quickly and was in bed waiting when Monica finally emerged from the bathroom in red lace crotchless panties, a bra, and red stilettos. She went to the stereo system mounted on the wall and put on her Kelly Rowland CD. She then went to the table by the door and lit the candles there. A dull light illuminated the spacious room. There was very little light, but there was enough for Monica to see King's erection from across the room. She unclasped her bra and stepped out of her panties. King made a move to get up, but Monica waved him back down.

"I'm in control tonight, Mr. Mills," Monica said.

"Anything you say, Mrs. Mills," Kochese said, smiling.

His hardness seemed to grow more from knowing that Monica wanted to take control of his body. She sashayed to the side of the bed and took his penis in her hands. It was hot and throbbed violently. She sat on top of him and rubbed the head of cock against the moist slit of her wetness. King moaned, wishing that she'd put it in. Instead, she leaned over, reached into the nightstand, and grabbed two silk scarves. Monica tied Kochese's hands to the large bedposts of the headboard. Again, she went onto the nightstand and grabbed a tube of massage oil. She coated her hand generously and began slowly stroking his manhood. Monica guided his cock inside of her, twirling her hips seductively, the entire time watching Kochese's facial contortions of pleasurable bliss. She felt the swell of his oncoming orgasm and removed his stiffness from her. She slithered up the length of his body and positioned her love nest above his face. His tongue darted out swiftly, barely grazing her clitoris before she shuddered and came.

Monica settled in, and King's tongue penetrated her soul, reaching into her deeply. She felt the hot wetness of his tongue flicking and twirling, driving her to the brink of the ultimate orgasm. She moaned softly, gyrating tempestuously against his chin. She rose up off his tongue to get a view of his face. Kochese's chin glistened from Monica's wetness. His radiant blue eyes beamed and flashed pure excitement as she settled back into position. His tongue found her clitoris again. He began to flick his tongue gently until Monica could no longer contain herself.

"Oh my God, Kochese, you make me want to fuck your face!" she moaned.

She bucked and thrashed wildly until she squirted violently, spraying her hot, wet juices onto Kochese's face. Monica collapsed next to him, still trembling. Her breathing was heavy but measured as she struggled to catch her breath. She gathered her strength and climbed on top of Kochese and slid his manhood deep inside. It seemed as if she could feel him deep in her stomach. Kochese thrust his body upward, and Monica could feel him bury himself deeper and deeper.

"Oh, baby, you're hitting my spot!" she squealed in delight.

Kochese and Monica both came to orgasm at the same time. Monica collapsed on King's chest and kissed him passionately.

The bright lights shining through the window woke Monica from her sex-induced slumber. King lay beside her, snoring and unaware that Monica had played him. She was intelligent enough to realize that fantastic sex had that heavy sleep effect on a man. King stirred, but he didn't wake as Monica got out of bed to look out of the window. DPD, DEA, and ATF officials lined King's front lawn. Had Noisy Boy been there, he would've surely given King a warning, but there was only Monica.

Before Monica could grab her gun to arrest King, he sprang from bed with a start. "What the fuck is going on, baby?" he shouted. "You don't see the lights? Shit, shit,

shit. I'm not going to jail. Put some clothes on. We gotta go!"

"Baby, let's just turn ourselves in."

"Baby, I love you, but you're crazy as a muhfucka if you think I'm going out like a sucker. Fuck that. Naw, I'm going out like a G!"

They both dressed quickly. King threw a few pairs of clothes into a bag, grabbed his .45 caliber pistol, and jammed it into his waistband. He held Monica's hand and led her through the hall, down the stairs, and toward the garage. They'd just run through the foyer when the front down came crashing down from the battering ram.

"Kochese Mills, this is the DEA. Turn yourself in. Show yourself, show yourself!!" an agent yelled, but Kochese and Monica had already made it to the garage and jumped into his Range Rover. Kochese hit the button on his garage door opener, and the door sprang to life. An agent stood sure-footed, planted firmly with his M16 pointed at the vehicle. King punched the gas with the full intention of running him over, but as he approached the agent, he dove out of the way, firing rounds into the side of the Range. King slammed the pedal, heading for the gate, while sirens and lights blared and flashed behind him.

"Where are we going, baby?" Monica asked.

King didn't answer. He just kept driving, recklessly weaving in and out of traffic. His eyes darted from the road to his rearview mirror. Monica had never witnessed King like this before. He looked worried and afraid. Monica looked back. The squad cars and black Impalas were behind them but not close enough to catch them.

King whipped into King's Kennel and parked in front of Evelyn's Dress Emporium. He didn't bother to turn the vehicle off. It was as if he thought that the small building was somehow impervious to the hailstorm of police that was about to hit it. Kochese cursed himself silently. He'd forgotten the keys to the shop in his haste and went back to retrieve them. Monica seized the opportunity and pushed redial on her cell phone. Muldoon was the last person who she'd talked to, and her phone had GPS tracking. King had obviously given them the slip because she didn't hear sirens or see any lights approaching. If she knew Muldoon the way that she thought she did, he would hear them talking, know that she was in trouble, and track her phone.

Kochese's hand shook profusely as he tried to open the door. The last thing that Monica needed was for him to be on edge. She touched his hand as if to steady it, and he calmed slightly, at least enough to insert the key in the keyhole. They entered the dress shop and went to Kochese's secret underground lair, where his mother sat in eternal slumber. Kochese hit the light switch and went to a closet underneath the stairs. He grabbed an AK-47 assault rifle and handed Monica his .45 caliber. He ran to the top of the stairs and listened. In the distance, Kochese could hear the approaching sirens.

"They're coming, baby! This is it. If they come down these stairs, we're going out like gladiators, you hear me?" Kochese shouted.

Monica didn't speak, afraid that she might upset him some type of way. He was wound tight, and the last thing he needed was to be tested. The sirens were loud, like they were right on top of them.

"Kochese Mills, this is Senior Agent Muldoon. We have this building completely surrounded," came a voice from over a bullhorn. "You and Miss Bircher need to come out, or we're coming in, and if we come in, we're coming in shooting first and asking questions later."

Kochese's response was to slap a banana clip into his AK. They heard the approaching footsteps of the agents.

Kochese kneeled next to his mother and looked into her dead eyes.

"You said you hated me, but I know you never meant that," he said. "You loved me deeply, Mam. You just didn't know how to show it or express it. I understand that now. All I ever wanted was for you to hold me and make it better. I could have been a good boy, Mama." Kochese sobbed.

Monica watched, dumbfounded. His actions were strange to her. She had a firm grasp on death and the finality of it, so to see a man that couldn't let go was perplexing to her.

"I guess you're finally going to get what you wanted all along, Mama!" Kochese screamed. "I'm going to make these white folks kill me! Is that what you want? Is that what you want, Mama?"

Monica needed to cry. She needed to be an Oscar Award-winning actress if they were going to make it out alive. She thought of Pop Pop, she thought of Jasmine, she thought of her mother and father, and the tears flowed. The more she thought about the few people in her life that loved her, the more the tears rolled. Monica walked to where King knelt and stared down at him. She loved him—she was *in* love with him—and the thought of losing him to either death or prison was too much to bear, and she crumpled to the floor next to him. Sobs of grief racked her body.

"Do you love me, Kochese?" Monica asked through her sobs.

Kochese looked at her through watery eyes. "You know I do, baby. Why you ask me that?"

"I don't want to die, baby. We just got married, baby." She cried harder. "We're too young for this shit, baby, please. Is this how you want your mother to see you go out? If they come down here, they will not only kill you and I, but they will blow your mother's body to pieces, baby!"

A voice boomed from beyond the stairs. "You have thirty seconds to comply, or we're coming down!"

Kochese looked at Monica and then at his mother, and then to Monica again. He shook his head and smiled. "You better be glad that I love y'all. I love my two favorite girls. A'ight, man. Don't shoot. We're coming up!!"

Monica took the AK from Kochese and laid it on the floor next to the .45 caliber. She grabbed Kochese, pulled him close to her, and kissed him passionately. Their kiss seemed to go on for an eternity.

"You're going to always be my husband, baby, no matter what happens," Monica said to Kochese. Then she screamed, "All right, sir, we're coming up!"

Chapter 30

A King Dethroned

Stripped of his kingdom, Kochese sat in the small, dank cell, fuming. Since his arrest, he hadn't had contact with anyone on the outside. His collect calls to Drak and the triplets had mainly gone unanswered, and he had no idea what was happening with Monica. King had no idea how he would pay for an attorney because, knowing the Feds, they would certainly seize his assets. At the arraignment, he'd been charged with multiple murders, conspiracy to commit murder, conspiracy to defraud the U.S. government, money laundering, and tax evasion. By the time they'd finished, the public defender they'd assigned to him was sweating like a Hebrew slave. He was a rookie attorney who was overworked and underpaid. Kochese watched nervously as the young man fumbled through his briefcase, trying to prepare his case. His appearance was disheveled, and he seemed to pour sweat with every word he spoke.

He'd looked at Kochese with worry and dismay. "Mr. Mills, I have to be honest with you. The severity of your charges is great, and there is a good chance that you'll face the death penalty. They are calling you a serial killer, and I don't think that I'm the man for the job."

Although King could appreciate his honesty, it only made the kingpin more nervous. That had been days earlier, and he hadn't heard from him since. He'd tried to bribe a guard who he knew from the outside, but the correctional officer had only laughed in his face.

"Where the fuck you gonna get money from, nigga?" the guard said. "The streets are talking, saying that the mighty King Kochese has been dethroned, playboy. Rumor has it that yo' ass ain't got two wooden nickels to rub together, so no, thank you, pimpin'. I think I'll pass."

Kochese couldn't remember the last time that he didn't have any answers. He was a sitting duck as long as he was behind bars, and he knew it. He tried to filter the noise out in the dayroom, but between the television and the constant chatter, it was no use. Kochese walked to the dayroom and picked up the phone to try a call to Drak again.

"Say, look out, white boy. Get away from the phone. I'm about to use it as soon as *All My Children* goes off," a stocky, dark-skinned black kid said.

"First of all, muhfucka, I ain't no fuckin' white boy, and second of all, what kind of grown-ass man sitting around watching goddamned soap operas?" Kochese barked. "Get the fuck away from me before I make you swallow your own face."

The kid moved toward Kochese, but he was stopped by an older man who whispered something into his ear. The blood seemed to drain from the boy's face instantly.

"Aw, man. King Kochese, man, I didn't even know that that was you, dawg. If you need anything, buddy, just say the word, and you got it. I'm Dinky, by the way."

"Dinky, is it? Okay, Dinky, I ain't no dog, so don't call me buddy. And as far as anything I need, I need you to get the fuck away from me. That's all I want from you, Dicky—I mean Dinky."

He dialed Drak's number and immediately started to curse.

"We're sorry, the mobile number that you've called has been disconnected or is no longer in service," he heard on the other line.

Kochese banged the receiver against its cradle. He couldn't grasp why he couldn't get one single person from his organization on the telephone. He'd tried his best to be a good boss, but people were only as loyal as the dollar in their pocket. Maybe the Feds had already begun to hand out indictments.

"Inmate Mills, you have a visit. Inmate Mills, you have a visit," a voice said over the loudspeaker.

Kochese stepped to the heavy glass and steel door that led out into the hall. The gears of the door whirred and buzzed as they slid open. Two correctional officers led Kochese into the visitation area. It was a small concrete block room with a rectangular stainless-steel table in the center of the room. The guard showed Kochese to a chair and chained his wrists to a set of shackles bolted to the floor. Moments later, two older white men entered the room and seated themselves across from him. One of the men opened a briefcase and pulled out some papers. He was nicely dressed and appeared to be an attorney. Kochese recognized the other man immediately. His intense blue eyes burned a hole into Kochese's soul as he stood to greet him.

"Hello, Kochese, my name is Hayden Cross," he said, extending his hand.

Kochese stared at the man for a long while. He'd evidently forgotten that Kochese had come to him as a teen, and he'd rudely slammed the door in his face.

"I know who the fuck you are, Mr. Cross. The question is, what do you want?"

"Regardless of whether you like it or not, I'm your father. I had many sleepless nights after you left my house, son, and I feel like I owe you."

"Man, you don't owe me shit. You're my sperm donor, not my father."

"That may be true, but I want to help you if you let me. You're going to court in the morning. I had your case expedited, and you won't be going to trial with a rookie public defender. Those Federal boys will eat his ass alive. No, you will have Mr. Talbot here."

"How did you do that? It's nig—I mean, there are dudes that have been waiting for months to go to trial."

"That's one of the advantages of having a shit load of money. Plus, your case is federal, and my company, CrossTech, pours millions of dollars into federal campaigns, so you have no worries. Let me handle this."

Kochese studied his father's face. Was this guy serious? The way Kochese felt, he needed all of the help that he could get. He wasn't in the business of trusting people, but if Hayden Cross was willing to use his money and power to help him, then so be it.

"I will have a nice suit waiting for you in the morning so that you're presentable at trial," Hayden said. "In that suit pocket will be a note with a surprise. Follow the instructions included in that note, Kochese."

He stood and extended his hand to Kochese, who this time, shook it vigorously. Aside from the crow's feet and slightly graying hair, looking at Hayden Cross was like looking in a mirror.

Kochese had found it difficult to sleep the night before, but once he'd dozed off, he'd slept peacefully, knowing that his case had been bought and paid for. An elderly correctional officer with brown-stained teeth smiled at Kochese warmly. She looked like someone's grandmother and was far too old to be walking the catwalk in a federal holdover.

"Mr. Mills, you have court, baby. Somebody done brought you a nice suit, so I gotta get you on down to the visitation area to change clothes."

Kochese could only smile. She was so sweet and nurturing. Her dialect was deeply Southern and very inviting. The entire time she led Kochese to the visitation area, she was reprimanding him about the ills of being in jail.

"You're a handsome young man, honey, and you seem to be real smart," she said. "Don't waste your life running in and out of this place, sugar."

Kochese simply nodded. Had it been anyone else that so blatantly intruded in his business, he would have cursed them, but Miss Matty was different. She only wanted what was best for everyone, regardless of skin color. She showed Kochese into the desolate visitation area. Lying across the table where he'd sat last night was a navy blue Armani suit, baby blue shirt, and a nice silk tie and scarf ensemble. Kochese reached into the inside jacket pocket and pulled out a small white envelope. There was a note inside the envelope that read:

> *Kochese,*
>
> *In the lining of your jacket, there is a .25 caliber pistol that's fully loaded. I want you to unload the clip in the courtroom. Don't shoot anyone, just create a diversion, and my team will handle the rest. See you on the other side.*
>
> *Signed, H.C.*

How would he make it through security with the weapon? How would he get to the gun with shackles on? Kochese didn't know what to make of the letter, but he was all out of answers. Instead, he would listen for a change. He dressed slowly in the high-priced clothes and sat at the table with his feet kicked up. He wondered how

Hayden had known what size he wore because the suit and shoes felt tailor-made. He subconsciously shrugged. *Oh well*, he thought. Kochese heard the familiar jingle of keys being inserted into the door that would eventually bring him his freedom.

"Mr. Mills, you're due in court in twenty minutes. Are you ready, sir?" the guard asked.

Kochese only nodded and extended his wrists for the shackles that he knew would come. The officer looked at his wrists and then at Kochese.

"There will be no need for that, sir."

Kochese nodded, but he was confused. He looked around to ensure it wasn't a trap because he was being treated more like a celebrity than an accused murderer. He walked in front of the guard, totally aware of his surroundings. The dull sliding thud of the guard's work boots lulled Kochese into a relaxed state of tranquility.

Moments later, they were standing in the center of the foyer leading to the maze of courtrooms at the Lew Sterrett Justice Center. Kochese's step faltered slightly as he approached the metal detectors but relaxed as he made eye contact with the guard manning the detector. She winked and smiled at Kochese, signaling for him to come through her line. She made eye contact with two men as Kochese approached, and they immediately started to brawl and argue at the top of their lungs, feigning an impending bout of fisticuffs. The noise drew the attention of the other guards on duty. They didn't notice Kochese and the guard slip around the side of the metal detector instead of through it.

The courtroom wasn't packed by a long stretch. Kochese had imagined it would be filled with his peers and curious onlookers who'd come to witness his fate, but it wasn't like that. The judge sat on high, staring down at Kochese as he stood with Mr. Talbot. The courtroom walls were stark white except for the mahogany trim bordering the white tiled floors. The judge's bench was the same texture of mahogany as the border and crown molding that lined the spacious room.

The court reporter sat to the right and just below the judge, positioned so that she could see and hear every word spoken in the federal court. The jury that stared back at Kochese wasn't made up of his peers. No, the jurors were older people who loathed his kind. The sneers and incredulous looks made him uneasy, but he steadied himself. He had already moved the pistol from the lining of his jacket to the outside pocket for quicker access, and he patted his pocket for reassurance.

The bailiff stepped forward. "Court will come to order," he bellowed. "The United States versus Kochese Mills. The Honorable Judge Frederick T. Bachman is presiding."

The judge ran down a list of Kochese's charges. He went on for what seemed like an eternity before asking how he wanted to plead. His answer was not guilty, of course. Kochese was waiting for some type of sign from his attorney that would let him know when to start blasting his pistol. That signal never came. Instead, the Federal prosecutor painted a detailed picture of the monster that Kochese had become. He said that the world would be a far better place by giving Kochese Mills the death penalty. And as evidence, he began his slide show of gruesome pictures.

"This, ladies and gentlemen, is Kochese Mills' trophy case." He pointed to a picture that showed an array of Ken dolls nailed to his wall with name tags. To add validity to the images, they'd also pulled the crime scene photos of each murder and showed them. "Had we not found this homicidal shrine, these killings would have gone unsolved. There is no limit to the extent that Mr. Mills will go to continue his criminal enterprise. Murder and mayhem are common for this psychopath!" The prosecutor huffed, pointing to a bucket of bloody, dismembered body parts.

"Objection, Your Honor, there is no need for name-calling," Mr. Talbot said.

"Overruled, Mr. Talbot. The fact that your client is on trial for multiple murders has given him a name worse than that," Judge Bachman said. "Continue, Mr. Prosecutor."

"This man is so sick that he keeps his mother's mummified corpse in the basement of a dress shop named for her. Although her death was ruled a suicide, I wouldn't be surprised if she wasn't murdered by her own son."

"Man, I didn't kill my fucking mother. I loved her!" Kochese screamed.

"Control your client, Mr. Talbot," Judge Bachman said, slapping his gavel.

"Sorry, Your Honor, it won't happen again," he said, putting his hand on Kochese's forearm and pulling him to his seat.

"Your Honor, if it pleases the court, I would like to call David Krutcher to the stand," the prosecutor said.

The judge nodded. "Mr. Krutcher, if you're in my courtroom, show yourself."

Kochese smiled deviously. He didn't know a David Krutcher, so he had no worries. Whatever information this person had would certainly be inaccurate because he had always been cautious with whom he chose to share information. He swiveled in his seat, as did everyone else in the courtroom, in search of this mystery witness. King Kochese's eyes widened and then became narrow slits of icy rage as the witness passed his table.

"Do you swear to tell the truth, the whole truth, and nothing but the truth, so help you God?"

"I do," he said.

"Can you please state your name for the court?"

"Yes, sir, my name is David Krutcher."

"And in your professional capacity, can you state your occupation and job title for the court?"

"Yes, sir. I am a Special Agent with the DEA or Drug Enforcement Agency."

"And how long have you been employed with the DEA?"

"Um, between office work and fieldwork, just under thirteen years."

"Objection, Your Honor. Is there a point to all of this?" Attorney Talbot said.

"I'm sorry, Your Honor. It has relevance to the case, I promise," the prosecutor said.

"Make it quick," Judge Bachman said. His demeanor spoke volumes to the prosecutor. Barring a miracle, there was no way that Kochese Mills wasn't facing, at the bare minimum, a life sentence in federal prison.

"Now, Mr. Krutcher, what is your specialty in the DEA? What type of assignments do you perform?"

"Well, for the first two years, I was in training, and for the last ten years, I've been in the undercover division of the DEA, the last five of which I've been in the employ of the defendant, Mr. Kochese Mills."

"And could you please tell us who Mr. Mills believes you to be?" the prosecutor asked.

"I was able to infiltrate Mr. Mills' organization as his trusted confidant, known to him as Drak."

And so it went. The prosecutor and Mr. Talbot assaulted Drak with a barrage of questions. At one point, Mr. Talbot went so far as to accuse Drak of being just as guilty as Kochese because he had also committed murder to make his case. Kochese smiled. Drak had played him beautifully. The truth was, Drak had never actually pulled the trigger or committed *any* crime, for that matter. Instead, he had ingeniously gotten others to do his bidding. Even with Baby Face, now that King thought about it, Drak had grabbed Face by his wrist when he stood him up to throw him overboard. He'd probably done that in an attempt to check his pulse, to ensure that he was dead before throwing him to the sharks. Kochese caressed the pocket that held the .25 caliber. He locked eyes with the bailiff, who gave him a nondescript nod, but Kochese didn't move. He would've loved to put a bullet into Drak's head, but that wasn't the plan.

"Your Honor, we have one last witness if it pleases the court," the prosecutor said. The judge waved his gavel as if to instruct the young, overly eager federal prosecutor to get on with it.

"We would like to call Monica Mills to the stand, Your Honor."

A heavy hush fell over the courtroom, so much so that it was clearly audible when Kochese spoke.

"She can't do this, can she? She's my wife. How can she testify against me?" he asked.

Mr. Talbot dropped his head to his hands. When the prosecutor had added her name to the witness list, he hadn't made the connection. The name Cross had been etched into his mind because Hayden Cross had instructed him to fight his hardest for his son. Monica entered the courtroom in a pine green skirt and blazer, with a sheer emerald green blouse. Her emerald green, eel skin six-inch stilettos completed her ensemble. It was next to impossible for Kochese to be angry at Monica. She looked beautiful, and he was madly in love with her.

Monica's attire was all business. Her normally long, flowing hair was pulled back into a bun, giving her the look of a sexy librarian. She took the stand, staring at the prosecutor and carefully avoiding eye contact with Kochese. She answered all of the questions thrown her way precisely and to the point. By the time Monica was finished giving her testimony, she'd painted Kochese's character as a gun-toting, heartless monster, surpassed only by Jeffrey Dahmer and the boogieman. To hear her tell it, Kochese was a pied piper of men and women, luring them into his fold with charm and riches. She testified that Kochese had no problem disposing of his workers like trash if it suited his fancy.

"One more thing, if you don't mind, Mrs. Mills," the prosecutor asked. "Could you please explain to the court why you're here testifying against your husband today?"

Monica locked eyes with Kochese, and for a split second, she felt her eyes well up with tears. She remembered the love that he'd shown her, the tenderness of his touch, and the intensity of his lovemaking.

"I'm here because I'm not his wife. My name is not Monica Mills or Monica Bircher. My name is Monica Dietrich, and I am a rookie DEA agent. I was doing my job, nothing more, nothing less."

Kochese's mouth dropped, and the courtroom buzzed and hummed with inaudible whispers. Judge Frederick T. Bachman slammed and banged his gavel. "Order in the court, order in the court! If this courtroom doesn't stifle, I will have you all cleared out of here!"

Kochese couldn't believe his ears. He had given Monica all of him, and she had played him. She was no different than any other woman.

"You swore you loved me! So I was just a job to you? You're going to pay for this, bitch!" he screamed.

"Mr. Mills, control yourself—one more outburst like that, and you will be removed from my courtroom and held in contempt," Judge Bachman said.

Kochese sat down heavily. Monica had knocked all of the wind from him. She had seemed so genuine, and it had all been a charade. Kochese leaned in and whispered into the barrister's ear. "Let me take the stand, Mr. Talbot," he said.

"I don't think that's a good idea, Kochese."

"I don't care about good ideas. I don't want to go out without speaking my mind," Kochese whispered loudly.

Mr. Talbot nodded his approval reluctantly and rose to address the judge. "Your Honor, if it pleases the court, I'd like to call my client, Mr. Mills, to the stand."

Monica exited the witness stand and took a seat next to Drak near the rear of the courtroom. "I didn't know that you were an agent, Drak," Monica said.

"Well, I knew you were an agent, Monica. My job was to gather intel, and after you came in, my job was to keep you safe. And the name is David."

Kochese's words caused them both to look up.

"I'm not perfect, and my childhood was crappy, but that's no excuse for my actions," he said to the courtroom. "I've lived my whole life wondering why my mother didn't love me. I've lived my whole life knowing that my father was one of the richest men in the state of Texas, and while he and his family ate steak every night, I went to sleep hungry. I don't apologize for my actions, because I am what they made me. There is nothing you can do to me that the people I loved or wanted to love haven't already done. I'm a condemned man. I know that."

Tears flowed freely from his eyes as he set his gaze upon Monica and said, "Miss Dietrich—or whatever your name is—I loved you, and I still love you. I'm sorry that we didn't meet under different circumstances. Oh my God, I swear you're the best thing that has ever happened to me. I want you to know that I forgive you for betraying me, and I wish you nothing but the best. I hope that you can live with yourself, knowing that my blood is on your hands. Take care of Noisy Boy, baby. He loves you."

Kochese reached into his jacket pocket and removed the small pistol. A gasp crossed the confines of the courtroom as Kochese put the gun underneath his chin and pulled the trigger. The .25 caliber dropped to the floor, and his body followed. As his lean, muscular frame slumped slowly into the witness booth, he heard Monica's soft, sweet voice somewhere from beyond the abyss.

"I love you, Kochese Mills. You will always be my husband."

Kochese heard screams, crying, shouting, and movement. He gasped one more labored breath, and then there was only darkness.

Chapter 31

New Beginnings

"Here's to Monica Dietrich on a case well won!" Muldoon said, raising a cup of apple cider.

"Here, here," her fellow agents cheered.

Drak walked to Monica and hugged her tightly. "You did a wonderful job, Agent, and we're all very proud of you. Don't beat yourself up about Kochese. It's not your fault. I know you loved him. Hell, if it's any consolation, I loved that fool like a brother, but we did our job."

Monica nodded. She understood perfectly, but it didn't ease the pain.

Muldoon walked up and put his arm on Monica's shoulder. "Well, Agent, what's next? Shall we sign you up for the next case?"

"Honestly, sir, this case drained me emotionally, and I need a break. Maybe I'll see if I can have an intra-agency transfer and try my hand at profiling. After trying so hard to get into Kochese's head, I think I'd be good at it. Besides, my sister Jasmine is coming home today, so the transfer will allow us to spend some much-needed time together."

Monica exited the complex and smiled brightly. Bird was leaning against his Dodge Charger with Noisy Boy on a leash at his feet. As Monica approached, the puppy wagged his tail vigorously. Monica kneeled and scratched Noisy Boy behind the ear. He licked her hand and jumped in excitement but was careful not to put his paws on her clothes because he knew that she hated that. Bird's hand was still bandaged, and his arm was in a sling, so when Monica leaned in to hug him, he somewhat flinched. Monica laughed as she hugged him.

"Nobody's going to hurt you, Calvin, you big baby," she said.

"Yeah, whatever. Anyway . . . so I know you're probably tired of hearing it, but what's next?" he asked.

"Come on. Let's ride, and I'll tell you on the way."

Moments later, they were on the freeway headed toward Pleasant Grove to the Buckner Home for Youth. Noisy Boy's head was hanging out of the back window, sniffing the air, slobbering, and drooling along the back of Bird's car.

"Calvin, I think I'm going to transfer to the FBI and become a profiler. That way, I can be home every night with my sister Jasmine. What about you?"

"Shit, believe it or not, the Feds let me keep my cash, contingent on the basis that I pay back taxes on my drug money. I think I might buy King's Kennel from the auction, change the name, and start some legitimate businesses. Find me a wife, make some babies, keep my nose clean, and stay my ass out of South Dallas. You interested?"

Before Monica could answer, Noisy Boy brought his head back into the car and growled ferociously at Bird.

"Well, I guess that's your answer. Noisy is the only baby I need," she said, laughing hysterically.

Bird laughed nervously and pulled the car into an empty parking space near the front entrance of the main building.

"I'll be right back, Bird." Monica disappeared into the red building with the huge glass doors. Her heels clicked and clacked against the clinically white tile floors.

Jasmine stood with her doctor smiling broadly. She was beyond excited. Eleven years was far too long to be confined anywhere, let alone in a mental institution. The sisters embraced for a long period before Monica held her sister at arm's length.

"Well, Jazzy Bell, are you ready for this?"

"As ready as I've ever been," Jasmine said.

As they walked out into the brisk autumn wind, Monica stopped and faced her sister. "We've been given a second chance, Jazzy, and we're going to make the best of it. The world is yours for the taking, so whatever you want to do in life, I've got your back one hundred percent," Monica said.

"That's so sweet, Monica, and thank you. I won't let you down."

"I know you won't. Now, what do you want to do first?" Monica asked.

"I know this might sound crazy, but I want to go to Good Luck Hamburgers to get a hot link basket. Then I want to go home, soak in a hot bath, and put on my pajamas. And after I'm good and clean, I want to put on a pot of coffee and spank your ass in Monopoly like I used to when we were kids."

Notes